HOLIDAY MEMORIES. . . .

Everyone has their holiday traditions, from family get-togethers to parades and barbecues to Easter egg hunts. Now let thirteen top storytellers play your hosts for the holidays, offering a whole new look at these traditional days in such memorable stories as:

"For These Things I Am Truly Thankful"—Before he even had a chance to get to Thanksgiving dinner he'd had a terrifying look at the darker side of the feast. . . .

"Brotherhood"—For the workers—and the management—at Kensington Steel this Labor Day would be one they'd never forget. . . .

"The Secret Sympathy"—Carnival was a time of celebration, but for two soul mates it would prove both an end and a new beginning. . . .

HAUNTED HOLIDAYS

Edited by
Martin H. Greenberg
and Russell Davis

DAW BOOKS, INC.
DONALD A. WOLLHEIM, FOUNDER
375 Hudson Street, New York, NY 10014

ELIZABETH R. WOLLHEIM
SHEILA E. GILBERT
PUBLISHERS
http://www.dawbooks.com

First Printing, October 2004
1 2 3 4 5 6 7 8 9 10

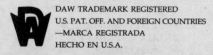

ACKNOWLEDGMENTS

Introduction © 2004 by Russell Davis.
For These Things I Am Truly Thankful © 2004 by
   David Niall Wilson.
Jewels in the Dust © 2004 by Peter Crowther.
Birthday Jitters © 2004 by Julie E. Czerneda.
The Dead Don't Waddle © 2004 by Esther Friesner.
Brotherhood © 2004 by David D. Levine.
Die, Christmas, Die! © 2004 by David Bischoff.
New World's Brave © 2004 by Daniel M. Hoyt.
Season Finale © 2004 by Bradley H. Sinor.
Voices in an Empty Room © 2004 by Richard
   Parks.
Memories Underfoot © 2004 by Ruth Stuart.
Judgment © 2004 by Kerrie Hughes.
Cover Me © 2004 by Nancy Holder.
The Secret Sympathy © 2004 by Brian A. Hopkins.

Contents

INTRODUCTION

by Russell Davis

I SUPPOSE I should start this introduction with a small confession. I need to admit something . . . a bit unpleasant. I don't like holidays. At Christmas, I cheer for the Grinch *before* his heart grows however many sizes, I've vowed to wait for the Easter Bunny with my twelve gauge handy, and I remain steadfast in my personal vow not to participate in holidays that have been made up so that retailers and card companies make more money—you know, days like "Sweetest Day." And with this attitude, you're probably wondering why I'm editing an anthology of holiday stories. Well, as the saying goes, there's a reason for the season.

I know I have to tolerate the holidays. I'm stuck with them. So are you. (It's okay to admit it, you know. It's just us here. When was the last time you got out and really partied down on Arbor Day?) But, I thought, if I'm stuck with them, couldn't I have them . . . my way? Perhaps a little darker. Perhaps

with a little of the shiny-new rubbed off and a little
more grimy, ten-o'clock-news reality rubbed on. Perhaps someone (maybe someone like me . . . or you)
really will get that damn rabbit before he leaves chocolate and hard-boiled eggs all over my house . . .
and yours.

Oh, my. Now that's a nice image, isn't it?

And it must be a nice image, or at least a pretty
decent basis for an anthology, because when I started
asking people if they were interested in writing a
horror or dark fantasy or supernatural story for this
book, they responded with something I could only
describe as joy. One writer, who shall remain safely
anonymous, asked how *many* holidays he could
haunt. I said all of them. All but me.

What's that, you say? Is there a holiday, perhaps,
that I *do* like? Well, now that you mention it, yes,
there is. I like Halloween. That's the kind of holiday
I can support without reservation—the one time of
year when it's perfectly legit to scare the hell out of
someone. Especially kids. (In my house, Halloween
lasts pretty much all year. A few weeks ago, I convinced my six-year-old daughter that she had a great
grandfather who was a vampire. His name? Nos Fer-
atu. Man, was my wife mad.)

Since plenty has been written about Halloween,
and there've been more than enough anthologies
dedicated to the subject, and I happen to like that
holiday just the way it is, the only rule the writers
had was to stay away from Halloween. I did get one
story involving Samhain, "Judgment" by Kerrie
Hughes, which isn't quite the same thing, but all the
others aren't even close. Inside these pages, you'll
find stories about holidays ranging from Columbus
Day to birthdays to Christmas. Some involve social

holidays, some political, some cultural; some of the stories are sad, a couple are humorous, but all do exactly what I'd hoped. Add a little twist to the idea of every holiday being a happy one.

So, with that out of the way, let me invite you to read this book—not in a single sitting, but rather, throughout the year.

If you're turning thirty-something and feeling a bit down, you might try Julie Czerneda's "Birthday Jitters."

If Thanksgiving is just around the corner, you should definitely give "For These Things I Am Truly Thankful" by David Niall Wilson a read before you head out to buy your groceries.

If you're a bit irate that the bank has chosen to close on Columbus Day, you might relax with Dan Hoyt's "New World's Brave."

Whatever the occasion, whatever the reason, whatever the season . . . I hope you find that these stories, and all the others included, offer you a brief respite from the continued cries of desperate retailers and demanding family members. You might even get an idea or two for how to deal with them next year.

From all of us, to all of you, please let us wish you the *happiest of holidays*.

FOR THESE THINGS I AM TRULY THANKFUL

by David Niall Wilson

*David Niall Wilson has been writing and publishing hor-
ror, dark fantasy, and science fiction since the mid-
eighties. His novels include the Grails Covenant Trilogy,
Star Trek Voyager: Chrysalis, Except You Go Through
Shadow, This is My Blood, and the upcoming Dark Ages
Vampire clan novel Lasombra. He has over one hundred
short stories published in two collections and various anthologies and magazines. David lives and loves with Patricia Lee
Macomber in the historic William R. White House in Hert-
ford, North Carolina, with their children, Billy and Stephanie,
occasionally his boys Zach and Zane, four psychotic cats, a
dwarf bunny who continues to belie his "dwarfness," a pit
bull named Elvis and a fish named Doofish.*

IT WAS LATE, and the hum of the neon sign outside the coffee shop was the only sound. Adam
didn't know why he stopped. Coffee was the stated
purpose, but really, after eighteen hours and a pot
and a half, it wasn't likely to help much.

Adam's stomach ached with hunger, but he focused on coffee. The stench of grease from the
kitchen in the back helped push his appetite aside.

It would be daylight soon, and he had to decide whether he needed to do some more thinking, or less. Not that the images crowding his head left much room for debate.

The place was alight with fluorescence. Grimy white tubes of energized gas lit the grill, the counter, and its row of stools. White metal ceiling lights lit every booth.

Adam hesitated. There was a blonde woman, forty-ish, her hair pulled back but escaping in frazzled ringlets over the scarf that held it, seated near the center of the counter. No one else was present except the thin, dark-haired kid running the grill and the register. He wasn't cooking at the moment. Eyes downcast, the woman nursed a cup of coffee and smoked quietly.

Adam moved to the counter and took a seat several stools away from the woman, but not at the end. He didn't want to seem rude, just needed to think. In the corner, a twenty-inch television with a grainy picture flickered. News. Nothing good there, never was. For the moment, Adam ignored it, but the glow of the screen brought back images of his computer monitor, and that was a memory lane he wasn't ready to stroll down just yet.

The dark-haired kid moved closer. He had a dirty towel over one arm, and he watched Adam as if he'd interrupted the Superbowl. The boy didn't offer to get anything, just stared and waited.

"Coffee," Adam said. "Black."

The boy turned away, and Adam turned his attention to his hands. He didn't want to watch the news. He didn't want to think about his computer, or the words he'd read on the screen so few hours before.

He wanted it all to go away. He wanted sleep. He wanted to order a cheeseburger but couldn't bring himself to eat.

The coffee slid in front of him with no perfunctory conversation and Adam dropped two dollars on the counter without glancing up. He didn't feel like talking. The volume on the television was low enough that he could barely hear the hum of voices. It was irritating, but he ignored it.

It had started so simply. He'd been seated in his cubicle, whiling away an idle hour on the computer, surfing for something interesting. Adam thought he might be a writer one day, so he cruised, now and again, for author's sites. Earlier that afternoon, he'd found one. The site was the journal of a disgruntled ex-grocery store employee. It was called Food Hell, and Adam had found himself morbidly fascinated from the first sentence.

"Even though it's not important, my name is Christopher."

It wasn't the story of the job that had made the words stick with Adam, it was the information embedded between the lines. It was the image that would not fade of his local grocery store as some surreal, otherwordly place with secrets no one who eats grocery store food should know. It was the stacking of outdated food near the front. It was the changing of labels in the back. It was wondering what that stock boy you pissed off might have done to your product before delivering it to you in aisle ten with a smirk.

It was the girl behind the deli counter who sold pornographic pictures of herself at work and talked loudly about the symptoms of her STD.

It was the way they shifted the lighting to hide wilted vegetables and sprayed water on them to glitter by day.

Adam had not slept. It was Tuesday. He had one day until Thanksgiving and thankfully he'd taken the next couple of days off from work. He wasn't sure he could have coped with the office after what he'd read. Adam worked for an accounting firm, and they handled the accounts for most of the local grocery chains. The logos and names, invoices and ledgers would all draw his thoughts back to that damned computer screen, and he didn't want to read anymore. He also didn't want to eat.

Behind his counter, the young grill cook polished the formica with a stained towel and stared at the fuzzy television screen. The blonde continued to stare at her own hands, and to smoke.

Jesus. Was it possible to have a smoking area in a place this small? Was it legal? Adam smoked, so it was a moot point as far as he was concerned, but still, there was something about the bobbing ash on the end of the woman's cigarette that was morbidly fascinating. She was shaking, or trembling. Maybe crying. Adam couldn't be certain from where he sat, and the kid behind the counter obviously didn't give a damn. There was a trail of ashes on the counter in front of her, not quite reaching the ashtray most of the time, and the fan on the ceiling dispersed the detritus of her tension to the air.

Adam turned his attention back to his coffee. Thanksgiving dinner was at Gail's parents' house. He wouldn't see her until the dinner. She worked nights and was taking extra time to prepare for December midterm exams during the day. It had been nearly a week and they planned to stretch the dinner into the weekend and unwind together. Right at that moment, if Adam had unwound, he'd have spun out like a top and dug a rut in the floor.

He was supposed to bring the potato salad. That was his concern. Clean clothes, be on time, potato salad. His hand trembled and the coffee cup shook. He'd intended to buy the potato salad at the deli, then carry it home, repackage it neatly, and let them all pretend they thought he'd made it. Now he wasn't so sure.

Christopher, the writer on the Internet, hadn't been specific about which grocery he'd worked in. The piece had the odd quality of bending one's mind to the contours of their own world. Somehow, Adam knew it was the superstore down the street from his condo that was in question. It had to be. He'd seen the girl behind the deli counter, and he'd imagined her. . . .

Adam shook his head to clear that thought. Suddenly, the image he'd always carried of that young girl, winking at him, was tainted. He could imagine that he'd seen sores at the edges of her lips. He could see a sort of rheumy, yellowish tint in the whites of her eyes. He remembered her veins standing out oddly, or had that been the lighting? What could they do with lighting to hide that?

The volume on the television set suddenly increased. Adam snapped from his thoughts to the present and turned, lifting his coffee and taking a long gulp. There was a man on screen, seated behind a desk. He wore all white and was presented against a white-walled background. Framed certificates lined those walls.

The man was talking about smoking. The boy behind the counter was staring pointedly at the blonde woman, who, despite the increased volume of the television, and the message it preached, had not looked up from her untouched coffee, or her cigarettes. When Adam glanced at her, he saw she'd tapped another from the pack, though its predecessor still glowed red with each puff.

As he watched her, words seeped into Adam's subconscious. Carcinogens. Asbestos. Pesticide. Sweepings off the floor of cigarette factories and traces of so many things it boggled the mind. Adam slowly swiveled his gaze back to the screen. The man behind the desk was gone. In his place a colored diagram pulsed. Dark, black masses seeped through what appeared to be a throat passage and human lungs.

The blonde's smoke drifted up toward the fan, past the television screen. The smoke on the screen flowed down. Hers flowed up. Adam's throat constricted. His coffee was forgotten. He imagined the taste of insecticide, too-recently sprayed on tobacco leaves and never cleaned away. He imagined the factory where the cigarettes were rolled, huge conveyor belts, dust in the air—germs. Coughing, diseased workers, fighting to make it through the day, oblivious to the miasma of poison they layered on each flat sheet of paper, each pinch of tobacco.

Adam couldn't breathe. He rose, nearly overturning the table near him. The boy behind the counter stared at him, and even the blonde broke eye contact with her hands to glance in his direction. Adam held one hand to his throat. His eyes watered, though he couldn't be certain which of the myriad poisons in the air was causing it. The room wavered, but he caught himself against the wall, closed his yes, and tucked his chin, breathing as much as possible through the filter of the soft cotton of his collar. He had to get out.

Without a word—ushered through the door by the boy's voice calling out, "You crazy, man?"—Adam rushed into the street, gripping his shirt collar and nearly tearing the fabric in his efforts to cover mouth and nose. The air outside was clean and crisp. The stars had faded, and the faint orange light of dawn backlit the skyline. Adam stood, shivering, coated in sweat. It wasn't cold, but he shook like a scared rabbit.

He leaned over to placed his hands on his knees for support as he caught his breath, and the motion crinkled the cellophane wrapper of the Marlboros in his pocket. His breath stopped for a beat, then he exhaled, righting himself and clawing at the pocket of his shirt. The material gave way with a loud rip and he whipped his hand out, sending the cigarette pack twisting and turning through the air. It fell with a soft plop in the gutter, the cellophane catching in the light breeze and waving gently.

Adam turned away and staggered down the street. He wasn't far from home. There was the park to cross, and then a quick cut over from Forty-second Street. He held his head low and as he went, his steps quickened. The surreality of the coffee shop faded, and reality encroached with cold fingers of pain tugging the edges of his mind over the brink into a full-fledged migraine. What was wrong with him?

He knew he had to sleep. One way or another, he had to get his act together before Thursday. Clean clothes, on time, potato salad—the mantra of his future.

The park was deep in morning shadows. There was something strange in that, as if the shadows that had stretched out from trees and benches in the evening were retreating, drawing in on themselves in defeat. It was comforting, and Adam's breath came easier. He told himself that he was just tired. He told himself he'd worked too long, too hard, and that these were symptoms.

Halfway through the park, he heard approaching footsteps. It was still pretty dark, and though he wasn't exactly in Central Park, Adam had enough sense not to discount trouble. He sped up. The steps behind him were steady and rhythmic, coming closer with each stride. Two choices: run, or don't. Wait and see who it is, deal with it when they catch up, or run and hope he could outdistance them.

Adam decided and took off with a lurch. He wasn't athletically inclined. The last time he'd run more than a block had been to catch a city bus, and that had nearly sent him into cardiac arrest. Still, he ran. He felt the flat, hard heels of his shoes slapping the pavement and pounding the soles of his feet. They weren't made for this, and he knew his feet would pay the price when all was said and done. The sound of his own breathing, and the leather slap of his shoes had drowned out the pursuing footsteps, so he couldn't tell how close they were. Could be right behind him, reaching out to snag the back of his jacket. Could have turned off and taken another route through the park. Could be stalking him, eyes narrowed and concentrated, waiting for the right moment to tackle and pound, stabbing him for the meager contents of his wallet and the Bulova watch on his wrist.

Adam glanced over his shoulder. At first he saw

nothing, then, turning the corner behind him, almost at his heels, he saw her. It was a young woman, dark hair pulled back in a ponytail, jogging. He cursed his own stupidity and turned back to the trail. Too late. His leg caught a fallen branch and the world tilted. His hands caught the earth, breaking the fall, skin peeling back in long scrapes across his palms. His knee hit painfully, and he skidded about a foot in the soft grass. Behind him, the footstep's sped, and he heard a voice calling to him.

"Hey, you all right?"

He barely heard the words. To the side of the trail, directly in front of him, an overflowing trash barrel had caught his eye. Food wrappers, beer cans, bottles and food scraps overran the rim and littered the earth. The same earth he was pressed closely into. The same earth that filled the scrapes on his palms. Adam tried to answer. He tried to lift himself, but could not bring himself to touch the ground.

How long had the trash been there? What was in it? Where had it come from? Other images intruded. Couples strolling through the park, arm in arm, sharing fluids. Pets, wild animals, strays, urinating on the ground, tromping it in with their feet, spreading it around. Long muzzles tearing at the trash, mixing it with their own saliva and dribbling it across the ground. Adam rolled over convulsively, nearly tripping the young woman who stood, staring at him in alternating concern for him, and for herself. His eyes were wide, wild and void of coherent thought. His body was shaking, and he waved his hands in the air as if trying to warn something away, or rid himself of something. Or fly.

With an effort he wouldn't have believed possible if it had been suggested to him, Adam wrenched his body from the ground without the use of his hands, and without a word, fled across the park. The young woman stared after him, shaking her head.

The water steamed and streamed from the showerhead, and Adam scrubbed. The nerves in his hands screamed each time the scalding water or the strong soap reached too far into the scrapes in his pals. His skin was pink from friction, but he couldn't stop. He could still see that trash barrel, could feel the odd burning in his palms. He could feel poisons and chemicals leaking into his system. He knew he was acting crazy, but still, he wasn't ready to stop.

Eventually, the water ran cold. Adam shut the valve and stood in the center of his tub, staring through the water-streaked curtain, its pastel flower design fogged by steam. He reached for the curtain, then he stopped. Was that a smudge of something dark, running down the curtain? Had he only shifted the filth to the plastic, where it could reenter when he tried to leave the tub. His arm jerked back, and he stood, naked and shivering, wet and wide-eyed.

Carefully, with the back of one fingernail, he brushed the top edge of one ring to the side. He worked it over slowly, being careful to make no contact with the offending curtain. He could hose it down later, scrub it with a brush—maybe toss it in the washer. Right now all that mattered was getting out, getting dressed, and trying to sort out the maddening rush of thoughts that suddenly crowded his mind.

"It will pass," he told himself. His hunger had grown so familiar he hardly noticed. He wasn't hungry in the sense that he wanted food to pass his lips, only in that his body was protesting the lack of fuel.

He was weak, and just the effort of stumbling from the bathroom to his bedroom for clothes nearly made him faint.

Despite all of this, he was focused on Thursday. If he could make it into a home where they cared about him, to a room where Gail would be waiting with open arms and a ready ear, he could do anything. He could pull it all back together. Maybe he could even eat, if he didn't ask where the turkey had come from. If he didn't think about the machinery that processed the wine, or the workers on assembly lines, some sick, some bored, some just clumsy. If he didn't think about how insects and vermin crowded around any place there was food.

If he didn't think at all—he could eat.

Adam dressed slowly. He coated his skin carefully, two layers of socks, long pants, long-sleeved shirt. Pants tucked into lace-up boots. No time to worry over what might be inside the material, or growing in the sweat-soaked interior of the boots themselves. There was only so much he could do to protect himself, but he was determined not to repeat the scene in the park. He had to go out, and he had to get potato salad, and he had to get back to his apartment. He had no one to call, and though he might have called to have the potato salad delivered, the thought of what an inconvenienced, underpaid grocery employee might do with food he or she was delivering was enough to eliminate this as a possible course of action.

He had to go out. Already he'd wasted his day. No sleep, and it was nearing six o'clock in the afternoon. An entire morning peeling away and destroying clothing, scrubbing and scrubbing his skin, his hair and his hands, scrubbing the floor where he'd entered the apartment, where he'd walked and touched. Pulling suspected foods from his refrigerator and running them, one after the other, down the drain, followed by bleach and powdered cleanser and more hot water. Then scrubbing his tortured hands again. The palms were raw, but he was convinced, for the moment, that they were clean.

He'd had a bad moment at the sink, remembering the plumber who'd fixed the gooseneck beneath the cabinet a month before. The man had been filthy, and his tools had reeked of grease and things better left unnamed. This had led to thoughts of the pipes themselves, which led to the sewers, and to the water company, and to a thousand employees, each with their own problems, their own hatreds, their own schemes, and all of this contributing to the final outcome—the water that flowed through the pipes, put together piece by piece by the same hands that pieced together the output of the toilet. Filtered miles away, the water flowed through aged pipes, collecting minerals and filth, to reach the spigot where he ran it hopefully over his dirty hands.

Somehow, he'd gotten past this. There had to be limits. If he couldn't use the water, he couldn't wash his hands. He *had* to wash his hands, and he couldn't use straight bleach, no matter how appealing that was, because in the end, the bleach itself was poison. He developed it into a mantra. The water is fine. I've used the water all my life. I've been drinking the water all my life. I've bathed in the water, been swimming in the water, some science teacher in a long forgotten classroom had told him he was 98% water himself. He had to trust something, he would trust the water. For now. There was bottled water. There were filters.

Now he had to go out.

In the odd, off-kilter universe he'd suddenly dropped into, the only important thing was potato salad, and the only way to get that potato salad was to buy it. Adam had the culinary skills of the long-term bachelor. He had microwave experience, and boiled a really mean pot of water. Potato salad was beyond him. He knew the grocery four blocks away on Taft was open 24 hours. All he had to do was stand, make his way out to door and down the street, and make his purchase.

With vague ideas of coming back to scour a Tupperware container, where he could air-seal his purchase, Adam slipped out into the late afternoon streets.

Excerpt from FOOD HELL—Internet Journal
"At eleven o'clock is when the bright, daylight grocery changes to full fledged 'food hell.' The lights in the store that are still lit are dimmer, and about ¼ of all the lights in the store shut off. The store never closes, but they apparently are too cheap to run the lighting 100% all evening. When it happens, I feel like I've just come down from some sort of drug. (Or just took one for that matter . . .) Everything turns a shade darker, and that bag of Doritos doesn't shine like it did an hour before. Everything looks like it's been bronzed. I imagine that this is what a goldfish sees when someone pisses in its tank."

Five and a half hours after he left home, Adam was still standing outside the front doors of the grocery store. He'd made five assaults on the interior, each time making it a little closer, but never quite bringing himself to enter. He felt as though he was being watched, and, after hovering outside the building for as long as he had, he probably was. He'd been over it all in his head a thousand times.

He didn't need to walk the aisles. He didn't need to think about the history of each can as it moved from field to factory, to cannery, to trucks and greasy, disgruntled drivers, who would deliver entire pallets to even more disgruntled grocery workers, who would do whatever they could to take their grievances out on the food before it left the building. He didn't have to do that.

He could enter at the right side of the front doors. The deli case was just to the right, past the produce. If he made it through there, carefully filtering the air near the fruit and vegetables by breathing through his outer layer shirt to avoid any lingering pesticides being washed away in the constant sprinkle of water. Water he would not think about because you had to trust something, and he had already decided he would trust water. If he could do that, he could be at the freezer racks, where most of the things he feared would surely be dormant in the frozen depths of the showcases. He could pick out a large tub of potato salad, make his way to the checkout and through, and get home. He knew he could do it. He'd mentally rehearsed every step.

At 11:12 PM, he finally worked up the nerve, possibly because the hunger was robbing the last of his failing strength, and he stepped through the front doors. He waited for the moment when a customer slipped out, and he could get through without touching the handles, or the glass. He had gloves in his pockets, but it wasn't cold outside, and he didn't want to attract attention by wearing them. He'd wanted rubber gloves.

Adam's hands shook, and he jammed them into his pockets, slipping to the right of the shopping carts and into the store proper. The produce racks loomed, and he gritted his teeth. It was just like the journal had said. The overhead fluorescents were dim, and if you counted along the length of the roof, every fourth or fifth light was out completely. The vegetables had a set of lights directed straight down on them, but even these seemed dim. It gave the rows of perfectly aligned grapes and oranges an otherworldly glow. To Adam, it seemed as if they were alive with some sort of pulsing light. He averted his gaze, tucked his nose down, and breathed through the cotton of his shirt. Another twenty feet, and he'd be at the deli counter, another five minutes, and he could be outside and on his way home.

He stepped past the bananas and a rack of prepre-pared salads, sealed in plastic. He wondered, briefly, who had sealed them. Where had they been "freshly made" and by whom? Under what conditions? Did the person preparing them have a good day? Did they cut themselves while chopping? Did any of their blood seep into the lettuce, or mix with the tomato juice?

He stopped, closed his eyes, breathed deeply, and turned to the deli. There was a girl working near the back of that section, shuffling from table to table with white-wrapped meat packages. The scent of that afternoon's fried chicken, cooked so long under heat lamps that it resembled jerky more than dinner, permeated the air. A line of ready-to-buy cakes proclaimed "Happy Thanksgiving" and sported any number of variations on the theme of pumpkins, turkeys, and autumn leaves.

He scanned the racks quickly. There were a number of presealed tubs near the center. Baked Beans. Pasta Salad. Three Bean Salad. He looked again, making his way quickly to the end of the case, then back even more quickly. Nothing. No potato salad.

Around the corner, he knew, waited the large vats of food from which these containers were filled. There would be stainless steel bins filled with friend chicken, steamed vegetables, baked beans and, of course, potato salad. He turned quickly, gazing down the aisle at the self-serve salad bar. It had been closed for the night. The stainless steel glimmered in the dim light, empty. With a soft moan that he did his best to stifle, Adam slipped around the counter and stared down through the smudged, greasy glass.

The potato salad was bright mustard yellow. He knew this. Splotches of white showed where the potatoes had been sliced and blended in. Adam could almost taste it, and this caused a watering in his mouth and racked his frame with a series of deep shivers. He fought through the dual waves of hunger and nausea and stepped a little closer to the counter. Raising his eyes, he caught the girl behind the counter staring at him oddly. He tried to smile, failed, and stood there, waiting for her to speak.

For a moment it seemed she'd got back to what she was doing and ignore him, but at last she turned and stepped closer.

"Can I help you?" she asked.

Adam didn't answer. He searched her face. He knew about herpes, knew about all sorts of STDs he'd been taught about in school. He scanned her lips for sores. He watched as the low-wattage lights shifted yellowly across what should have been the whites of her eyes. Or were they really yellow? He glanced at her hands, but they seemed clean enough, wrapped in a clear layer of latex. But what had the gloves touched? What sort of meat had she handled, and when? How long would the fluids from that afternoon's chicken take to sicken and fester?

"I . . ." He started to speak, clamped his mouth shut, biting his tongue painfully and jerking at the pain.

"Are you all right?" she asked, stepping back a bit from the counter. "If you're sick, you shouldn't lean too close to the food. . . ."

She didn't seem to know how to handle the situation, and that is probably what saved Adam from having security called.

"Potato salad," he whispered. She stared at him blankly, obviously not hearing him, and he repeated it, louder and with as much force as he could muster. "Potato salad. I need . . . potato salad."

She stared at him a moment longer. He was watching her again, analyzing each movement. Disease was a tricky thing, and you could not be too sure. She reached for the large spoon stuck like a blade into the mass of potatoes and mustard.

"How much?" she asked.

Adam glanced at the price, eyes wild. Questions, more questions, and why should she ask him how much? The price was clearly marked and . . .

He stopped. He breathed. "One quart," he said simply. To himself, he added, *Jesus, are you losing your mind?*

The girl quickly grabbed an empty tub from the top of the pile beside her and began scooping the potato salad in quickly. She obviously figured that her best bet to be rid of him was to get his food prepared as quickly as possible. Adam watched carefully for the spoon to touch any other surface, for her to touch the food with her gloved fingers, or run them around the inner rim of the tub. She did not. It was going to be okay. In moments, the seal was in place, properly burped, and she was sliding it across the countertop to him. On top of the tub she marked the price, $4.58, in black magic marker. Adam nearly panicked, then realized the chemicals could not seep through the plastic tub. He could remove the lid with no danger.

He pulled the gloves from his pocket, put them on carefully, and reached for the tub. All the while, she watched him nervously. He watched her just as closely. She was a pretty girl, late teens. She wore a touch of makeup, perhaps a bit more than the job demanded? She was well-built, but had a sort of worn, frazzled look. A look that Adam loosely associated with street people. Prostitutes. Dancers in late-night sleazebag bars. He wished he could remember the name of the food in the journal. It was on the tip of his tongue, and though her name tag clearly read "Tina," he knew it wasn't the real name that mattered. It was the nickname, the name the other store employees gave her behind her back. The name earned by the flaunting of disease and the peddling of naked self-photographs. He watched, her, and suddenly, he knew. It was her. It was this store. It had to be this store, and this girl, and he couldn't eat that potato salad. He wanted to have children. He and Gail had plans, and this—this tramp—this rotted, diseased—thing—would not prevent that with a dose of chlamydia.

"Could you put that in a bag, with a photo?" he

blurted suddenly. He was angry, so suddenly angry that the vein just over his eye was pulsing, and he could feel it, could feel the hot blood coursing through in short heavy beats.

"Excuse me?" she said, stepping back a bit farther.

"A photo," he repeated. "You know what I mean. The ones you sell, the *good* ones. I like lots of lace." He was leaning closer now. His hand gripped the tub of potato poison tightly. "I like it if I can see the sores. You do have sores, don't you? All over, I bet. I would like a photo of you, naked and oozing, to show the manager. To show the world."

"You're crazy," she whispered. Then she screamed.

Adam whirled. He still gripped the tub of potato salad in one gloved hand. The small scattering of people still shopping at the hour turned to gape at him, and at the girl, screaming behind the counter. One aisle over, a young man in a black T-shirt with his hair spiked at odd angles and sporting a blue store badge had pushed his pallet truck out of the way and was coming at a run. From the manager's office, a metallic voice crackled.

"Alpha twenty—Deli."

Alpha twenty? Something from the journal itched at his mind, but Adam had no time for it. They were converging on him now, several young men in blue work shirts, the spike-haired kid with the name tag, and at the far end of the aisle, he saw a fat old man in a gray security uniform round the corner. The guy had one hand resting on something at his belt—a nightstick? A gun?

The doors might as well have been a million miles away. Adam tried to run, but his legs ignored him until the first of the young men was within about ten feet.

"Now, take it easy," the kid said, hands held out in front of him. His jeans were filthy, covered in so many stains and foods that Adam was sure they were swimming around the boy's legs, alive with filth.

Adam moved. He lurched to his left, toward the front doors, clutching the fouled potato salad to his chest like a football, praying it wouldn't pop open. The boy made no move to stop him, and he breathed a little more easily. Then he saw why. Two others had blocked his way, and from behind him, heavy footsteps approached. Wheezing, heavy breath—diseased breath, he thought.

He glanced over his shoulder. The security guard was drawing near with surprising swiftness. He had one hand wrapped tightly around the handle of a slick, black nightstick hanging from a loop on his belt.

"Just . . ." the man was laboring with each breath, obviously unused to physical exertion. "Just a minute there," he wheezed. "You just stop where you are."

Adam turned, saw the two young baggers closing in on him from the front, and did the only thing that came to his mind. He drew back one arm and launched the potato salad at the guard. It was a good shot, not too low to do any good, or high enough to hit the face. It struck the older man's chest, bursting open in a viscous, yellow explosion. The man started back, caught one foot in the slick salad, and went over backward. Hard.

Adam turned to the exit, slipped down the length of a fruit rack, and made a dash for the door. He might have made it, but the kid from the back, the one with the spiked hair, launched a running tackle that brought him down just inside the door. Adam felt the greasy, filthy floor against his cheek and wrenched around, trying to get away from it, trying to keep his clothing between himself and any surface. His shoulder was ablaze with pain, dislocated, or broken, but he couldn't worry about that. He had to move.

Hands grabbed him roughly from behind. Many hands. Filthy hands. He felt something cold encircling his wrist and yanked to free himself, but the pain in his shoulder drew a scream of agony. He tried to speak, tried to breathe, but then, he saw their faces, looming so close, thought about their breath—about where those lips and teeth had been—the air above him suddenly aswarm with germs and bacteria, a whirling cloud that dragged his mind, thankfully, into darkness.

The steady click click of heels on cement drew nearer, and Adam listened in alarm. His arms were secured tightly by the sleeves of the straitjacket. His shoulder had been set back in place, but it throbbed, and even the heavy dose of painkiller they'd forced down his throat could only dull the pain. The sun streamed through a window down the hall, but Adam's cell was dark. He eyed each shadowy corner warily. Who had been in this cell? What diseases might they have had? Who cleaned it?

They had offered him a phone call, but how could he call anyone? The phone had been used by whores, by drug addicts, by filthy, crawling, diseased men and women, crawling with God knew what. How could he bring such a thing so close to his own lips?

The steps drew abreast of his cell door, and a

round, red face appeared from the gloom, pig-close eyes staring at Adam from beneath the brim of a guard's hat.

"You okay in there?" the man asked.

Adam said nothing. It was a stupid question, and he didn't want to encourage more. He had to get out of this place.

"Heard you had you some trouble over 't the grocery," the man continued, stepping closer. He was fat, and his voice was nasal. Everything about him made Adam think of pigs.

"I been to that place," the guard chuckled. "Been there plenty. You get out, you go back and check out that chick at the deli. The man was leering now, and Adam was afraid he'd begin to touch himself, right there. "That girl," the guard continued, "Tina? She's hot. Sells pictures, too, if you get to know her. I work extra hours as a security guard, been in the freezer with her a couple of times, you know what I mean?"

Adam began to squirm. He imagined the filth crawling over the fat guard's body. Imagined the diseased blood flowing so close—only a filthy layer of skin between them. The jacket was too tight, and he could not move. With a growl, Adam smacked his head into the wall. It was heavily padded with canvas and matting, but the pain felt good. It cleared the images of cold sores, rimming the guard's mouth. It cleared the image of the girl, Tina, and her sore-crossed skin and yellow eyes.

"Hey," the guard called out. "Hey, now . . . you stop that!"

Adam did not. He pounded, and he pounded as the world faded to gray. The guard had opened the door, and Adam nearly went wild, trying to pull into the corner, away from the guard, away from his touch. He stopped pounding his head and glared up at the man, drawing his legs in to kick out. Anything to escape. He was shaking as the guard retreated.

"I'm gonna go get someone," the man muttered. "Crazy as a squirrel at a nut farm. Damned psychos anyway."

The footsteps receded, then stopped. Adam kept his eyes closed. He pressed his lips together, determined to wait until the air had cleared as much as possible before breathing. He thought, for just a moment, of Gail, and the potato salad, but he couldn't worry about that now. He had to get out.

The guard's voice floated back a last time.

"Hey, fella," he said. "I almost forgot. It's Thursday. Happy Thanksgiving."

As the footsteps receded and the cell fell silent, Adam began to crash his head into the wall once more, praying the padding had been washed. Wondering who had sewn it in place, how many others had touched it, where the jail bought its food and who prepared it. Wanting to eat, and certain he could not. Ever. Pain exploded in his head, again and again, wiping the images away. For this, he was truly thankful.

With thanks to Adam Greene for Food Hell.

JEWELS IN THE DUST

by Peter Crowther

Author, editor, critic/essayist and now, with the award-winning PS imprint, publisher, Pete Crowther has produced seventeen anthologies, almost one hundred short stories and novellas (two of which have been adapted for British TV), plus Escardy Gap (written in collaboration with James Lovegrove) and Darkness, Darkness: Forever Twilight Book One, the first in a projected cycle of short SF/horror novels. He's currently working on the second installment, plus a mainstream novel, a couple of anthologies, several new PS titles and another TV project.

> *Dear, beauteous death! the jewel of the just,*
> *Shining nowhere but in the dark;*
> *What mysteries do lie beyond thy dust,*
> *Could man outlook that mark!*
> From *Silex Scintillans: "They are all gone"*
> —Henry Vaughan (1622–1695)

ABIGAIL RUTHERFORD SWEPT into the room in a blaze of maroon cotton and myriad wafts of scarves whose designs dwarfed even the ambitious creations of Jackson Pollack—comparatively pedestrian efforts as far as Abigail would have it—and whose colors would have rivaled even Joseph's fabled coat.

"Today's the day!" she announced with a bravura wave of an arm that was skinny and wattled, the fingers of the hand at the end slender enough to pick locks, pushing the sweet scent of lavender before her like a summer tide.

Tommy looked up from the comic book spread out between his elbows on the floor, the gaudily-colored pages a mystery of shape and form and secret actions in nighttime cities, strangely-garbed and muscular heroes braving death—and worse!—as they swung between concrete towers and over the glittering streets far far below. "Really?" he asked, pulling himself to a kneeling position.

"Really!" Abigail confirmed.

"Yay!" said Tommy.

He leaped to his feet and did a little skip and jump around the comic book.

"Careful," Marianne Rutherford cautioned her son with a big smile. "You'll be wanting another copy of that magazine if you mess up the pages." She turned to her mother-in-law and tilted her head to one side as she always did when she was offering a change of mind. "Are you sure, Abby? I mean, *really* sure that today's the day? It's just Saturday—a fine May Saturday I grant you, but just another Saturday."

Abigail did a twirl and burst into a fit of coughing which soon spread into laughter. "As sure. As I'll. Ever be," she said, pausing for breaths between each point. She leaned against the wall, smiling at her grandson with thin lips that carried a swipe of lipstick, cheeks that bore the trace of hastily-applied pink-colored powder, and eyes that carried the sky in them, complete with cotton-candy clouds. "And it's not. Just another. Saturday. It's Derby Day."

"Derby Day!" young Tommy exclaimed, his face a glade of smiles.

"That's right," Abigail said, her voice not quite able to match the volume of her grandson's. "So, scoot, young fella," she added, ignoring the quizzical look on her daughter-in-law's face. She clapped her hands as though shooing errant cats busy chewing the plants in her beloved garden, the three rings—engagement, wedding and eternity—giving out the faintest *clink* before settling once more.

"Make haste!" she urged.

"Bring sodas, bring potato chips," she advised.

"Run and jump and greet the day!" she instructed.

Tommy disappeared in a flash, the swinging to and fro of the room door on a steadily decreasing fulcrum the only sign that he had ever been there at all. That and the sound of small feet pounding up the stairs and a small voice calling out to the gods of childhood and eternal summer.

Marianne looked across at the window.

It was still early outside—early in big-wide-world terms, where activities among the windblown fields and hedgerows commenced long before they did inside the house. Everything was new out there, as though each thing—every glimmering ray of sunlight and every tiny drop of dew—were a one-off, a never-to-be-repeated infinitesimally small theatrical performance. New and only ever *now*.

Inside the house, it was different.

Here, within the labyrinth of walls and windows that was the home they all shared, everything was familiar: radio news shows that forever reminded lis-

teners of the time and what the weather was going
to be like, and the sound of bacon frying and Mister
Coffee percolating, each mingling with calls for missing neckties, socks, and comic books, and all of them
forever underpinned by the soft susurrant hum put
out by the old amalgam of wooden joists and nailed-
on clapboard stretching itself to meet the onslaught
of another day. Every one of them a repeat performance. Like scenes on the VCR, rewound and replayed forever without deviation.

Time stolen rather than spent.

Time waiting to die.

To Marianne Rutherford, the world outside looked
momentarily immense, unpredictable, and somehow
achingly wonderful, its sound signatures harder to
place, complex rhythms and discordant refrains.

A haven.

A release.

An escape.

Marianne turned around and mentally shook off
the feeling of cramp unfolding in her stomach as she
took in the full creative excess of Abigail's outfit.
"That's quite a combination," she said, a mischievous
grin on her face as she stood up and planted a kiss
on her mother-in-law's cheek. "One thing's for sure:
we're not likely to lose you." She took hold of Abigail's shoulders and held her at arm's length. "My,
oh, my, don't you look the bee's knees!"

Abigail shuddered, her breath coming hoarse and
sounding wheezing, deep down inside her body.
"The bees' knees. And the cat's PJs." She returned
the smile and affected a small slap on Abigail's arm.
"Got to. Look my. Best. On Derby Day," she said
between gulps of air. "For Jack."

Abigail fought off the frown that threatened to engulf her face. "Right," she said. "For Jack. On Derby Day."

Marianne felt Abigail's bony shoulders stiffen as she turned her back around again, immediately cursing herself when she saw Abby wince and try to cover it up.

In truth, the dress hung awkwardly from Abigail's scrawny frame. It fell all the way to her ankles— ankles puffed up with water from the steroids. Marianne recalled those previous occasions when the dress came out—"red letter days," was how Abby referred to them, by virtue of the fact that the dress was the last present from her beloved Jack—and how, in those suddenly seemingly distant days of another life, the dress extended only to just below Abigail's knees. Then the garment itself had seemed to be alive and proud, like a peacock unfurling its tail feathers; now it looked equally as tired and spent as its owner.

"Well," she said, backing Abby gently to a chair, "I think you look wonderful and I'm sure Bill is going to think so, too."

Bill came into the room with a big grin on his face. To a degree, it managed to cover the darkness below his eyes. "You gonna make some sandwiches, honey? It's the Big Day."

Marianne gave her husband a mock salute. "Yeah, Mom already told us. Derby Day," she said, with just the slightest of upward movements of her eyebrows. There had been so many Big Days this seven or eight months, as the weeks had fallen from the calendar at almost the same rate that the pounds had fallen from Abigail Rutherford's once-ample frame.

Thanksgiving had been the first one, when Abigail had spent the full day out in the garden, taking in

the fall air as she waited to be called to join her
beloved Jack. But that night, as they all sat down to
one of Marianne's turkey dinners, the table resplendent with sweet potatoes and corn on the cob, sausages rolled in strips of bacon, bowls of peas with
knobs of butter melting over them like flower heads,
Abigail had announced that she didn't think today
was going to be the Big Day after all. Patting her
son's arm, she said, "But I'm guessing it'll be soon,"
her sentences full and flowing, before the tumor
eventually took away her breath.

Then Christmas Eve and Christmas Day followed,
with New Year's Eve and New Year's Day itself coming on hot behind them. And January saw Martin
Luther King's birthday and even Martin Luther King
Junior Day . . . but still Abigail made it through to
midnight, her carefully chosen clothes returned to the
wardrobe in the small room she occupied in her
son's house.

Groundhog Day came and went and, with it,
drifted Lincoln's Birthday and Valentine's Day—a
particularly fitting one for her and Jack to be re-
united, Abigail had thought. By now, the chemo had
taken a toll and she was increasingly tired.

Then Presidents' Day, and Washington's Birthday—"All of them great men," Abigail had proclaimed to Bill, "just like your father. And I reckon
that today. Will definitely be. The day he calls for
me to join him."

But it hadn't been. Nor had the day that Daylight
Savings began—"That's because. We lost an hour,"
Abigail had explained as Bill and Marianne had
tucked her up in her bed, the shadows playing
around the walls like mischievous elves. "Your

dad . . . he needs. The full twenty-four hours. To get me." And snuggling down beneath the sheets, she added, "But it'll be. Soon. Secretary's Day," she said sleepily. "I was a secretary when your dad met me." And she closed her eyes and smiled at the memory. "My, but he was handsome. Still is, for that matter."

By now, the cancer had spread throughout her body. It was just a matter of time.

But Secretary's Day turned out not to be the Big Day, though it was the day that the breathing apparatus was delivered to the house and, taking her first swig from the oxygen tank, Abigail winked knowingly at Bill and Marianne. "See, I told you it was going to be a big day today," she confided in them. "Just not *the* Big Day. But it'll be soon. You mark my words. Maybe it'll be Mother's Day."

But today, the first Saturday in May, Mother's Day was still more than a week away. But Abigail seemed convinced. Convinced because it was Derby Day.

"Sandwiches coming right up," Marianne said, affecting a stiff-handed salute as she opened the refrigerator. She stared at the shelves of packages and jars, cold cuts, butter cartons, and fruit juice bottles, individually wrapped cheeses from the deli on Sycamore, tubs of yogurt, taramasalata and hummus, small hillocks of salad greens, cucumber, and tomatoes. "What'll it be, O great one?"

"Everything!" Bill said. "What say you, Mom?"

Abigail chuckled appreciatively. "Sure . . . let's have everything. Let's have—" She took a deep breath and shuddered. "Let's have sandwiches fit . . . for a king and his queen," she said, her words labored, her hand clenched but for the index finger pointing upward and circling. "Fit for placing. Before. A visiting. Dignitary. From far-off. Alpha Centauri. Come here to spend. The afternoon." She chuckled and added, "And maybe get a little tan."

Marianne laughed appreciatively.

"Can we have peanut butter?" Tommy asked in a nasal whine as he reappeared laden with more examples of four-color comic book wonder. "And that tart jelly stuff?"

"Tart jelly stuff?" Abigail said, screwing up her face. "Sounds yucky!"

"He means the boysenberry," Marianne said as she transferred more of the contents of the fridge onto the breakfast counter. "He likes it spread with peanut butter and slices of banana."

"Ugh! Gross!" Abigail said, rolling her eyes around and around at Tommy. "Who'd be nine years old!"

Bill loaded water into the kettle and placed it on the electric hob. "Let's have coffee, too. Real stuff, not the instant."

"And make it leaded," Abigail added. "None of that decaf. Not today. If I pee myself, then at least it'll keep me cool."

"Mom!" Marianne said in time with Tommy's sniggers. She was cutting through cheese-topped bread rolls, setting them all out across the counter, tops next to bottoms. "I can see where we're heading with this," she said. "It's Decadent Day."

Tommy frowned as he watched his mother work. "I thought it was Derby Day," he said to no one in particular.

"It sure is, son," Bill said, and he ruffled his son's hair. "What your mom means is that it's both of them. Two days all rolled up in one."

"So what's a deck-a-dent day?"

"Dec-a-dent day." Abigail said before spelling it

out and then repeating it as though it were a mantra. She slumped tiredly onto a stool and took a deep breath. "It's a day when. We don't let anything matter, Tommy. A day when. None of the normal rules. Apply."

"I'm not sure that's a good idea, Mom. We have to have—"

Abigail nodded. "Your father's right, Tommy. We have to have. Rules. Or the world . . . well. It just wouldn't. Hang together." She smiled gently at Tommy's father and then quickly looked away. "Everything would just fly off. In confusion. Like . . . *whoosh!*" She swept her arms up in the air to either side and then collapsed forward coughing.

As his father took hold of her and gently patted her back, Tommy said, "You mean like gravity?"

"That's right," Bill said softly between *shh* and *there* and *okay now* sounds as he continued to pat and rub, "like gravity." Eventually the coughing subsided.

"You okay, Gran?" Tommy had thought about it before even asking.

Maybe if she *wasn't* okay they wouldn't even leave the house. And he so wanted to go out and picnic, feel the grass springing up beneath his sneakers, trying to get right inside with his toes. It had been such a long time since they'd done anything at all, what with Gran's constant coughing and that gizmo tank of air she sucked on while she was watching the game shows on TV.

As he watched her, waiting for a reply, Tommy suddenly noticed—just for the most fleeting of seconds—how thin she'd gotten; like she could get through doors when they were still closed. It looked to him as though Gran could do with a whole heap of peanut butter, banana slices, and boys-and-berry jam sandwiches to build her up again, and maybe a couple of chocolate spread ones and a carton of vanilla yogurt or strawberry and caramel mousse from the Safeway store.

"I'm as fine as wine. And as frisky. As whiskey," came the reply, though it was a little wheezy and not altogether convincing, the memory of a voice rather than the voice itself.

Tommy hoped his father hadn't noticed. He looked around at his mother and saw she was watching him as she loaded cold meats onto buttered bread and spread that gungy brown stuff that had a fancy boy's name—Hugh Muss—and looked like his poops when he was sick and they were all runny. He saw her smile at him, a strange smile, kind of sad and yet not sad.

Marianne watched her son watching her. For just a second she thought of herself back at nine years old, tried to imagine what the world looked like through those young eyes. "You all ready?" she said, breaking the eye lock and placing a cheesy top on a mound of lettuce, sliced ham, and pickle. "I'm gonna be done here in a few minutes and we don't want to be waiting while you get your things together."

Tommy shrugged and held out the confusion of comic books. "I got things to read," he said triumphantly.

"And you've brushed your teeth?"

Tommy thought for a second. What the heck did brushing his teeth matter? They were going out to eat, weren't they? He certainly didn't want all the sandwiches to taste of peppermint. Boy, parents could be a little wacky sometimes.

He nodded. "Before," he added with a jerk of his head. "When I got washed up."

"Clean shorts?"

He looked down at his shorts, saw the dangling figure of Spiderman hanging from his belt, and then noticed the stain on his left leg just below the pocket and the bulge of his Bart Simpson handkerchief. He shifted his leg slightly and lowered the comic books to cover it. It wasn't a big stain. "Can we take the frisbee?" he said, changing the subject, and he skillfully shifted the need for an answer from his mother to his father who seemed to have stopped patting and rubbing.

"Can we, Dad?"

"Sure. We can do anything today."

" 'Cos it's a deck-a-dent day, right?"

Everyone seemed to find this amusing and all thoughts of clean shorts went off on the wind.

Abigail sat up front alongside Tommy's father, a place usually reserved for his mom. The fact was that Gran was the only one Tommy's dad would let up there, like she was the President's wife visiting for the day. There was a lot of huffing and puffing as Bill and Marianne helped Abigail into the seat and fastened the belt across her. There were a couple of *Sorry, Moms*, followed each time by *That's okay, son*, or, *That's okay, Marianne, it's just me sitting awkward*, and then she was in place, wheezing like a train or the air-conditioning pump before Bill fixed it last spring.

Tommy slid into the back of the old Chevrolet, the familiar smell of creased and worn leather drifting up to meet him. He slid his comic books onto the shelf behind the seat, tossed the frisbee on top and pulled his cap on tight. "We taking the roof off, Dad?"

Bill Rutherford plopped into the driver's seat and looked across at Abigail. "How about it, Mom? You up for a little fresh air?"

Tommy's grandmother patted her son's knee. "Let's go. The whole way. Let's take off the sides. While we're at it—" She glanced around at Tommy and did that spinning movement with her eyes. "—And let's. Let's take off the hood. And the trunk lid. Let's just strip ourselves. Strip ourselves down. To the bare essentials. What say you, Tommy?"

Tommy chuckled. "Sounds good to me, Gran," he said.

Marianne slid in next to Tommy and put an arm around him. "You think we should, honey?" she said, aiming the question at Tommy's father. "Mom's gonna get cold."

Tommy saw his father look into the rearview mirror. It was a strange look, aimed at Tommy's mom. It said, this look, that nothing mattered today. Today, nobody was going to get cold. Today, nobody was going to get *any*thing bad.

"Sure," Tommy's mom said, responding to that wordless glance as she pulled her son close, squeezing him under his armpit sending him into paroxysms of wonderful agony. "We're gonna be fine and dandy back here, curled up like a couple of hibernating bears. *Woo-woo-woo!*" She squeezed him some more.

"Mom . . . MOM . . . don't! *Please* don't."

She stopped and Tommy immediately wished she would do it again, but Dad had started the engine and the roof was starting back on its pulley system.

The early summer sky revealed itself in thin slices as the canvas roof whined backward.

Clouds rolled.

Blue shone everywhere.

Birds flew and the air was thick with a million zillion microscopic bugs and gnats, each of them bound for distant lands—lands such as the trash cans over by the back porch, or the drain hole beneath the leaders at each corner of the house. Those things must smell like chocolate syrup to those tiny things, Tommy thought, and just for a moment, he regretted the odd occasion when he had joined in with the other guys in the schoolyard, removing wings and legs from creatures that wanted nothing more than to be able to languish on a nice turd or deep into the potato peelings and coffee grounds inside a bag of garbage.

The roof reached its destination and gave out a thick grumble. Bill got out, walked to the back of the car and leaned on the canvas, first at one side and then at the other. At Tommy's mother's side, Bill leaned over and gave Marianne a kiss on the cheek. Tommy watched for a second and then looked away. He had seen something in that small affection—he had seen tears in his father's eyes. It made him feel a little anxious—the way he did when Miss Gradzsky announced a surprise math quiz and the only homework he'd done had been to catch up on what The Avengers were doing in this month's issue.

The comic books!

He turned around to the back shelf and saw it was now securely covered by the folded roof. Oh, well, he wouldn't need them until they got to where they were going. Which was—

"Where we going anyway?" he asked as his father

fastened the seat belt and slipped the gear lever into reverse.

"Oh, that's a mighty fine point," Bill said over his shoulder as the car drifted back out of the drive and onto the road along the front of the house. "Where'd you think, honey?"

Marianne didn't answer right away. Tommy turned to look up at her and he saw that she, too, had those same tears in her eyes. "Well, it's got to be Mom's choice," she said. "It's her day, after all."

Tommy leaned forward and stood up behind Abigail's seat. "Where we going, Gran?"

Abigail looked across at her son and, in a soft voice, she said, "All the way. We're going all the way today."

Bill smiled and swallowed hard.

Tommy leaned forward. "*Where* we going, Gran?"

Abigail slapped her knees and breathed in deeply. "Well, I reckon we should go down to Morgan's Meadow, down by the stream." She shifted around so she could see Tommy's face. "But before it gets too wide so's you can't go paddling."

"Neat!"

Abigail closed her eyes and laughed. "Yes, neat!"

Tommy knelt up on the seat and leaned on the folded roof as they backed out onto the road. Then, with a slight clunk of gears meshing, they were on their way. He watched the road dovetail onto itself, cars parked at the roadside shifting by and coming together as they moved farther away from the house.

"Honey?"

"Yeah?"

"Is she asleep?"

Bill looked to his side at the crumpled-up figure. "Yeah, I think so."

"So's Tommy." Marianne stroked a lick of hair from her son's forehead. "She okay, d'you think?"

Bill shrugged. "Right now, all we can say is she's here."

He signaled right and turned out of town, passing the junkyard and heading for Walton Flats. "You know," he said, settling his arms on the steering wheel, "I got to thinking this morning."

"Sounds ominous."

"No, nothing too . . . nothing too morbid."

"This while you were still in bed? I woke up one time and could feel you were awake."

"How could you feel I was awake?"

"I don't know," Marianne said, suddenly wondering how it was that she *did* know but totally convinced that she did. "Your breathing changes when you're awake."

Bill was silent for a minute and then said, "No, it was while I was shaving."

"Mmm. And what were you thinking?"

He made a sound that was part laugh and part apology for what he was about to say. "I was thinking about now . . . the absolute now that we have right at this very instant."

"While you were shaving, you were thinking about us in the car?"

"No, I was thinking about the now that I had *then*."

Marianne glanced down at Tommy and shifted her arm. Tommy grunted and moved closer to her.

"I was thinking about *all* the nows, every single nanosecond of time that we kind of close our eyes to because we're thinking about what's coming along, either looking forward to it or—" His voice trailed off.

Marianne reached out a hand and rubbed her husband's neck.

"I was thinking about how, when we have everything we could possibly want in the world and we're with the people we so dearly want to be with, about how . . . oh, it sounds silly."

"No, it doesn't. Go ahead. Tell me what you were thinking."

"Well, I was thinking wouldn't it be great if we could just freeze that frame. If we could just stop everything from moving on and changing."

"You mean—" Marianne glanced at the back of Abigail's head and heard a soft snore. "You mean Mom?"

"Yes, but more than that. Everything."

"What else is there? What else is bothering you, honey?"

"Thata's just it. Nothing was bothering me. And then—" He nodded sideways at Abigail. "—we had the visit to the doctor, then to the hospital, and then the operation, and the radiotherapy, and then—now—the shortness of breath, another visit to the doctor, the x-ray . . . and here we are. Waiting."

They had been told that Abigail had three to six months, though the likelihood was that it would be closer to three. Then, as the breathing worsened, even that prognosis seemed to be a little overly optimistic. They were looking at weeks, the doctor had told them, Abigail nodding, a small smile of acceptance on her lips.

"I'm not sure I'm foll—"

"Well, it was all that—*all* that—that kind of started

me thinking about how brief it all is. The time we have, you know? But how, if we added every single fraction of time together and truly appreciated it, life would be almost endless." He slowed to make a left turn.

"But it still wouldn't *be* endless," Marianne said. "Mom, and *my* mom and dad . . . they wouldn't always be with us. And Tommy would still grow older and he'd still find his own life and his own adventures."

"Yes, I guess that's it."

"What's it?"

"What you said . . . about adventures. That's what life is, just one big adventure."

"Oh, honey," Marianne said, her voice soft and low. "It'll all work out okay."

The car slowed down and Bill prepared to make a left onto the strip leading onto the meadows.

Tommy sat up quickly, his head narrowly missing Marianne's chin, and said, "We here yet?"

Bill turned the wheel and moved through a gap in the traffic, the car juddering as it moved onto the rough track. "Almost," he said. "Couple more minutes."

She could feel him in the car right next to her, smell his cologne and the grease he used to put on his hair. But she knew that if she opened her eyes he wouldn't be there. There would only be the car, and her son and Marianne and Tommy, and outside the window it would be a world where her husband no longer existed.

Oh, Jack, she thought, squeezing her eyes tight, *I'm causing them such sadness.*

They love you, Abby. The wind whispering through

her hearing aid sounded just like his voice. Sounded just the way he always spoke to her. *Be happy with that. Your time will come. And it won't be—*

She felt small hands on her shoulder, rubbing it gently. "Gran? You awake?"

She lifted her head to make out she'd just woken up and hadn't heard the conversation her son and Marianne had been having, but the truth of the matter was she didn't sleep too well now, and her dreams—such as they were—were filled with images of the cancer turning itself over and over inside of her.

"You bet. I'm awake," she said. She turned to look across the meadows and, just for a second, she thought she could see horses, lots of horses, being led in a procession by men so small they could have been boys. But it must have been the sunlight through the trees and refracting through the window glass, because there were no horses and no men.

"You gonna park down by the river, honey?" Marianne asked.

Bill didn't speak.

"Honey?"

"Oh, yeah, sorry. I was just thinking how deserted it is."

"And on Derby Day, too!" Tommy added. "Maybe everyone's gone someplace else."

It was true. Since they had pulled onto the dirt track leading through the meadows, they had not seen another car nor even kids out walking or sitting listening to their radios, or playing with balls.

"It's nice. It's not—" Abigail ventured stiltedly, "—too crowded."

But there *were* people there, weren't there? She could see them . . . there behind the trees and just

around back of the bushes . . . could see their striped
jackets and their boaters, the occasional flash of pink
parasol. She squinted her eyes and concentrated, but
the meadows were empty.

Bill pulled the old Chevrolet up onto the grass
alongside a thin pathway that wound its way down
to the riverside. The air was filled with the sounds
of summer, of sunshine and of water burbling its
way over the ancient stones of the riverbed. Bill got
out and pulled the seat forward for Marianne before
going around to let Abigail out. Tommy ran his feet
on the carpet like a train, his hand clasped on the
bright yellow frisbee and his lungs greedily gulping
in the outside air.

"Just hold your horses there a minute, Scout, while
we get your gran out," Bill chided.

Marianne went around to the trunk and got out
the hamper, setting it down beside her on the grass.
Then she lifted a pile of old sheets and rugs.

Tommy pushed the now vacant seat forward and
made to slide out, but the sight of his father holding
onto his gran stopped him in his tracks.

Bill held onto Abigail tightly and Tommy could
see her thin arms dithering from side to side, like a
butterfly not sure of whether it wanted to settle on
this flower or maybe this one, and her hair blowing
in thin wisps in the gentle breeze.

"You okay, Mom?"

"I'm fine, son," came the reply. "Just as fine as
wine."

"Not too cold?"

Now with a firm hold on the Chevy's door, Abigail
straightened up and smoothed out Tommy's dad's
collar. The smile she gave him was a secret smile,
knowing and sad. Tommy frowned and though he

hadn't made so much as even the tiniest noise, both of them turned to look at him. "We're just fine," she answered, with that big grin and a hunch-up of her shoulders that suggested being a part—along with her grandson—of some great and exciting plan. "Aren't we, Tommy?"

"We sure are," Tommy agreed, and just to prove it, he lofted the frisbee high into the sky, tracing its path with his hand over his eyes as though he were saluting it.

"Tommy," Marianne shouted, "will you come and take some things, please? Let's get this picnic on the road!"

Jack came to see his wife after they had eaten.

Bill had gone down to the riverside with Tommy, and Marianne—who had started out with such fine intentions to read the daily newspaper—had succumbed to the aftereffects of the food and the sunshine, her eyelids drooping slowly until they had closed completely.

Abigail watched her son and grandson while she listened to their distant voices, mingled in with the sound of her own breathing and Marianne's soft snores. It was as though they were in a different world, the two men—a world that Abigail was able to look into and hear but one which she could not actually visit.

He's a fine boy, Jack said hunkering down beside her.

"Land sakes!" Abigail said, the words coming out as a hiss, her hand up to the collar on her sweater, fingers trembling over the chain he had bought her those many long years ago.

Shh! he whispered, glancing at Marianne.

"You gave. Me a start," Abigail said.

He shifted around so that he was in front of her and smiled. *You look as handsome as ever, Abby . . . mighty handsome, if you don't mind my saying.*

Abigail shook her head and made to reach out to him. But Jack pulled away. *Uh-uh,* he said, *that's not in the rules.*

"Can't I. Touch you?"

He made a tight-lipped mouth and shook his head, his eyes mischievous as ever. *Not yet, anyway.*

"But I thought—" She lowered her voice when Marianne shuffled onto her side. "I thought. You'd come. For me. I thought. Today. Was the day. The special day."

All days are special, Abby. What's so different about this one?

"Well, I figured you'd come for me today." She hung her head down and said, "I'm sick, Jack. Terrible sick."

I know that, Abby.

"I'm going. To die."

Yes, you are.

"And soon."

Right again. And soon. But not today.

Abigail looked up at her husband and just for a second, he looked seventeen years old again and then he was thirty-something. Then in his fifties. Then he was a young buck of twenty-two. Seemed like he couldn't stay put for more than a minute at a time.

"So when—" she asked, "—exactly?"

Jack shrugged. The sound of laughter drifted over from the river and Jack and Abigail turned to look. Tommy was doubled up in hysterics pointing at his

father. Bill was standing pulling up his trousers—
even from here they could see that Bill had somehow
gotten into the water.

They're going to come back, Jack said, turning back
to face her. *I have to go.*

"But you didn't. You didn't. Answer me, Jack.
When?"

*I don't rightly know, Abby. But someday soon. Maybe
tomorrow; maybe next week*— he shrugged again. *Like
I say, soon. But it might not be a day that has anything
written beneath it on the calendar. There'll be nothing
special about it.* He looked back at Bill and Tommy,
slowly making their way up the embankment toward
them. *And certainly nothing special about it for them.*

With Jack's attention momentarily distracted from
her, Abigail wondered whether she could shoot out
her hand and take a hold of her husband's wrist . . .
whether doing so—her living skin joining up with
her husband's ghost's—might mean she would die
right there and then.

But the laughter drifted up to her and into her
head like the fizzy bubbles from a bottle of 7 Up,
and she turned, her hand halfway out in front of her
but stopped short of its target. Bill waved to her and
she raised her hand and waved back, feeling suddenly weak but somehow strong as well.

"They can't see you," she said as she looked back
at him.

Jack nodded. *But I'm gonna have to go anyway.*

"Do you. Do you have to?"

He nodded again, this time with a deep sadness
etched into his face—his seventy-eight-year-old face,
the one she had watched those years ago, lying so
still on her pillow as he drifted away from her, fighting to stay another few minutes.

Like I said, Abby, all days are special. And, right now, these last days you're spending with Bill and his lovely wife and that fine boy . . . these days are special to them. These days are like small gems . . . like jewels in the dust. Make them count. Every single one of them.

And then he reached out and touched her cheek.

Fire and ice.

Soft and hard.

Dark and light.

A thousand sensations shot through Abigail Rutherford's face and coursed up and down her body, setting her fingers to tingle and her toes to curl.

I was never real good with rules, he said.

"I love you so much, Jack," she said, her words coming out in a stream without any pauses for breath.

I love you, too, Abby. And then he was gone.

Tommy was the first one to appear, the sound of his pounding feet waking Marianne in a fluster.

"What's the matter? What's happened?"

"Dad—" Tommy could hardly speak from a mixture of exertion and laughter. "Dad fell in the river!"

"I didn't fall in the—"

Marianne got to her feet. "Bill? Are you okay, honey?"

"I'm fine." He flapped his trousers at her and gave a weak smile. "Slipped off the stepping stones, that's all."

"You should've seen him, Mom! Gran, you should have—"

Abigail nodded and made a mock-scowl. "He was never. Real good. On his feet. Your father," she said. She pulled the blanket from around her shoulders and threw it over toward her son. "You make sure. They're dry. You'll get. Rheumatics."

Tommy frowned. "Room attics?"

"Hush now, Tommy. Let's get your father dried up and back home."

Drying his feet while Marianne and Tommy loaded the picnic things into the trunk, Bill sensed he was being watched. He shook his head. "Could've happened to anyone, Mom," he said.

"I know. But it was. Always you. It happened to."

He wiped out his shoes and, pulling a face, slipped them onto his feet.

"You had a nice time?"

She nodded emphatically. "I've had a wonderful time."

"How you feeling?"

She lifted a hand to her cheek and rubbed the spot where Jack had touched it. It felt warm. Special.

"I'm feeling. Just fine," she said. "It's been. A great day."

Bill nodded and, just for a second, he frowned.

She reached out then and took her son's hand. "A special day."

For the rest of her life—a rich, happy and fulfilled life . . . and one which turned out to be a little longer than she had once hoped—Abigail Rutherford treated every day as a special day, savoring every minute and every hour as though it truly was her last.

Which, of course, is what we all should do.

BIRTHDAY JITTERS

by Julie E. Czerneda

Canadian author and editor Julie E. Czerneda has been a finalist for both the John W. Campbell (Best New Writer) and Philip K. Dick (Most Distinguished Science Fiction Novel) awards, as well as winner of two Prix Aurora Awards, the Canadian version of SF's Hugo, for her novel In the Company of Others *and her short story, "Left Foot on a Blind Man," published in* Silicon Dreams, *edited by Martin H. Greenberg and Larry Segriff (DAW Books). Julie has published eight science fiction novels with DAW Books, the most recent being* Survival, *the first novel in her Species Imperative series. As editor, Julie's* Space Inc. *anthology, also from DAW, explores daily life off this planet. Julie's first horror piece, "Birthday Jitters," is also her thirteenth short story sale. Coincidence or omen? One ponders.*

I KNOW THE terrible truth about birthdays. My enlightenment came the day of my twenty-ninth, on my way to what I believed would be another very happy celebration of the event, complete with presents, cake, candles, and the requisite gathering of loved ones.

Loved ones. Little did I know. . . .

*   *   *

Roland Fargus knew. Roland. Great name for a hermit, if a hermit's what you call a man who spends his days treasuring pieces of dry cardboard and scrounging for burger corpses in the trash behind Mickey D's. I'd have joined my town pals in the ever popular Friday night sport of hazing the homeless, if the sad old guy hadn't been my uncle.

Uncle in name, anyway. None of the newest generation of Farguses knew he existed; the rest of us had no trouble forgetting. And, other than the embarrassment of Roland the Wretched, we had a tight family, a good one, real pillars of the community. People in town and throughout the surrounding three townships either knew a Fargus or were related to us. You couldn't escape that characteristic round face, upturned nose, or, in the case of mature male Farguses, retreating hairline.

It took work to keep such a big family tight, but no one minded. Holiday gatherings were our points of contact; meals our glue. Thanksgiving brought everyone to the big table at our house, except for the overflow of acned teens whining about sharing tables with preschoolers. It was at our house because my dad was the oldest Fargus not ensconced in Trillium Manor. Not that he'd have been lonely there—the Manor had almost a full floor of Farguses. We were justly renowned for the ripe old age of our various greats: aunts, uncles, parents. There was a saying in our family: survive the tricky thirties and be guaranteed a century plus. Seemed true enough.

Don't get me wrong. My family didn't hog all the Fargus' entertaining. Christmas dinner alternated between the homes of my three aunts, while Easter remained a source of ongoing power struggles between those of my cousins old enough to have tables of their own. Regardless of host or cook, every Fargus family supper was a feast, agonizingly perfect and perfectly attended. Fail to show up and you'd get a worried delegation on your doorstep that night, complete with leftovers and chicken soup. The old joke about needing a doctor's note to be excused from a family gathering wasn't too far from the truth.

Not that anyone complained about attending. Free food and good company. What more could you ask? Roland's willing and successful avoidance of the warm, comfy fold was the only puzzle to any who spared him a thought. How could anyone prefer to live on handouts and garbage?

We did family birthdays best of all. I remember kids in my class would beg to be invited to my parties. Mom would let me pick a theme. Knights and dragons, ocean creatures, Halloween ghouls. It didn't matter what I asked, our backyard—or basement, if it rained—would undergo the required transformation into castle, undersea world, or haunted mansion. Mom would appear with a cake that might have been sculpted by some Hollywood prop guy. No matter its shape or size, the cake would glow with a candle for every year. And there'd be an extra cake, with more candles, for the family dinner later that night.

The candles. The cakes may have come from a mix, dressed up with homemade icing, jam filling, and those sprinkles you can bite without risking a tooth, but the candles always came from a battered old tin kept in the pantry. My aunts and mom each had their own. Ours, with its well-worn images of puppies, flowers, and children, was the nearest thing we had to a family heirloom, having passed through two generations of Farguses already. Its shining gold interior was stuffed with waxy spears of pink, or blue with white swirls, or sequined in silver and gold, or whatever suited the theme. The box never failed to provide the right candles for any birthday, no matter how challenging the decor.

Growing up and leaving home might have ended theme parties, but it didn't mean losing a truly Fargus birthday. You were always welcome back. If you were starting your own household, well, Mom or one of my aunts would take the new addition to the family aside shortly after each became official and gently emphasize the importance of continuing family traditions. There had been one or two newcomers who had scoffed, or who turned out to be chronically forgetful. Somehow, the appropriate mother-in-law would sense when insincerity or inability risked her offspring's birthday rites and a cake, with candles, would arrive on the Day. They were, of course, gracious enough to provide this service for the offending or lax in-law, so protests were few and futile.

I didn't have a partner to look after my birthday for me. I wasn't living at home, either, the morning of my twenty-ninth birthday, being the proud renter of a basement apartment complete with cable. But I had the unfailing comfort of my mom's phone call, inviting me to the family party in my honor.

Not just mine, of course. I'd shared every one of my birthdays with my Great Auntie Myrtle Fargus-Smythe. My earliest birthday memory was of her seamed and puckered lips, vainly attempting to put out what had seemed an ocean of flame. From the family album, I knew it had been a mere eighty-two pink-and-white candles. But at the time, the heat from that cake had been terrifying. I'd had to be hauled from under a chair to do my duty and join the other youngsters in helping Auntie Myrtle blow out her candles. If the breath leaving my tear-dampened lips had done little more than add spit to the icing, my windbag cousins had more than made up for it—almost setting the poor woman's shawl on fire.

Yet in the photograph, she's smiling.

I shook off the memory, unsure why it made me uneasy. Of course she was smiling. Everyone smiled in their birthday photos. I checked my watch. Plenty of time for a quick jog before work. I wasn't to pick up Auntie Myrtle from the Manor until five PM, to give her time for a nap before her hairdresser arrived to freshen her "do." I hoped I still cared about my appearance that much when I passed a hundred and six.

And looked better, I thought, unable to restrain a shudder. Auntie Myrtle's cheeks had shriveled to the point where cake crumbs could be lost in their creases. Finding a safe place to plant a birthday kiss had become a challenge. It could have been worse, I suppose. Farguses aged like leather, wearing thin and growing stiff, but tough rather than brittle. Some of my friends had relatives in Trillium Manor who couldn't live anywhere but the first floor—the one with extra-wide fire doors and power-assist bathrooms. Trapped by their own flesh, with no casual trips home, most could no longer walk without help.

My cross trainers, complete with fresh socks, were prominently displayed in front of the TV. Magazine photos of the impossibly fit covered my sofa and chair, with a poster showing the opposite above the toilet. All part of my twenty-ninth birthday gift to myself—a resolution to do anything and everything possible to get off my rump and do something about my body.

It wasn't love; it was fear. Like most other Farguses of my generation, I'd finished college to find love handles and the beginnings of a potbelly waiting for me. It was abundantly clear I wasn't destined to be one of the lean no-matter-what-they-ate Farguses. I was going to be one of the lumpy ones, the ones who were more likely to have certain issues as they aged. Heart attack. Diabetes. Kidney failure. Cancer. The ones who didn't pass their thirties.

My parents scoffed at my sudden interest in fitness, insisting I was perfect as is, calling me a solid, promising young man.

Solid. Thinking rather wistfully of sunken cheeks, I grabbed my shoes and headed for the door, determined to control my fate.

Roland Fargus happened to be along my jogging route, his squalid cardboard tent nestled against one pillar of the highway that humped over our town, leaving a shadow and little more in its wake. The few people who took the off-ramp headed for the golden arches, ate, used the bathrooms, then jumped back on as if our town didn't exist.

I suppose that's why I looked for him when I ran by each morning. Our family treated Roland the same way. It wasn't something I judged, just an irony I couldn't shake any easier than the flab riding my butt.

As usual, he was bent over a can. I ran early, before the traffic began filling the streets with noise and stench. Roland was up and digging through trash bins before they were emptied for the day—and before there were passersby to shout at him. Or worse.

I'd learned it was safe to stare; he never acknowledged my existence either, seeming as aloof as the traffic overhead. I grew to think of him as one more landmark to pass along my route, a sign I was two thirds of the way done with each morning's self-torture.

Until today. For some reason, the pounding of my feet rolled Roland's head in my direction, the movement as deliberate and slow as a pet chameleon sizing up a cricket. His pale eyes glittered within a mass of filthy hair twining from forehead to chest. A nose, sunburned and peeling, marked the middle of his face. Startled, I lost my rhythm, my feet tangling themselves so I almost stepped into the oily edge of a puddle. Then I heard him say: "It's not going to save you."

My feet landed in the puddle and stayed there. "P–pardon?"

Roland's voice had a rasp to it, as if used so seldom it had lost the polished shape of vowels. "The running. The sweat. Your time's almost up no matter what you do. Poor bastard."

I'd been ready for mockery, would have understood and deflected spite without a thought. His pity stung. "Why do you say that?"

"Because it's true. Do you know who I am, Bobby?"

Bobby? No one called me that—not since my first day of school, when I'd proudly written "Robert Fargus" all by myself and insisted the family use my full, grown-up name. Which meant Roland had been living like this longer than I'd imagined. "You're my uncle. Roland Fargus," I said, now wishing I'd worn a more dignified T-shirt than my faded Spiderman.

Perhaps my acknowledgment surprised him. He straightened and took a step closer, tilting his head as though to see me better. It shifted a mat of hair, showing me the squint lines at the edge of one eye. "You always were a nice boy, Bobby," he said at last. "I'm so sorry."

"Why?" I demanded as he turned to leave, presumably heading for the shelter of his hideaway, with its floor of newsprint and twisted sleeping bags. "Why do you feel sorry for me?" I fought to keep it polite, to avoid sounding scornful. He was family, after all.

His eyes fixed on me again. They glistened, as if moist. "No reason. Nothing. I shouldn't have said anything. Run all you want—" His left hand waved into the distance, hurrying me along. "I'm a crazy old man—didn't your father tell you?"

Roland's fingers were spotless, the nails as tidy as my own. I stared at them, my preconceptions of his life and choices fragmenting. Why so much effort to keep clean while living like this?

He noticed my attention and tucked both hands inside the shapeless parka that sheltered his body from neck to knee. "There's nothing I can do for you, Bobby," my uncle almost whispered. "I was afraid to speak out when you and your cousins were young, when it might have made a difference. It's too late now."

"Afraid of what? What difference?"

"Afraid of—" his voice faltered, then gathered strength again. "They left me alone because I left them alone. I know it made me no better than them. I've traded your lives simply to keep my own existence. Such as it is. You'd better go. Talking to me for long— it's not a good idea."

I clutched at what made some sense. He was a crazy old man, which meant he was someone who needed help, whether he knew it or not. I'd been raised properly. And he was family. "What's not a good idea," I said firmly, "is your living like this, Uncle. Come with me. Please."

He was already shaking his head so violently the tangles writhed over the fabric of his parka, making a sound like terrified snakes. "Never. I won't go back. I'm only safe here."

"You call living like this safe!" I eased my tone, tried to make it persuasive and gentle. I'd never been good at talking to children or pets. "Uncle. It would mean a lot to me. Today's my birthday—"

"Dear Sweet Jesus." Suddenly his too-clean hands were fastened on my arms, nails digging in to hold me; his face, contorted and wild, pressed close to mine until his breath entered my nostrils, hot and reeking of old onion. "You can't go back. You can't! They'll suck another year out of you. It might be your last! The bright little vampires will steal your life! Stay with me, Bobby! Don't go!"

I should have listened then, but I couldn't. Panicked by his closeness, by the hysteria in his voice, I shoved Roland away from me as hard as I could. Yet even as I staggered down the street, I found myself shocked not by what he'd said or done, but by the strong, solid feel of him.

Roland might be living out of cans, but he was no gaunt scarecrow. And I didn't know a Fargus his age who wasn't.

What was going on?

*   *   *

My timing stayed off the rest of the day, so I wasn't surprised to find I was too early to pick up Great Auntie Myrtle. Rather than sit in the main floor waiting lounge, where anyone without wrinkles was a magnet for bored, nosy residents, I took my car around the block a few times. I didn't intend to swing wide on my third trip. Or to make the turn onto Industrial Road. But there I was.

Roland was sitting on his "porch," as if waiting for me.

I pulled up along the curb and stopped the car. It didn't seem right to leave it running, adding fumes to the already potent air under the overpass. Then, it didn't seem right to stay inside, on a cushioned driver's seat, with Roland patiently sitting on his triangle of styrofoam. I found myself walking around the car, oddly unconcerned if any of the vehicles passing by carried folks who'd know me on sight, and leaned on the part of the front fender that didn't have rust. "Sorry I pushed you, Uncle," I told him, hearing an almost sullen note in my voice. It had been a while since I'd had to apologize.

"I scared you, Bobby, talking crazy." Roland's eyes slid away from me. "You look fine. Off to your party, then?"

"After a stop at Trillium—picking up Auntie Myrtle."

This brought his eyes back. "The Old Hag still steals the limelight on your day, does she?" He barked a laugh at my sputtering protest. "You don't have to be on your best behavior with me, Bobby Fargus. I was there for your first five birthdays, in case you remember. I do—you hated sharing the family party. Who wouldn't?"

It was akin to heresy. I smiled anyway. "I admit,

there were times—but I'm a little old to worry about sharing my birthday these days, Uncle."

"And you think one day it will be your day, don't you? Yours alone? You think you'll outlive her?"

They weren't innocent questions, not with that searching look, not with that gentle pity. My fear from this morning, from every morning, rushed back. Did he know somehow? "Of course I'll outlive her. Not that I wish any ill to my great aunt—your aunt," I emphasized with as much dignity as I could muster with a dry mouth, "but she's already very old." Even for a Fargus, one hundred and six was a significant accomplishment.

"Oh, she'll keep getting older. Just like the rest of them in the Manor." Roland rubbed his hands over his knees, as if trying to remove the stains from his pants. "But not you. You're almost done." He didn't wait for me to think of something to say to this, but lifted his arms in a hopeless gesture. "It's the birthday parties, Bobby. That's when they steal your time."

If he'd stood and approached me . . . if he'd said anything that made any sense at all . . . I would have jumped back in my car and been out of there for good. But in the back of my mind, I felt I'd failed him earlier. I'd fail him even more going to sit at that table without taking him with me, if I ate more than I needed, while he gnawed on brown-tipped apple cores and stale pizza crust. What my parents would have to say—I shuddered, but gathered my courage. "A lot of people don't like birthdays," I began. "You should think of it as a chance for a decent meal."

Roland's hands tightened on his knees, but gave no other indication of violent tendencies. I'd watched enough reality crime on TV to know the signs. "I want you to keep listening to me, Bobby," he said in a calm, reasonable voice. "Listen just for a couple of minutes, without arguing or leaving. Will you do that?"

I checked my watch. Great Auntie Myrtle would be in her rinse. I'd listened to customers babble about their kids and dogs far longer to make a sale. Roland was family. "Sure," I promised, my brain ready to disengage as long as necessary.

"Good. Good. What I'm going to say—it's fantastic. You'll find it hard to believe. I know I did. But I swear to you, Bobby, it's the truth. More than that. It's the only way to save yourself, if you still can."

"I'm listening, Uncle."

His hands lifted and spread as if holding a platter in the air between us. "It's something about the candles. The ones they put on the birthday cakes. I don't know how they work—if there's some kind of curse on them or magic mumbo jumbo at work— You promised to listen!" as I involuntarily shuffled my feet.

I stopped shuffling and nodded. "Birthday cakes. Candles," I repeated numbly.

"Right. That's when it happens. When a child blows out the candles on his cake, the year of life he might have had goes, too—but not into smoke. No. It goes to the others. They steal it for themselves." He hunched, peering up at me through his mat of hair. "Not everyone, mind. It's just us. Just the Farguses. It's our family tradition." His beard twisted over where his mouth had to be, as though his lips fought that barrier to get out the words.

"Tradition." We certainly had enough of those, I thought, glad of the firm reality of the car behind me. An abhorrence of my cousin Sam's overspiced pumpkin pie I could understand. But candle phobia? No wonder the crazy old coot didn't want to come to a birthday party. "Are there any other traditions I should worry about, Uncle?" I asked, proud I wasn't laughing out loud.

"I know you don't believe me, Bobby." Roland got to his feet but thankfully stayed by his hovel. "It took me years to comprehend myself. But I couldn't ignore the evidence—"

"There's evidence?"

"Ever notice how you feel after blowing out the candles? That sense of anticlimax? Maybe a faint moment of exhaustion?"

"Anyone over sixteen fusses over their birthday—"

"No. The weariness is real. They keep you sitting, hand you gifts to open, so you won't stand up and realize you really are different from the way you were the moment before air left your mouth, before they stole your time."

For no reason beyond duty, I made myself argue with him. "Everyone in the family has a cake with candles—"

"When was the last time you saw one of your elders blow out their own? What a nice family tradition—to let the children help—" Roland spat, cratering the blackened dust. "There are two kinds of Fargus, Bobby. The ones who take and the ones who can't. They know who's who early, believe me."

"They?" I said weakly.

"Who is in charge of birthday parties? Who bakes the cake? Who puts on the candles?"

Mom? I blinked at the unbidden image of my mother and aunts conspiring in their kitchens over icing and dried violets, whispering arcane spells over

layers of chocolate or vanilla, lemon or orange, spice
or carrot. I saw the cake sitting before my Great
Auntie Myrtle and remembered the terror of its carpet of flame, waiting to consume my breath. "This is
utter crap!" I protested involuntarily, forgetting my
duty to humor the old man.

"Is it?" Roland seemed to draw strength from my
disbelief, his own voice firming and growing stern.
"I thought so, too, boy, until the day I decided I
didn't want to celebrate getting older. I refused to
take part in birthday parties of any kind. And you
know what? That next year, I began to feel better,
stronger. But it wasn't as easy as that—you can't
just refuse."

I couldn't argue with him there. Roland's self-
exile from the family couldn't have been easy; we
Farguses took our gatherings seriously. "What happened?" I asked, curious in spite of my better
judgement.

"I avoided the family, stayed away. Made it clear
none of them were welcome. It wasn't good enough.
They tracked me to my job. Cupcakes with candles
would appear on my desk, follow me down the halls,
trap me in meetings. From the family. This—" an
eloquent wave at his cardboard-and-bag castle "—
this was the only way to finally escape them."

"Them?"

"Why do you think your mother and aunts get
teary at birthdays? They know what they are doing—
some still care about us. Not the old ones—they are
happy as can be with the curse. How do you think
they keep on living, when most of us don't?"

*The family gift—pass the tricky thirties and live and
live and live.*

"Good genes," I countered, my hands damp against

the fender. "Some of us have them. Some of us don't."

"Like you? Think a bit of a pot means you're doomed to die in your thirties? Hah! Look at me, Bobby." Roland unzipped his parka and dropped it to the dirt. Underneath was a body mirror image to my own, if more heavily rounded at belly and thigh. "I'm ten years older than your father. I passed the tricky thirties decades ago—because I escaped the hags and their candles. You can, too—"

My cell phone interrupted him. I reached for it like I'd reach for a rope if drowning, desperate for a sane voice. It was my mother. "Robert? Where are you? Aunt Myrtle called to say you weren't there to pick her up yet."

"I'm on my way, Mom," I told her, then looked at Roland. Even as I opened my mouth to ask, he shook his head violently. "Be there in five," I said instead and closed the phone.

"I have to go—"

"Good-bye, then, Bobby. Just do yourself one favor. Pay attention tonight. For your own sake. Watch them."

I felt trapped into nodding a polite acknowledgment, for all the world as if the two of us had been neighbors meeting over a hedge, discussing the best way to discourage dandelions.

Not curses, candles, and my life.

"There you are." Somehow, my mother managed to make the phrase welcoming and ominous at the same time. I kissed her cheek then helped guide Great Auntie Myrtle through the front hall, around the piles of shoes determined to trip latecomers, quite sure my guilt showed.

They couldn't know where I'd been and no one chastised me for being late. This was my birthday party, after all, and a young man of twenty-nine, I was reminded by several amused relatives, was likely to have his thoughts elsewhere. Their cheer and warmth helped me relax, and sometime between the last piece of fried chicken and the usual tussle to get little Nancy to stop hiding her peas under her plate, I'd almost managed to put Roland Fargus out of my mind.

Almost. Every so often, a rich mouthful threatened to gag me; I shivered when the windows began to rattle under the driving rain. I knew I shouldn't have left the old man. I should have brought him home, here, to his family. I'd let his bit of inane fantasy get under my skin and he was the one suffering for it.

"Happy Birthday to you . . ." The song startled me from my thoughts. I looked up to see my cake approaching.

The candles were dark blue this year, their tiny flames steadfast and true against the breeze of my mother's triumphant passage through the dining room. This year's cake was a tall concoction of frothy white icing, with my name in melted chocolate across the top and more chocolate drizzled down the sides. I'd seen something similar on the cover of a magazine at the grocery store. My mom and aunts liked to keep up on styles.

"Make a wish, Robert." My mother set the cake before me, its pedestal plate holding it at just the right height.

Have you ever had an idea, or maybe it was something you'd seen or read, that spread itself like a blight over what you thought was normal? I stared at my cake, and suddenly saw each candle as a tiny vampire, waiting to suck another year away. I couldn't blow them out to save my life.

Or maybe that was the point.

"Robert? Do you need Nancy's help?"

Any other day, I would have heard this from my aunt and laughingly defended my right to my own candles. Instead, I stared across the table at the round, friendly face I thought I knew and saw a monster, ready to sacrifice her offspring.

Without hesitation, I inhaled, then blew out the flames with one breath.

Nothing. Only a round of congratulations from those at the table and a pout from Nancy, who'd lunged forward too late.

Roland was insane and I was crazy listening to him. Knowing this, I couldn't help trying to stand up right away. My mother's hand dropped on my shoulder, pushing me back down even as she planted a kiss where the hair thinned over my temple. "Sit, dear, sit. Cut the cake. You don't want to slow down your presents!"

All normal. All as birthdays should be, in a loving family. But I felt my heart pounding as I put the knife to the icing and pressed it through the soft, clinging layers. My mother collected the candles as they tipped and threatened to fall, gathering them all into one hand with soft exclamations of pleasure.

"Where's my cake?" The volume my great aunt could produce from her frail form never ceased to amaze me. "Did you forget my cake, Rebecca?"

The usual chorus of denials counterpointed my mother's calm: "Patsy's bringing it, dear. Let Robert finish—"

"I'm not getting any younger, you know!"

"It's all right, Mom," I said, putting down the

knife. Auntie Myrtle rarely waited this long to demand her half of our party—it was a sign of my mother's determination and fortitude that my cake at least arrived first.

Or was it?

Damn Roland. His crazy lies were ruining my party.

They dimmed the lights for effect, not that you'd notice. One hundred and six candles produced enough illumination to pick out the expectant eyes around the table, to spark from every piece of glassware and waiting fork, and bring out the colors of both sweaters and wallpaper. I presumed the batteries were pulled from the detectors—my Aunt Patsy was squinting against the smoke filling her face and rising over her shoulder. I heard Great Auntie Myrtle give a sound like a purr beside me.

I knew she would be smiling, showing no teeth whatsoever.

My mother was herding the youngest to our side of the table, a tricky maneuver at best with the huge cake on its way to the same destination. "Gather 'round your great auntie. Careful now. Robert?"

I pulled my chair back slightly from the table and turned it so I faced Auntie Myrtle. Sam's youngest, Mike Jr., immediately crawled onto my lap, presumably after a better vantage point. I ignored him. I ignored the arrival of the cake, despite the wave of heat wafting toward me. I ignored the singing and the clatter of plates.

Instead, I watched the woman clapping her gnarled hands with glee.

Pay attention, Roland had urged.

The song ended. Five little Farguses puckered up and blew happily at the carpet of flame, Mike Jr.

managing to miss completely. The candle flames danced and flickered in answer, some going out, others fighting to burn longer. Laughter and more breaths.

All the while, I watched.

I watched Auntie Myrtle's eyes sparkle. I watched her tiny tongue dart out to moisten her nonexistent lips.

I watched her complexion begin to glow with a blush that wasn't the reflection of fire.

Answering to instinct, I wrapped my arms around Mike Jr., resting my cheek against his soft hair, smelling baby shampoo and chocolate. He squirmed free to join the other children waiting for their share of cake.

"Robert?" Softly, from my mother, her tone making the word both warm and warning. I looked up to find the eyes of everyone over forty fixed on me. My Auntie Myrtle, for once, wasn't smiling at all.

"I'll have ice cream with my piece, please," I said.

I won't say I believed Roland's wild story about the candles and our family's tendency to either die too young or live too long. Not even when I woke the day after my twenty-ninth birthday and had to lie back down again to still the irregular racing of my heart. I blamed it on too much to eat and drink, swearing to keep to my fitness regimen and watch my diet.

It couldn't be because my own family was stealing my health.

The doctors had their own explanations. High blood pressure. Congested veins. A heart forced to work harder than it should. I was sent to one specialist after another, began taking pills to lower my blood pressure, pills to calm my nerves, pills to lower my cholesterol, pink ones, blue ones. They came in as many colors as candles.

I kept running. Desperately. Daily. In any and all weather. Roland was gone, his cardboard settling under the assault of rain then snow into the shape of a corpse. Every so often, I'd pick up two coffees in the drive-thru on my way to work. I'd follow the shadow of the overpass, stopping at likely trash bins, but never found him. I'd leave the extra coffee with someone faceless and cold, feeling as though I looked into a mirror.

Roland's disappearance ate at me. Had I driven a poor old fool away to his death?

Or had a wiser man than I known to flee for his life?

Whether I believed Roland or not, somehow I missed Easter supper at Sam and Mike's. I managed to schedule a trip out of town over my mother's birthday. Thanksgiving came and I spent it with a girl I'd met at a bar who was avoiding family of her own.

Well before Christmas, I'd changed my phone number so I didn't have to make excuses anymore.

My family was remarkably restrained. I had no visitors. There were postcards from whomever of my relatives had taken a trip, but no messages other than "hope to see you soon." Perhaps losing Roland had taught them a lesson. Perhaps I was going to be granted the right to decide my own way of life, make up my own traditions. My own fate.

Ever feel the approach of your birthday on the back of your neck, as if fingers of bone sought your life's pulse?

As mine grew closer, I worried over what Roland had told me—how the family birthday cakes found

him at work. I could have tried telling my coworkers
I didn't want a celebration this year, but they'd plot
something anyway. After all, who didn't object to
their thirtieth? Who didn't try to stay twenty-nine as
long as possible?

Who didn't fear time?

The pills, the diet, the running weren't enough. I'd
left it too late. That's why Roland had pitied me. I
was no longer well enough to pick up and move
away; I couldn't survive on the streets. All I could
do was believe in Roland, believe he'd survived his
tricky thirties by avoiding the candles. If that was
enough, I could save myself.

But how? And what about the others? Mike Jr.,
Nancy, all the other children?

Then, I *knew*.

I had to destroy the threat at its source.

Splash!

I winced and paused, clutching the remaining
games in my arms. My mother had gone outside to
refill the bird feeder, but she had impeccable timing
when it came to catching me in the wrong. This . . .
was wrong.

Gathering myself, I slipped the next cartridge into
the dark, gleaming liquid. Our tidy storeroom left
me no choice. My excuse for being here was to finally
pick up the box of vintage Nintendo games I'd left in
the basement. I'd mumbled something about a new
gaming store taking trades—my parents wouldn't
know the difference.

I did. The beloved adventures of my youth disappeared into the sump, as if the sacrifice of health
wasn't enough to appease time.

The box was the key. Once it was emptied, I carried it up the stairs, listening for my parents. Nothing. I tiptoed into the pantry, pulling the door almost closed before turning on the light. Subtle smells of cereal and spice competed with cleanser. The shelves were always full. When I was younger, I'd believed elves restocked them while we slept, especially close to a holiday, when treats briefly outnumbered staples.

It was darker magic I sought now. My hand went unerringly to the second lowest drawer on the back right side. I'd helped my father install all the latest hardware and shelving, including this set of wide pullouts. The tin box winked at me from behind its wall of icing sugar and shortening. With a shudder, I grabbed it and stuffed it into the Nintendo box.

Step one accomplished.

I'd been afraid to incinerate the tin box and its contents. For all I knew, setting the candles on fire would only suck more life from those of us vulnerable to their theft. Instead, I'd run my car over the box until it oozed colored wax and pieces of string, then shoved the remnants into the dumpster behind Mickey D's.

Fire would do for the rest. I licked my lips as I drove, prodding the lump of the latest cold sore to afflict the inside of my mouth. I focused on such things rather than what I had to do. I wasn't a monster.

Yet.

If only I'd been able to find Roland. My hands twisted on the steering wheel until its Naugahyde wrap squeaked in protest. This was a job for two. More than enough guilt for two as well. Or would sharing it only double it?

I pulled into the driveway of Trillium Manor as always, but didn't stop at the entrance or head for visitor parking. Instead, I made the sharp right into the narrow lane that led around back. The plow didn't fit back here—or else the custodians were too lazy to bother. The headlight sparkled on the icicles draping the brick wall. My car slipped and bounced along bones of ice; I didn't dare slow down or I'd be stuck for sure.

Fire melted ice.

I shrugged away guilt and anticipation, settling for a numb attention to detail as I turned the car around. Better to take three tries than dig a tire into a snowbank. Better to leave the engine running than risk a stall. Better to put on gloves before opening the trunk than have gas stinking up my hands.

I kept my face down, trusting the hood of the shapeless old coat I'd found in a garbage bin. If anyone was awake, the items I carried to the rear service door should appear innocuous on their own: a recycle bin full of newspaper, a can of gasoline, and a crowbar.

I didn't need the crowbar after all. The cheap padlock hung loose beside the door; perhaps frozen. I opened the door to a choking blast of warm, moist air, redolent of the dumpster behind Mickey D's but with an added tang of urine and bleach. Doing my best to breathe only through my mouth, I heaved the can and bin into the room and closed the door behind me, blinking as my eyes adjusted to the brightness.

I knew my way. This was where we moved in our senior Farguses, at least the piece or two of furniture that would fit inside a room already crowded by bed and dresser, the box of photographs, the bags of clothes. The rest was scavenged by the next generation, what wasn't tossed aside adding to possessions that would be scavenged in turn by their offspring. I'd become conscious of such cycles lately.

And planned to break one.

Straight ahead through doubled doors: the elevators and stairs. Left corridor: the laundry rooms, quiet at this time of night. Right corridor: waste disposal, including the garbage chute to every floor.

My destination. I staggered to the door, shoving it wide with the recycle bin, then pushed the bin into the darkness beyond. I let the door swing closed behind me as I groped for the switch.

The lights came on before I touched it. "Whadda you doing here, Bobby?" demanded a familiar, rasping voice.

"Uncle Roland?" I gaped at the apparition beside me. He was wrapped in a floral comforter that had seen better centuries. Behind him, on the floor, was a familiar pile of cardboard and sleeping bags, as though he'd simply moved his hovel indoors. "I looked for you everywhere."

"Didn't look here, did you?" He'd washed sometime in the last month, so his hair was merely dark with grease as opposed to matted. "Murph lets me come out of the cold,. Doesn't explain why you're down here. After hours. And with that." He poked the recycle bin with a bare toe. "What are you about, Bobby Fargus?"

"I have to stop them. You can help me!"

"Help—" Roland let the blanket fall from his shoulders, his fingers combing hair from his eyes as if that helped him see me better. Then his hands went still. "You can't—you can't mean to—"

I blinked to clear my own vision, the moisture

burning my chapped cheeks. "It's the only way to end this—to save us. They all have to die."

"Bobby, no! Why? Because of what I said? I'm crazy, Bobby. Look at me!" Roland beat both fists against his own chest. "I'm a nutcase. Certifiable! I should be locked up on the third floor of the Berton Institute, for cris'sake. You mustn't believe anything I say."

"Why do you defend them, Uncle?" I asked, feeling suspicion fall around me like the kiss of cold, wet snowflakes. "What's changed? What did they offer you?"

His mouth worked to protest, to say something. A curse, perhaps. It didn't matter.

I needed the crowbar after all.

Roland helped me, in his fashion. His cardboard bed was dry and warm. Doused with gasoline, it ignited into a pillar of virtuous flame. Licking its way up the walls, impatient for the draft coming down through the chute door. A door I'd propped open, feeling more mechanically inclined than usual.

I left him there, arranging his arms around the gasoline can. A fitting epitaph for the man who'd revealed the truth to me, however confused he'd been at the end. I hurried out the door into the corridor. I'd filled my car before coming—it should still be running, waiting to take me home, where I'd hear the news tomorrow about the tragic fire, and the loss of an entire generation of Farguses, their leathery bodies so much carbon, and the crazy old homeless man who'd killed them all.

Three more steps to safety. To health. To a future. Before I could take the third, I was blinded by spray and deafened by alarms. I yanked the hood over my head and stumbled forward, arms out-stretched. A red light flashed from all directions.

I'd failed. It remained to be seen how completely. My hands were dripping wet and slid painfully down the metal edge as I tugged the door open. Steam rose from my clothes as the cold air hit. I ran for my car as I'd run from my fate.

Only to have my feet betray me on the ice. Falling, twisting, I looked up and saw faces pressed against dozens of lighted windows, faces that watched until my head hit the ice and I knew nothing more. Faces of family.

The case was never in doubt. There were more than enough witnesses, each delighted to have an excuse for an outing. Others had seen me jogging by Roland's summer hovel, under the highway. What no one understood was why. Oh, they asked. The police, the media, those doctors. At first, I refused to explain, but the nights locked in the ward held things worse than anything I'd seen on television, worse than I could have imagined.

And there was always the chance someone might have believed me.

Candles and family curses. I'd destroyed the evidence; they refused to examine my aunts' tin boxes. I should have kept silent, but it all came out. At least, I'm no longer in a prison ward. I'm on the clean and sanitary third floor of Berton's Institute.

Helpless.

But safe. I have to believe it or go as mad as they say I am.

"Don't scrunch your eyes like that, Mr. Fargus. I know you're awake."

I might be awake, but I didn't have to acknowledge my jailer. But she had other ideas. My eyes shot open as flecks of chilled water hit my face. "Don't do that!" I snarled vainly into Nurse Brocket's too-close, too-smug grin. She straightened, replacing her pink plant mister in its holster with the smoothness of a gunfighter, the bottle surely uncomfortable against her thin hip, and slid the wheeled table over my lap. "I've already had the slop you call supper," I protested, twisting my wrists against the straps holding me to the chair.

"I know-o," she chortled, a sound so unlike her ear-threatening habitual whine that it rated the raising of heads by the other chair-bound fools lining this wall. I glared at them, but without success. Those who weren't drooling couldn't focus at the best of times. "I have a surprise for you. Look!" Nurse Brocket whirled away from me, only to turn back more slowly. Slowly, so her motion didn't do more than bend the tip of each tiny flame rising from the object in her hands.

There were thirty candles on that cake, guttering with spite, like so many fierce little eyes watching me with hunger—and expectation.

"Here you go, Mr. Fargus. From your mother—

"Happy birthday!"

THE DEAD DON'T WADDLE

by Esther Friesner

Esther M. Friesner is the Nebula Award-winning author of thirty novels and over one hundred short stories. She is also the editor and creator of the popular Chicks in Chainmail *anthology series. Her most recent publication is* Death and the Librarian and Other Stories. *She lives in Connecticut with her husband, son, daughter, two cats, and no groundhogs.*

MITCH SMALL SLAMMED the front door behind him and stalked out to where his brand new Lamborghini Diablo waited gleaming under the driveway spotlights. Only the sliver of a new moon showed in the wintry heavens as he jammed the pedal to the metal and tore away in a spray of slush. One part of his brain continued to curse out Loretta and all her tedious whining about marriage, marriage, marriage, while the other ninety percent of that underworked organ bitterly calculated how much damage his grand exit was doing to the Diablo's glossy flanks and tender underbelly. Pennsylvania winters could be rough, and most municipalities fought them tooth, nail, and rock salt. Magically, Mitch managed to rationalize matters so that everything—the argument, the salt damage to his pampered car, the bitter January weather—was strictly Loretta's fault.

"Stupid bitch," he growled as he barreled through the streets. His progress was a living lesson in how traffic regulations were for lesser creatures. Mitch hadn't become one of the best corporate lawyers at the firm by doubting his well-deserved place at the center of the universe. The race was to the swift and the battle to the strong, but the rest of the world was to the arrogant. His inborn sense of entitlement transformed every blazing red traffic light in his path into merely a polite suggestion that he slow down *just* a hair (but only if he *really* felt like it), while octagonal stop signs got about as much attention as a poppy seed in a tar pit.

"Who the hell does she think she is, trying to make me feel guilty, for God's sake?" he snarled as trees and houses and strip malls streamed past the car's rapidly fogging windows. "Guilty for *what*? I didn't do anything wrong! I didn't force her to move in with me. And I damn well know that I never told her it was just for a year, so we'd have time to plan a really nice wedding. She made it all up; it's—it's *entrapment*, that's what it is! So *what* if her ditzy friend Janice claims she was right there when I *allegedly* said that stuff about marrying her some day?" (Mitch liked words like "allegedly." They made him feel warm and complacent and vindicated inside.) "The main thing is *I* don't remember it. So it never happened. And if they both swear it did, big deal! Like *that* makes it binding? Hell, it doesn't even make it believable! The bitches will say *anything* to get married, and their skanky girlfriends will do whatever it takes to help them land some poor, unsuspecting

bastard. Lie? Ha! Lying's small potatoes to those har-
pies when they've got that bigass diamond ring in
their sights. They lie as easy as breathing."

He was still going on about the untrustworthiness
of women in general and Loretta in particular when
he saw the welcoming pastel lights of the all-night
donut shop glowing like a caffeine-fueled beacon in
the distance. Mitch's mouth was dry from his recent
rant, so he pulled into the almost deserted parking
lot.

He drank a cup of coffee that was black, bitter,
and burned. It was a perfect match for his black
mood, bitter attitude, and the conviction that he'd
been badly burned by Loretta's refusal to see reason
(a.k.a. *his* point of view). The waitress who filled his
order was a pretty little thing, just on the cusp of
losing that prettiness to the stresses of earning a
nickel-and-dime living on the graveyard shift. By a
perverse stroke of luck (courtesy of the Petty Vengeance Fairy), she was bored, she'd just broken up
with her boyfriend, and she hated the owner of Al's-
All-Nite Donuts with a vindictive passion worthy of
a Borgia.

All it took was a wink and a donut. The next thing
they knew, they were going at it mightily in Mitch's
car. The Lamborghini Diablo might not provide the
same level of romantic accommodation found in
larger vehicles, but Love will find a way, and Lust
is pretty damn smart about downloading driving directions from the Internet.

"Oooooh," the waitress cooed, stroking the lush
upholstery when the two of them were done. "Is this
real leather?"

"Only the best," Mitch assured her, grinning ear
to ear. In his mind the cheap quickie was already

transforming itself into a glorious marathon love-making session that would leave porn stars everywhere taking envious note. His afterglow was a compendium of equal parts animal satisfaction and gloating that he had by-God *showed* that bitch Loretta that she wasn't the only fish in the sea. Already he was planning how best to let her know ("accidentally," of course) how quickly he'd managed to replace her.

The waitress leaned forward to check out the Diablo's gleaming dashboard. "Wow," she said in that same hushed tone of voice most people reserve for visits to St. Patrick's Cathedral. "How fast does this thing go?"

"Why don't I show you?" Mitch was feeling benevolent, otherwise he never would have made such an offer. It would take him days to banish the smell of lard and powdered sugar from the Diablo's interior, and the longer this little chippie hung around, the harder the task of deodorizing the car was going to be. Still, she'd done him a favor: he felt that he owed her *something*.

Shortly thereafter, Mitch and the waitress were careening down one of the more rural roads in the hill country surrounding his home suburb. Al's-All-Nite Donuts would need a new sign, or at least a subtitle reading *Except One-Hour Joyride Breaks*. Hopped up on a double-double espresso that his new ladylove had brewed specially for him before they took off, Mitch took curves on two wheels, straightaways at the speed of uh-oh, and no notice whatsoever of anything but the gleeful desire to show off his magnificent car. For Mitch Small, to go racing through the night in a glossy, brand-new Diablo with a willing woman by his side, smugness draped around him like a custom-tailored suit, meant that all was right with the world.

THUD!

"What was that?" The waitress squealed and jerked her head in all directions like a panicky chicken.

Mitch stopped the car. To his credit, he didn't waste time falsely claiming, "I didn't heard anything." He'd heard that THUD all right, heard it loud and clear. How could he ignore a sound that could only mean the worst possible thing to any driver worth his license?

Something out there had dinged his precious car. The nerve!

Mitch reached over and opened the glove compartment to extract an industrial-sized flashlight, then got out to investigate. Sure enough, there was the evidence, a bloodstained dent on the left-hand side of his front fender. Whatever had hurled itself so mercilessly against the innocent Diablo had done damage.

"Son of a *bitch*," Mitch snarled, clenching his teeth in rage. The flashlight beam swept the snowy road, searching for the culprit. In spite of the cold, the waitress stepped out of the car, curiosity getting the better of good judgment.

"What was it?" she asked, hugging herself and shivering. "You think it was maybe a—? Oh! There it is, I think. Over there." She pointed to a small, dark object huddled by the side of the road.

Mitch swung the light around to where she was pointing, then stomped over to check it out. The waitress scampered after him, clinging to his back and peering over his shoulder.

"Oh, God. Oh, God. Oh, God, I think you killed someone's *doggie*," she moaned.

"Serves 'em right for letting the hairy little fuck run loose," Mitch replied.

"How can you *say* that?" Her voice rose to exasperating heights, with an irksome nasal twang that Mitch had not chosen to notice until now. "Sometimes people can't help it when their doggies get loose. Sometimes the poor things get lost, you know? Oh, my God, what if it belongs to some little *kid*? Jesus, she'll be heartbroken! I had a doggie when I was eight, a doggie named Jojo, and one day he got out of our yard and—"

"Will you shut *up* for two seconds?" Mitch snapped. "Do you honestly expect me to give a rat's ass about some mutt you had when you were eight?"

"But he *died*!" the waitress wailed. "He ran out into the street and a truck hit him and he *died*!"

"So *what*?" Mitch countered at the top of his lungs. "If you had the little hairball when you were eight, he'd he dead by now anyway. Dead or fifty." He didn't have any basis in reality for putting in that last barb—she didn't look a day over twenty-nine—but he was fed up, cold, and angry. He had to strike out at something.

The waitress gasped and drew back her hand to slap him. Mitch let her raise it as high as she could before calmly saying, "Touch me and you walk home." He got more satisfaction out of watching her slowly lower her hand, defeated, than he'd gotten out of all their time making rather constricted whoopee in the Diablo. He laughed in her face.

The waitress (he still hadn't bothered to ask her name; why bother?) turned away. Suddenly, she got a good look at the small, furry body by the roadside. "Oh, wow!" she exclaimed. "It's not a dog after all. I think it's a gopher or something."

"Are you nuts?" Mitch changed the angle of the heavy flashlight's beam, the better to determine precisely what sort of creature he'd rammed into eternity. Not that he cared about the luckless beast *per se;* he just wanted the pleasure of telling the waitress her ID of the victim was wrong. He got his wish.

"That's no gopher," he condescended to inform her. "It's a woodchuck."

The young woman crept closer, squatting down carefully for a closer look. She shook her head. "Can't be," she said. "It's the middle of winter. They hibernate."

"So maybe the poor bastard had insomnia, okay? Look, I know a woodchuck when I see one!" He gave the body a casual kick with the tip of his shoe.

The waitress let out a little scream. "Oh, my God! He's not dead yet!"

"Yeah?" Mitch tilted his head, looking skeptical. "Where'd you get your medical training? Watching reruns of 'E.R.'?"

"I swear, I saw him move," the waitress maintained. "I saw him breathe. Maybe we could still save him. We oughta take him to a veterinarian." Automatically, without a thought to the possibility of fleas, ticks, or germs, she laid on hand on the creature's slowly moving side.

A beatific smile suffused Mitch's face. "Sure we should," he said. "Why don't I wrap him up in my coat, while we're at it, just so he's nice and comfy and doesn't bleed all over the seat? Oh, but wait just a sec: Maybe we should give him a little first aid before we do anything else. What's that they're always saying about open wounds? About how you should apply pressure?"

He lifted the flashlight and brought it down

swiftly, suddenly, brutally on the woodchuck's skull.
The waitress' shocked shriek echoed through the
frosty air almost as loudly as the sound of crunching
bone. She lost her balance and fell backward, sitting
down hard in the snow packed up along the roadside
by the plows. Her hand landed in the swiftly spreading crimson pool leaking from the unlucky animal's
body.

"Oops," Mitch said, grinning. "Too much pressure." He glanced at the waitress where she sat
stunned in the snow. He wrinkled his upper lip in
disgust at her soaked uniform. "Baby, I hope you've
got a cell phone to call yourself a cab, because no
way am I letting you back in my car like *that*." She
was still sitting there, staring at the woodchuck's
corpse, as he got back into his Diablo and drove
away.

The following week of Mitch Small's life went
swimmingly. The world was his oyster in a year free
of water pollution, hepatitis, and months with no R.
His impromptu session of Bludgeon Therapy with
the woodchuck reminded him that he was, after all,
a man of action: decisive, determined, and not some
marriage-hungry hag's boy-toy. The day after his encounter with the waitress from Al's-All-Nite, he
waited until Loretta left for work and then tossed all
her belongings out into the snow, topped the pile
with a bridal bouquet he'd had specially made for
the occasion, and changed all the locks.

He was still bent out of shape over the dent in his
fender, but the guy at the body shop was too stupid
to gouge him. He stuck the charges on the credit card
account Loretta once had loaned him for making on-
line purchases when he claimed he'd maxed out his

own cards buying "a very special piece of jewelry for the one I love." The relationship ended before she found out it was a solid gold signet ring for himself.

Mitch was just pouring himself a cosmopolitan when the doorbell rang. A frown touched his lips. That had better not be Loretta. He reached for the fireplace poker just in case. He doubted he'd have to use it, but if she'd come for a showdown and brought that dyke Janice for backup, who'd blame an honest man for protecting himself?

A glance through the peephole revealed that it wasn't Loretta on his doorstep after all: It was that waitress-chick from the donut joint.

Somewhere in the seldom-visited recesses of Mitch's Common Sense Command Center a small voice bleated piteously: *Do not open that door! That is a woman you treated with less respect than a pay toilet. You used her, you mocked her, you insulted her, and then you ditched her miles from anywhere in the freezing cold. I don't care how tight that blouse is she's wearing or how much thigh she's showing in that skirt or how wide she's smiling, this is not a safe person to let into your house! Okay? Got it? Am I making myself clear? Hello? Mitch? Anyone?*

It was good advice, and Mitch actually was on the brink of heeding it. Alas, at that very moment the waitress took a step back from the door, the better to frame herself in the peephole's fish-eye lens. With the finesse of a spokesmodel unveiling a hot new product, she hiked her skirt up just enough to reveal the whisper of a black lace garter belt, a murmur of deliberately forgotten underwear, and a silent shout of *Come and get it!*

Common sense got the boot as Mitch made a bee-line for the booty.

* * *

Of course she'd forgiven him for ditching her in the snow. Wasn't he the most wonderful man in the world? She should have known *so* much better than to annoy him with her silly little concerns about an animal too stupid to stay out of the road.

Of course he believed her. Didn't she sound sincere when she told him what a stud he was? Obviously a woman of such high intelligence and discernment would never lie, lest she forfeit his incredibly skilled-and-indefatigable amorous attentions.

It all made sense to Mitch.

When she told him she didn't believe in marriage, he asked her to move in.

January whizzed into early February in a delirious blur of wild lovemaking and free donuts. Mitch's bedroom was perpetually redolent of powdered sugar, cinnamon, and chocolate, with an underlying note of animal musk. There were times that Mitch hauled himself out of bed for a post-party bathroom run unable to focus his eyes. He was no scientist, but he was pretty sure that all of that high-impact bouncing must have some residual effect on a man's sight.

Why else would his eyes be playing tricks on him?

They weren't *upsetting* tricks; by no means. In fact, they were dreadfully commonplace, as optical illusions go. Mitch suspected as much and confirmed his suspicions when he spoke with one of his fellow attorneys. (Like Shakespeare, Mitch believed that *They do not love who do not show their love.* In his case that meant telling everyone at the firm all the sticky details of his stud sessions. Of *course* they were interested! They must be. It was about *him*, wasn't it?)

Mitch mentioned the "eye-thing" while recounting

his most recent stint in the saddle to a colleague so desperate to make partner that he'd have listened to a one-man Kirk-vs.-Picard debate without demur. "So at first I think that the brown, furry blob I'm seeing—just out of the corner of my eye, you know?—is the cat. Then I remember we don't have a cat. And whenever I turn my head to get a really *good* look at it, it's like it sort of waddles out of sight, around a corner. Man, I didn't know anything could waddle that damn *fast!* So it's gone, only it's there again when I look away. Weird, huh? Must've been a trick of the light. Either that or all the—" (Here he made a fist and executed wild, pumping motions with his arm, all the while doing his level best to imitate the sound of squeaky mattress springs) "—knocked a few brain cells loose. Heh. Lose enough and you're a dead man, but what a way to go!"

"Well, I don't think you could ever do *that* enough to kill off *all* your brain cells," Mitch's cornered audience remarked, his eyes all the while desperately scanning the horizon for some hope of rescue. (Midway through Mitch's saga he had realized that if listening to this soft-porn puffery were the price of partnership, it was too damn high.)

"Are you kidding?" Mitch whinnied. "Shows you how second-string *your* sex life's been. I tell you, some of the things she's been making me do—"

"*Making* you do?" Despite the knowledge that any questions would only extend his torture session, Mitch's victim could not help but ask.

Mitch brushed linguistic nitpicks aside. "Oh, it's not like she could *make* me do anything I didn't really want to do. I'm the *man,* after all. But sometimes she comes up with these ideas, and she does these *things* to me, and—well, let's just say she's got the talent to bring matters to the point where a *real* man *can't* say no. Not without blowing up like a plugged volcano."

"Er, sounds . . . dangerous."

"Nothing I can't handle." Mitch slapped him on the back. "It'd probably kill *you*."

"Lucky it's not me, then. I still need all my brain cells." It was out of his mouth before he could stop it.

Mitch scowled. "What did you say your name was again, sport?"

The victim hastily gave the name of his greatest office nemesis and scuttled away. Mitch's lip curled into an expression of rank disgust. Was that little shit making fun of him? Probably jealous as hell, jealous because the best sex *he'd* ever have would be the prepaid kind. Mitch left the office and went straight home, wishing with all his heart that there was a way he could make that sarcastic bastard see just what he (Mitch) was getting that he (sarcastic bastard) could never hope to get.

Inspiration of the why-didn't-I-think-of-this-before? variety struck just as he was pulling into the driveway. Instead of his usual "I'm home, sweetcheeks!" Mitch greeted his *inamorata* with "Hey, baby, bust out the videocam! It's showtime!"

The next morning dawned with that special, knife-edged brilliance that sometimes makes northeastern winters bearable. Sometimes.

Mitch Small woke up to find that in the course of the night his bedmate had managed to exercise Eminent Domain over all the blankets. Now she was completely wrapped up in the heart of her ill-gotten conquests with nary a wisp of hair nor a glimmer of crimson toenail showing. Mitch debated grabbing hold of the wooly cocoon and yanking her out of it, but immediately dismissed the notion as too much effort for a man in his physically depleted condition.

What a night! Some of the things she'd done to his body would have left the authors of the *Kama Sutra* with their jaws somewhere down around their ankles. Her agility was matched only by her flexibility and exceeded by her imagination. Mitch was smiling as he stood up to go to the bathroom.

Then he fell down.

Scowling and swearing, he pulled himself back onto the bed. What the heck was the matter with his legs? They looked . . . depleted. Where once there had been hard, taut reserves of muscle there was now an alien softness, a complete lack of tone. What was worse, as Mitch gave his thigh an experimental squeeze he became aware of a disturbing lack of power in his hands as well. His grip had all the firmness of boiled custard.

A low, persistent whirring noise distracted him momentarily from any further self-evaluation. Like an undersized refugee from *The War of the Worlds*, the videocam whined at him from atop its tripod.

"Oh, wow, the tape!" Mitch leaped to his feet and, for a wonder, stayed there. The memory of the previous night's gymnastics had a miraculously revivifying influence over him, the triumph of really dirty mind over matter. Staggering only a little, he managed to remove the cassette from the camera and bear it off to the living room where he popped it into the VCR and hit Rewind.

"This is going to be *good*," said Mitch as he settled back into the buttery soft embrace of his Italian leather sofa. The tape clicked to a stop. There was a thin, glittery trail of drool at the corner of his mouth as he aimed the remote control at the television and pressed Play.

There was a good-sized puddle of drool gathered in the lap of his robe by the time the tape had played itself out, but it was not salivation born of lusty enjoyment. This was the dribble of horror.

"No," he rasped, shaking his head slightly, as though he feared more vigorous effort would cause it to snap right off his neck and roll under the coffee table. Stranger things were known to happen. Proof of that had just unscrolled itself before his helplessly staring eyes. "No," he said again, and then, louder, "No!"

A stirring came from the bedroom. A sleepy, inquiring noise was heard; nothing you could call *words*, precisely. Snufflings? Yes. Grunts? Oh, certainly. Some people were little better than animals when it came to communicating with others before they'd had that first cup of coffee.

Mitch's head whipped around at the sound, a look of stark terror in his eyes. "It can't be," he whispered, afraid of raising his voice again, lest he raise other things besides. "It's—it's impossible. I must've been dreaming, feel asleep while the tape was playing. I fell asleep and had a nightmare. Yeah, right, that's it." He touched Rewind again and sat curled up on the sofa, every nerve wound tighter than a golf ball's innards. When the VCR sounded the *click* that meant it was ready to rock 'n' roll once more, Mitch just about jumped clean out of his skin.

"It didn't happen," he whispered as his trembling forefinger touched Play.

The first image on the screen was reassuring in its banality—a nice, clean, establishing shot of Mitch's bed, complete with bedmate.

"That's funny," Mitch muttered. "I thought her eyes were blue. And bigger. And not quite that . . . beady." He took a deep breath and continued to watch.

She was smiling: a sweet, inviting, altogether human smile. She had very good teeth—a trifle prominent, yes, but nothing beyond the powers of modern orthodontia to cure. She beckoned, and in short order Mitch saw himself join her in the bed.

What followed needed precious little explanation to those familiar with such matters. As for those still innocent, well, no explanation could ever justify an activity that looked so damned silly to the inexperienced eye. Sex was never intended to be a spectator sport.

Mitch begged to differ. He found something soothing in observing his own amorous gyrations. Maybe he wasn't the world's most imaginative lover—selfish people seldom are—but after what he thought he'd seen on the videotape the first time through, he was filled with a desperate craving *not* to see anything extraordinary this time. A vision of commonplace sex was just what the doctor ordered. He began to relax. He even ventured to smile.

"Nothing," he murmured. "It was a trick of the light, that's all. I didn't really see—"

The self-comforting words died in his throat. The figures on the screen had shifted position. The lady had taken control and the gentleman was deferring to her. His eyes were closed as his senses transported him to realms of pleasure that were as intense as they were exhausting. His hand groped for her hair.

And found it. It was pretty hard to miss, even with closed eyes. It was everywhere, that hair, thick and brown and luxuriant. The on-screen Mitch moaned happily, stroking it, all the while blissfully unaware that the hand caressing those plush tresses was nowhere near the lady's head, but rather . . . on her back. That was probably a good thing. At that moment, the hand rash enough to venture near the lady's head would have found itself in imminent peril of receiving one hell of a nasty bite.

Not that she'd *mean* to bite him, but with two front teeth like those . . . They'd changed, those teeth. Grown. Taken themselves way beyond the point where an ordinary orthodontist could intercede. Not unless he also held a degree in veterinary medicine.

Mitch felt the blood drain from his face and solidify in his gut. "No," he said yet again. (He was in no condition to come up with a snappier line of patter.) "She's—she's an *animal!*" And for once in his life, those words were not intended as a compliment to the lady.

He tried to hit the Stop button on the remote and found himself unable to do so. He was compelled to watch the tape out to its end, forced to see himself being put through one bizarre and arduous carnal encounter after another by something inhuman. His on-screen self was too blissed-out to care, too sapped to open his eyes and truly see who—*what*— was having its wicked way with him.

When the tape had almost spun itself out, the nightmare creature moved its round, beady-eyed head close to Mitch's ear. Its black lips parted in a hideous, buck-toothed leer and, in a voice that somehow evoked an unspeakable combination of *The Wind in the Willows* and *The Necronomicon*, it whispered, "*Now* aren't you sorry you left me by the side of the road like that, my love?" It rested one hairy paw on his chest and slowly, delicately, drew it downward.

The tape ended as the pain began. Mitch became aware of a dull, burning sensation just below his throat. He parted the folds of his robe and looked down. The long, glittering claw tracks still oozed red.

With a strangled scream of revulsion, Mitch leaped up from the couch and raced to the bedroom. He paused in his headlong rush only long enough to lay hands on his domestic weapon of choice, the fireplace poker. In his spent state the effort left him feeble and dizzy, but he was damned if he'd allow that—that—that *thing* to spend one more moment under his roof. Fighting to stay on his feet, he reached down and tore away the rolled-up blankets, all the while brandishing the poker and shouting, "Get up, you sneaky bastard! I don't care *how* damn much wood you can chuck, you're finished chucking around with me!"

The naked woman in the rumpled bed rolled over, rubbed her eyes sleepily, and said, "Huh?"

Half an hour later; Mitch sat watching the videotape melt in the fireplace. His lady friend had gone back to sleep after the two of them had viewed it, at his insistence. All that it had showed was a pair of healthy adult human beings at play.

Following the screening of the tape, Mitch and the waitress had what couples therapists everywhere would describe as "an open, fulfilling, and mutually satisfactory dialogue." This basically translated as: In future Mitch would wait until *after* gawdawful o'clock in the frickin' morning before waking a lady up to listen to a bunch of insane accusations. The lady, in turn, would not make sure that Mitch's superiors and rivals at the law office heard all about this. In detail.

She also told him she was leaving him. She was used to crazy boyfriends, but she preferred vanilla-flavored insanity; none of this *creative* shit. As soon as she caught up on her beauty sleep, she was going to get dressed and go.

"A woodchuck," she muttered as she sank back into slumber. "Do I *look* like a frickin' woodchuck? Man's fantasizing about *rodents*, for God's sake. Watching too damn much MTV or something . . ." The rest was lost in snores.

Mitch sighed and poked up the fire. The boiling videotape was making an awful stench as it melted. The fumes were probably toxic. He didn't care. He'd done the unthinkable, lost his cool, made a fool of himself.

"I'm tired," he said aloud. "That's the problem. I've got to rest, get a bite to eat, build my strength back up. Maybe it's a good thing that the bitch is clearing out. Jeez! I mean, it felt good and all, but the way she was putting me through the paces, she almost ki—"

A fugitive thought struck him—an impossibility, perhaps. At least he hoped it was an impossibility. Joking aside, you couldn't *really* kill a man by making him do *that* without respite or letup.

Could you?

The videocassette was really stinking the place up now. His head swam; he needed fresh air. He got up and lurched to the front door, throwing it open to sparkling snow, azure skies, and the crisp, refreshing tang of an icy morning. "Beautiful," he murmured, taking a step outside despite the cold. "Just beautiful."

"I'll say," came a voice behind him. "Clean outline, solid black interior, gorgeous contrast on the snow, no way anyone could mistake it for anything but the sign it is. I couldn't have done it any better myself."

A huge paw that reeked of the deep places of the earth fell heavily onto Mitch's shoulder. "Back to bed we go. You know the rules."

A plaintive note of helpless yearning escaped Mitch's lips as he was dragged backward into his own house and the door slammed shut behind him. He knew that he had looked his last on the sun; that the promise of that brilliant February morning outside was the last he'd ever look on the living world. In his debilitated condition there was no way he'd survive to see the springtime.

He knew the rules, all right: six more weeks of winter.

Special thanks to Tamara Fougner for the use of the zombie groundhog.

BROTHERHOOD

by David D. Levine

David D. Levine attended Clarion West in 2000 and hasn't slowed down since. His stories have appeared in such publications as The Year's Best Fantasy #2, The Magazine of Fantasy and Science Fiction, Interzone, and Apprentice Fantastic, and he is a winner of the James White Award, Writers of the Future, and the Phobos Fiction Contest. He lives in Portland, Oregon, where he and his wife Kate Yule produce the highly-regarded science fiction fanzine Bento. His web page is www.BentoPress.com.

GUS COLLINA DIED on a summer day, when the light slanted down through Kensington Steel's tall, soot-streaked windows and cut hard-edged columns through the filthy air. Outside those windows the Monongahela River oozed past the town of Monessen, water cooked brown and thick as pudding by the July heat; inside the plant it was hotter still, the year-round heat of the furnaces made even more intolerable by the blazing sun outside. It was one of those days where the sweat pools at the base of your spine, crawls across the palms of your hands under the thick leather gloves, and drips from your forehead onto the lenses of your safety glasses.

Gus was working the coil line that day, where red-hot iron ingots were rolled out into long sheets. He was just coming to the end of another double shift, pushing hard to meet the impossible quotas management demanded. After sixteen hours on the job he was bone-tired, but it was 1937 and he knew he was lucky to have a job at all, and so he kept on working. Until he stumbled, just a little, and one foot caught on the other. He put out a hand to steady himself—and touched the four-foot-wide band of steel, four hundred degrees hot and moving forty-five miles an hour.

Tony Collina saw him die. Tony was Gus' brother, two years younger, and he watched from a catwalk fifty feet away as Gus was pulled into the works without even time to scream. Tony prayed to Saint Sebastian, the patron of steelworkers, as his steel-toed boots rang down the steps and pounded across the gritty concrete floor, but even as he rushed he knew it was already too late.

They found nothing but blood. Every solid particle of Gus' body had been crushed out of existence between the turns of hot steel on the ten-ton roll at the end of the line.

Tony moved through the crowd of friends and relations at Gus' wake, accepting condolences as he passed the hat for Gus' wife—widow, now. Anna had two daughters, and a baby on the way, and no insurance or savings.

Gino Mattioli came through the front door still in his work clothes, his face filthy and bearing the red marks of his safety glasses. Not even death could slow the production lines at Kensington Steel. "Tony, I'm so sorry I missed the funeral. I came as quick as I could."

" 'S okay, Gino." Tony held up his hat, which rattled with silver and paper. "For Anna."

Gino's handsome face pinched into a scowl as he dug in his pants pocket. "Jesus, what a situation. How's she taking it?"

"Not well. My wife's with her now."

Gino pulled his hand from his pocket, stared down into it for a moment, then with an expression of resignation dumped the whole pathetic handful of change into Tony's hat. "Sorry, that's all I've got."

"Thanks anyway."

The two men embraced, the hatful of money jingling in Tony's ear. Before letting go, Gino asked, "How about you?"

"Me?"

Gino pulled back, held both of Tony's shoulders. "Yeah, you. How are *you* taking it?"

Fireworks of emotion exploded in Tony's chest like the sparks from a Bessemer converter. Tony had always been the shortstop to Gus' pitcher. They'd played together, fought together, got in trouble together, worked together. Gus had handled everything when Pop died of tuberculosis in '34, shielding Tony from the diagnosis as long as he could. Gus had been the best man at Tony's wedding, just a year ago. And now . . . all of a sudden, at twenty-seven, Tony was the papa of the entire family.

"I'm all right," he said. He turned away so Gino couldn't see his face. "I'm all right."

Gino squeezed Tony's shoulder. "I'd better go in and pay my respects."

"Yeah. You do that." He wiped his eyes quickly and turned back. "Thanks."

Gino walked into the living room, where Gus and Anna's wedding photo sat atop a plain pine coffin and a huge cross of flowers perfumed the air. Tony tried not to remember that the coffin was empty except for a pair of bloodstained and mangled steel-toed boots, tried not to think about how much the coffin and the flowers and the priest had cost, tried not to worry about how he was going to support Anna and her kids as well as his own Sofia and little Bella . . . tried not to wonder how many more men would die before this job was finished.

Gino finished praying and rose to his feet. He kissed his fingers and touched them to the coffin. "It's a damn shame," he said, looking over his shoulder. "That's—what, six already this year?"

"Seven."

"Jesus." He shook his head. "They're killing us. Honest to God, Tony, they're killing us with this schedule."

"I know. But if we don't make this deadline, you know they'll give the damn bridge contract to Inland and then every single one of us will be on the W.P.A."

"Now you're talking like management."

Tony pursed his lips, drew in a breath through his nose. "I have to go and give this money to Anna." But as he turned to go, Gino caught his shoulder.

"We don't have to take this. We can fight them. We can unionize."

Tony slapped Gino's hand away. "And we can lose our jobs. Or worse. Remember Republic Steel?"

Everyone knew how the Republic Steel strike had ended. On Memorial Day in 1937, a crowd of picketers were met by armed policemen as they approached the plant. Ten men died in the resulting melee, hundreds were injured, and the strike was broken. The newsreels called the strikers a blood-thirsty mob, but the steelworkers' grapevine said they were just a Memorial Day picnic crowd, including women and children, armed with nothing but placards. Either way, the strike had been a disaster for the union.

Gino's dark brows drew together as he stared hard into Tony's eyes. Then he turned away and waved dismissively at Tony. "Go on, then. Tell Anna, if there's anything I can do . . ."

"I'll tell her."

On the way to the back bedroom where Sofia comforted the grieving Anna, Tony passed through the kitchen. Warm smells of the lasagna and porcetta and ravioli brought by the aunts and neighbor women enticed his nose but the stove was cold. Cold as death.

Tony sat up in bed. "Who's there?"

At first, there was no sign of what had woken him. Sofia snored gently beside him, and little Bella breathed peacefully in her crib beside the bed. Similar sounds came through the door, where Anna and her two children slept in the living room. Six people made a tight crowd in the four-room company house, but Tony could not shirk his family obligations.

Just as Tony was about to settle back down and close his eyes, he saw something move. It might have been the curtains stirring in the fitful breeze, but no—it was at the foot of the bed. Something rippled in the stripes of yellow light cast by the streetlight through the Venetian blinds.

Tony's eyes snapped open and his heart pounded. "Anna? Is that you?"

"Don't you know me, you moron?" The voice was familiar, but it sounded like a long-distance telephone call from the bottom of a freezer, and the hair rose on the back of Tony's neck.

"Gus?"

"Who else?"

Tony squinted into the darkness. Was that a human figure perched on the footboard? Or was it just a shadow? Tony could see right through it to the Blessed Virgin on the wall behind it.

"You're not Gus," he hissed. He gripped the sheet so tightly he felt it start to tear.

The figure leaned forward, the stripes of light shifting across its face, and Tony thought he saw Gus' big ears and prominent Adam's apple. Just like his. "Who else would know about the deal you and I made with Walter Ailes?"

Goosebumps pricked Tony's forearms. "I never should have let you talk me into it in the first place."

The shadow seemed to shake its head. "I'm sorry about that, now."

Tony closed his eyes, pinched the bridge of his nose hard. "This is a dream, right?"

"Maybe. But even if it is, there's one thing I want you to remember when you wake up."

Tony let go of his nose, stared at the shadowy figure.

"You're going to have to decide who your real friends are, little brother. Ailes gives you money, but . . ."

"I have Anna and *your* kids to support! There's no way I can back out now."

"Don't make the same mistake I did." And then, without transition, Gus was gone.

Tony gazed on the face of the Blessed Virgin. Her

cheap printed smile was not very comforting. *It was just a dream*, he told himself. But then he put out a hand to the footboard where his brother's ghost had sat. The wood was cold under his fingertips, though the July night was sweltering.

Tony put the pillow over his head, just like when he was a kid, and shivered until he fell asleep.

Molten steel glowed orange-red as it seethed from the giant ladle into the ingot molds laid out at Tony's station. He pulled a bandanna from his pocket and wiped the back of his neck as he watched the pour, then stuffed it quickly away before guiding the ladle to the next mold. Hot air and sparks roared out of the mold as the steel poured in, burning the scowl on Tony's face.

Bruno the foreman slapped him on the shoulder. "You're wanted at the office," he shouted over the clang and rush of the plant.

The oak-and-glass office door closed with a thud, blocking out most of the sound from the plant floor beyond. "I'm Antonio Collina," he said to the suspicious-looking clerk behind the counter.

Walter Ailes, the plant's director of personnel, emerged from a back room a few minutes later. His hair and skin were very pale, and wire-rimmed glasses perched atop his hatchet-thin nose. Tony was ashamed of his own swarthy, grimy complexion.

"Thank you for coming, Mister Collina," said Ailes. "Won't you please come this way?" His skinny hand was cool and surprisingly strong, easily matching the pressure of Tony's callused fingers.

Together they moved from the concrete of the plant floor onto hardwood. Tony became increasingly uncomfortable as they walked, acutely aware of the gray grit embedded in his coveralls, his face, his hair. He was afraid to touch the clean cream-colored walls; he knew he stank of sweat and hot metal. "What's this all about, Mister Ailes?" Tony whispered. "You said never to come into the office."

"Yes. But Mister Kensington wanted to have a word with you." Ailes opened a heavy door on which OFFICE OF THE PRESIDENT was written in gold leaf.

The office behind the door was bigger than Tony's entire house, with high ceilings and oak bookcases full of ledgers. The desk, also of oak, was the size of the altar at St. Cajetan's. Behind the desk hung a portrait of OUR FOUNDER, Joseph G. Kensington. And below the portrait sat Joseph G. Kensington II, President of Kensington Steel. He stood and held out his hand.

Tony had never met a Kensington before. He was nearly as pale as Ailes, but his nose was round and pink and his jowls seemed to bulge from his high starched collar like a big bubblegum bubble. "Mister Collina, I was so sorry to hear about your brother Giuseppe."

"Thank you, sir." Kensington's hand felt like a bunch of uncooked sausages. Tony didn't want to grip it too firmly, for fear it would burst.

"I like to think of everyone here at Kensington Steel as family. And families stick together in time of hardship, do they not?"

"Uh, yes, sir."

Kensington wiped his hand with a white silk handkerchief, then dropped it in the wastepaper basket. "I am aware," he said, "that some members of the Kensington Steel family do not have the family's best interests at heart. Mister Ailes tells me that the weekly reports that you and your brother have written on these agitators' activities have been most informative."

"Thank you, sir." Tony gritted his teeth at the memory of the men who had lost their jobs as a result of those reports. But the extra six dollars a week in his pay envelope, which had been a luxury for a family of three, were a necessity for six. It would be even worse when Anna's baby came.

"I want to make sure that these reports continue. Despite the unfortunate circumstances."

"Of course, sir." *You coldhearted bastard,* he thought.

"We believe," said Ailes, "that there may be an increase in . . . antisocial activity, in the wake of your brother's death."

"I don't understand, sir." But Tony knew what he meant, and he felt sweat trickling down his sides.

"We are talking abut *unionization,* Mister Collina!" Kensington thundered. "Communists and anarchists. Bloodthirsty men who desire nothing less than the destruction of the American way of life!" His pink cheeks grew pinker.

"All we ask," said Ailes in a soothing voice. "is that you appear to cooperate with any attempt to unionize the men, and keep us informed of the organizers' actions."

"I, uh . . ." The room as suddenly hotter than the August sun and the proximity of the blast furnaces could explain. "Yes, sir." He would have to avoid Gino. If nobody asked him to join, he wouldn't have anything to report on.

"However, Mister Collina," said Ailes, and his words were suddenly as thin and strong as his fin-

gers, "please do keep in mind that you are not our
only such . . . reporter. If your reports are not complete and accurate, we *will* know it."

Six dollars a week. "You can depend on me, sir."

As Ailes was escorting Tony back to the plant
floor, a Serbian laborer came up to him with a large,
heavy box. "Where you want this, Mister Ailes?"

Ailes' face betrayed a sting of annoyance. "Put it
with the others."

"Yessir."

As the Serb turned away, Tony noticed the words
stenciled on the end of the wooden box: AX HAN-
DLES, TWO DOZ. Aghast, Tony watched as the Serb
opened a storeroom door. Behind that door were
more boxes of ax handles, and other things: tear gas
grenades, rifles, and riot guns with barrels the size
of beer bottles.

Ailes' eyes narrowed with anger. "You should not
have seen that, Mister Collina. I trust you will keep
this information . . . confidential?"

"Uh, yes, sir."

"Good. And I hope you will understand that we
are prepared to defend Kensington Steel from the
forces of anarchy." He lowered his voice and leaned
in close. "By *any* means necessary. Do you understand, Mister Collina?"

"Yes, sir."

Later, back in the noise and stench of the plant floor,
Tony recalled what Gus had said about deciding who
is real friends were. But that had just been a dream.
The six dollars a week was real, and it would keep his
brother's children from going hungry.

Even so, and even in the heat of the blast furnaces, Tony shivered.

Weeks went by. Tony filed his reports, usually nothing more than repeating his coworkers' grumbles and antimanagement jokes, and the money came in every week. He kept his conversations with Gino focused on baseball and their wives' cooking. After a while he started to relax.

Then, one night, he dreamed of Gus. They were playing stickball in the street by the house where they'd grown up, though they were both adults and wearing their steel-mill coveralls.

"Heads up!" shouted Gus, and hit a long high ball to Tony.

"Got it!" He reached for the ball, but it sailed past his outstretched fingers and into the bramble bushes behind Uncle Ottavio's house.

"It wasn't my fault!" Tony cried.

"I may have hit it," Gus said, "but you blew your chance to catch it. Now you have to go into those brambles and fetch it out."

The bramble bush was very dark and tall, and seemed to grow as Tony watched. "I'm scared," he said, and turned back to Gus.

Gus was covered with blood, and sharp points of broken bones emerged from his cheeks and forehead. The eyes were white and staring in his ruined face. "You should be."

Tony woke screaming. The sheets were soaked with sweat, and Bella began to cry. Sofia got up to comfort her, but as she patted and rocked the baby she asked Tony "Is everything all right?"

"Yeah," Tony said. "Just a bad dream."

Six dollars a week. He hoped he hadn't sold himself too cheaply.

The next day Tony sat heavily on a bench in the break area. He took off his hard hat and rested his head in his hands.

"You heard we lost another one?" said Gino as he sat down next to him.

"Aw, Jesus. No, I just didn't sleep well last night. Who?"

"Negro boy down in the coke yards. Pietro Dani— you know him?—he fell asleep running a crane and dropped a whole load of coke right on top of the guy."

"Jesus."

"We're not going to take this anymore. We're going to take action."

Tony's heart felt as though it had just stopped. "Don't tell me this, Gino."

"I know you don't want to hear it. But we've got to do something. We're meeting down at Polish Hall tomorrow night at eight. We've got a man from the C.I.O. to help us organize."

Tony swallowed. "No, thanks."

"Please. It's important. We've been talking about doing something for a long time, but Gus' death was what finally got us moving. It would mean a lot if you could show your support."

"Yeah," said Arturo Cavenini as he sat down on the other side of Tony. "You should come."

You are not our only reporter, Ailes had said. Could Arturo be one of the others? Now Tony would have no choice but to write Gino up. "I really wish you hadn't asked me."

"C'mon," said Arturo. "What can it hurt?"

Tony thought about ax handles, and gas grenades, and riot guns. "It can hurt a lot." He stood up to leave.

Then he felt a cold touch at the back of his neck, and heard a voice like a long-distance phone call in his head. *Go to the meeting,* it said. *Do it for me.*

"What's wrong?" said Gino. "You look like hell all of a sudden."

"It's nothing. Just gas."

Go, said the voice.

"Okay, I'll go."

A broad smile broke out on Gino's face. "Thanks, Tony. I mean it."

Tony shook his head to clear it, but the voice and the cold were already gone.

There were about seventy-five men at Polish Hall, shifting and muttering uncomfortably on the long wooden benches. Tony twisted his cap in his hands. *It's not too late to leave,* he thought. If he left before the meeting started, it would look funny, but then he could tell Ailes he didn't know who the ringleaders were. He felt like Judas Iscariot.

Tony's decision was made for him then, as the doors closed and Gino took the stage. "Thanks for coming," he said. "I'm proud to see so many members of our Kensington family here tonight." An ironic chuckle ran through the crowd. Tony felt sick. "This is a great night for the workers of Kensington Steel, because tonight we begin to reclaim our lives. For the last sixteen months we have struggled with double shifts, impossible production quotas, and tragic losses." He gestured at Tony, and a few men muttered, "Yeah." Tony managed a wave and a weak smile.

Gino began to pace back and forth, the stage floor creaking under his boots. "We've been cooperative. We've been polite. We've tried to work with management. But the situation just keeps getting worse. As you may already know, they aren't even going to give us Labor Day off." Tony found himself growling right along with the rest of the crowd. The news was a surprise to him. "Are we going to take that?"

About a dozen men yelled, "No!"

"Are we going to keep working double shifts for twenty-four dollars a week?"

"No!" This time it was most of the crowd.

"Are we going to watch our brothers die, one after another, until no one is left?"

No!" Tony yelled it, too.

"That's right!" Gino said. "Because tonight, we organize!" he raised his fist, and the crowd responded with applause and shouts of encouragement.

When the noise died down, Gino introduced Mike Kelley of the Congress of Industrial Organization, a beefy, florid man with a brusque manner and a thick working-class Irish accent. He spent the rest of the evening outlining a strategy for organizing a union, passing out packets of leaflets and buttons, and getting men to volunteer as shift captains and other key organizers. The mood of the crowd was upbeat as it dispersed into the night.

As Tony walked home, though, a weight settled onto his shoulders. For one thing, he knew he had to write up a report on the meeting. If he named names, men would lose their jobs; if he didn't, Ailes would cut off his money for shirking. For another thing, he knew that any serious attempt at rebellion would be met with well-informed, well-armed resistance. He wanted to run from the whole situation, but both

Gino and Ailes—for their own reasons—would expect him to continue attending meetings.

In the dark between streetlights, Tony spotted a beer bottle in the gutter. He kicked it savagely and it flew through the air to smash against the curb on the other side of the street.

The shower of glass fragments seemed to hang in the air for a moment.

Tony swallowed.

The glittering cloud of glass splinters did not fall to the pavement. Instead, it swirled into a manlike form. Gyrating like a swarm of bees, it churned across the street to where Tony stood paralyzed in the dark.

"What's wrong, little brother?" Gus' voice came as a scraping and grinding of broken glass. Tiny particles escaped from the swarm, pattering on the sidewalk and stinging Tony's face.

"G–g–g– . . ." Tony stammered, then clamped his jaws together. "Gus, I d–don't know what to do." He shivered in the hot August night.

"Remember who you are. Stick with your own kind."

"But if I stick with the union, I'll have to tell Ailes everything!"

"Yes . . ." The final s sounded like a bucket of sand being poured out.

"If they march on the plant and Ailes knows they're coming, people will be killed! Is that what you want?"

A tinkling chuckle came from the figure's midsection. "I'm not the only one who wants to see a few deaths in the Kensington family." Then the swarm of fragments clattered to the sidewalk, peppering Tony's shoes and pants. He slapped at a sudden pain in his cheek, and drew out a sliver of glass. His own blood on his fingers was black in the light from the distant streetlight.

"Gus, you bastard," he said. But there was no one there.

Gus had gotten him into this mess in the first place. Could his ghost be trusted?

The phone booth at the back of Johnson's Restaurant smelled of cigarette smoke and fried fish. Tony had to try three times before he got the nickel into the slot, and his fingers trembled as he dialed the number.

"Ailes here."

"Mister Ailes, I want out. I don't want to write reports for you anymore."

Ailes chuckled. "You don't want me to know about the meeting at Polish Hall, do you?"

Tony drew in a shuddering breath. "If you already know about it, what do you need me for?"

"God gave us two eyes and two ears for a reason, Mister Collina. I always like to keep several men on the hook . . . I mean, as reporters. Each provides a check on the others."

"I'm sorry, sir, but I still want out."

"I'm afraid that would be . . . inconvenient. To you."

"To me?"

"Yes. If certain reports, in your handwriting, were to be made available to the other members of your nascent union, the results might be . . . unfortunate."

Tony gaped into the phone.

"Do we understand each other, Mister Collina?"

Tony gulped. "Yes."

"Very well, then. I expect to see your complete and accurate report on my desk this Thursday as usual. Good evening, Mister Collina."

"Good evening, sir." But the line had already gone dead.

Two weeks later the crowd at Polish Hall was up to a hundred and fifty men. They planned a big Labor Day rally at Monessen City Park with all the wives and children, then they'd move to the plant entrance for the three o'clock shift change, to distribute leaflets urging men to join the union. The anger and resentment of men forced to work sixteen hours on a holiday would be sure to pay off in a big groundswell of support. They were excited and confident, and they chattered among themselves in Italian and English as they left the hall.

Tony accosted Gino as he locked the doors. "Gino, this isn't going to work."

"Sure it will! Management is playing right into our hands. Anything they try to do to stop us will just add to our support."

Tony could not meet Gino's eyes. He turned away and watched moths circling the streetlight nearby. "They know what we're doing."

"What do you mean?"

"They have spies. In the plant. In the union. And they're ready to hit us back. *Hard*."

Gino put a hand on Tony's shoulder. "Spies? Who? How do you now?" He tried to turn Tony around, but he resisted.

"I can't tell you. I just don't want to see anyone else get killed."

Gino's hand tightened on Tony's shoulder, then he

pushed him away with a disgusted sound. "You're just chicken. If we *don't* organize, more men *will* get killed. Like Gus. Remember Gus?"

Tony still did not meet Gino's eyes. "Yeah. I remember Gus."

"*He* wouldn't be afraid to do the right thing."

"Don't be so sure."

Gino stood silent for a moment, then turned and walked away. Tony listened to his footsteps fading away into the dark.

Labor Day dawned hot and clear, with a big blue sky relieved by a few puffy clouds. The carpenters and the plumbers and the printers were up early, preparing their floats for the afternoon parade. The steelworkers of Kensington who weren't on shift were up early, too, but they didn't have a float— instead they were cranking out mimeographed leaflets and painting placards.

By lunchtime, City Park was thronged with people. Women in their Sunday outfits carried picnic baskets; children laughed and ran across the grass. The smells of fried chicken and porcetta were everywhere.

Tony observed the festivities as though from inside a Mason jar. *Labor Day's going to be just like Memorial Day*, he thought. At best, the union organizers would lose their jobs; at worst, they'd lose their lives, and the lives of the women and children as well.

Tony had tried to convince Gino and Mike Kelley not to go through with it, but they refused to listen. He'd made clear in his reports that the workers intended no violence, but knowing Ailes he expected deadly force in reaction to any action at all. He'd even thought about leaving town, but where else could he find work?

So here he was, at City Park on Labor Day, feeling like the ghost at the feast. He would keep his own family away from the plant, and take any action he could to prevent violence. But he didn't feel very confident he could make much of a difference.

A great cheer erupted from the bandstand at the center of the park. "Come on," said Sofia. "We're missing everything!" She settled Bella more firmly on her hip and ran ahead with Anna's two girls, leaving Tony with the picnic basket and Anna with her very pregnant tummy to struggle along behind.

They laid out their picnic blanket in the shade of an oak, ate their roasted-pork sandwiches, and listened to politicians make speeches and brass bands play. For a while Tony could almost forget the coming confrontation. But at one o'clock Gino called through a bullhorn for all the off-shift Kensington workers and their families to gather to the left of the stage.

"Sofia," Tony said, "I want you to take Anna and the kids home."

"Why?"

"Just do it, okay?"

"But I wanna go with you, Uncle Tony!" said Lizzie, Anna's oldest. "All the other kids are going."

"Sorry, kiddo," he said, and swung her around by her arms. She laughed and laughed as she flew through the air, then he set her down and bent down to her level. "You be good for your mama and Aunt Sophie, okay?"

"Okay."

"I love you." He hugged her, and over her little shoulder he saw Sofia give him a look of deep concern. He straightened quickly and marched away, not wanting her to see the expression on his face.

The crowd around Gino was festive, men and women in their best clothes laughing and singing as they distributed placards and packets of flyers among themselves. Gino and Mike Kelley made inspirational speeches, they all cheered, and then they set off across the grass toward the Kensington Steel plant. Tony found himself carrying a sign that said WIN WITH THE C.I.O.

As the crowd walked down Fourth Street toward the plant, a shadow crossed the sun and the laughter dimmed a bit. It was only the smoke pouring from the plant's smokestacks, but to Tony it seemed like a bad omen.

They got closer to the plant. Even from a mile away the plant dominated the horizon, but now they were only a few blocks from the main gate and it seemed bigger than the world—a looming gray wall that, even from here, smelled of hot iron and sulfur.

The crowd walked on in silence.

One block from the main gate they could read the sign above it: KENSINGTON STEEL BUILDS AMERICA. And below the sign they could see a line of men.

"Finks," muttered a man next to Tony. Professional strikebreakers. Muscular, leering men armed with ax handles and riot guns. There were policemen in the line as well, carrying truncheons and rifles.

The leading members of the crowd of workers paused at the sight. The ones behind them came on, unknowing. Between the two groups a press of confusion developed.

One of the policemen stepped up and raised a bullhorn to his lips. "All right, you anarchists. This is as far as you go today. You are ordered to disperse."

The man next to Tony slowly bent down and set down his picket sign, then picked up a large piece of brick from the street. Others around him did the same.

A cop cocked his riot gun with a metallic *ch-chunk* that cut through the sounds of the plant.

Tony grabbed the wrist of the man with the brick. "Don't do anything stupid!" he hissed. But the man just shook him off in annoyance.

"You are ordered to disperse," the bullhorn repeated.

Tony began to back up, pushing his way through the crowd.

Then the tense silence was cut in two by the three o'clock whistle that marked the end of the first shift.

Despite the heat and humidity, Tony felt a sudden chill at the sound—but he did not shiver. Instead, insanely, he was comforted. For some reason it made him think of snowmen, and snowball fights, and snow forts. A protective cocoon of cold.

Tony and Gus stood together within a swirl of snow. They were wearing their winter coats.

"Don't run," said Gus. "I need you to stay here."

"And get killed?"

"You have to trust me."

"Trust you? Damn it, Gus, you talked me into this deal with Ailes, and then you *left* me!" Hot tears cooled quickly as they ran down his cheeks.

"I know. I'm sorry. I screwed up, okay? But from . . . where I am, I can see things I couldn't before. I can fix it. I *gotta* fix it. But I need your help."

Tony's breath huffed out of his mouth in big white clouds. At last he said, "What do you want me to do?"

"Just relax, and let me do all the talking."

Tony gazed on his dead brother's face for a moment more, then closed his eyes.

The shift-change whistle was just dying away as he opened his eyes again. He felt funny, like he was underwater. Cold water. But it was still a comforting kind of cold.

Tony's legs began to move, and he found himself pushing through the crowd until he stood between the two groups. His arms raised themselves in the air and he waved for attention.

"Put down your weapons," he said to the workers. Though the words came from his own mouth, they were a surprise to him, and his voice sounded as though he were talking over a long-distance line. "Too many have died here already." Amazingly, many of those who had picked up rocks and bricks did put them down. And even though Tony had not raised his voice, he saw men way at the back of the crowd reacting to his words.

Tony turned to the line of men at the factory gate. "Put down your guns and clubs. These people are not your enemies." Some of the finks lowered their ax handles, but the cops were more disciplined and retained their weapons.

Seeing this, the men in the crowd who had not put down their bricks gripped them tightly, and a few men bent down to pick up new ones. Despite the cocooning cold, Tony began to sweat.

Just then the first-shift workers began to pour from the plant's doors. But this was not the usual tired shift-change procession. These men were still wearing their work clothes and safety gear, running hard. One man screamed in horror.

Tony had no idea what was happening. Neither

did anyone else. Cops, finks, and workers looked around, uncertain of what to do.

The policeman raised his bullhorn. "You strikers are still under an order to disperse!" But no one moved.

The first men to emerge from the plant passed through the main gate. They ran wide-eyed and staring, intent on putting as much space between themselves and the plant as possible.

The bullhorn spoke again. "Pinkerton men, see to the disturbance inside the plant! Officers, disperse these strikers!" The finks turned and ran toward the steel mill; the cops moved forward, raising their weapons. Several men in the crowd of workers raised bricks over their heads, prepared to throw them.

"*No!*" Tony cried, raising his hands, and a wave of cold seemed to burst from him, rings of stillness spreading like ripples in a pond.

He faced the crowd of workers—his friends, his coworkers, their wives and children—and said "*Go home!*" As one they backed away from him. He turned to the policemen, and to them he did not even speak—he only stared at them, and they shrank back.

Without a word, the workers turned and walked away, back toward the park. They moved as though in a dream. The cops stood where they were, equally entranced.

Only Gino seemed to remember himself. "Mother of God," he whispered. "Tony, what's happened to you?"

"I'm not Tony," came the words from his mouth, and he strode purposefully toward the plant. Gino followed him.

When they reached the plant, the last few first-shift workers were just emerging from the doors, and most of the finks were already inside. The sounds of the working steel mill had never paused, but now they were joined by screams and gunshots.

"What the hell is going on in there?" asked Gino, but Tony just kept walking.

Soon they passed through the door of the plant. "By the Blessed Virgin," said Gino.

The steel mill was running at full capacity—ladles pouring molten steel, huge stamping mills pounding ingots into plates, rolling mills pressing out continuous sheets. But the men running the mill . . .

Some of them were gray and transparent, like half-developed photographs of themselves. Others were horribly burned, leaving flakes of charred flesh behind them as they moved. One man had a steel pry bar thrust through his chest, oozing blood from both sides. Everywhere were torn and mangled limbs, flayed skin, cracked skulls.

Those whose faces were still intact seemed to be having a wonderful time. Tony even recognized one of them—it was Marco Costanza, who'd bled to death after his arm was crushed by a falling girder. He was moving fine, hauling heavy bundles of steel rebar one-handed, though the other arm dangled uselessly at his side.

The dead men paid no attention to Tony and Gino, or to the strikebreakers. One of the finks stood stockstill, petrified by fear, and was crushed by a forklift driven by a headless machinist. Another fink fired his pistol at the gray shadow of a crane operator; the bullet ricocheted off the crane cab and grazed his skull, knocking him over.

"What the blue blazes is going on here?"

Tony turned toward the sound of the voice, to see

Kensington and Ailes emerging from the office. Kensington was puffing like a locomotive, his pink face glowing like a blast furnace.

The dead steelworkers all turned toward the voice as well. All action in the plant stopped. They began to move toward Kensington.

Kensington was clearly terrified, but to his credit he pressed on regardless. "You men will stop this . . . Halloween prank, or whatever it is, and get back to work this instant!" But the dead men closed steadily in around him. "Get back to work!" he gasped again, with no effect. "Get . . . back . . ."

A ring of burned, shredded, and broken flesh closed around Kensington, and from the center of it came a strangled scream and a sound like broomsticks breaking.

Tony turned his attention to Ailes, who was pressed against the office wall, arms and legs trembling. He was even paler than before.

"Mister Ailes," Tony said. "Nice to see you again. You have records. Files. Reports."

"Y–yes . . ."

"Take me to them."

Ailes turned and half ran, half stumbled through the office. Tony followed at a steady pace. Gino came behind him.

They entered Ailes' private office. "Here they are," he said, and pointed to a file cabinet.

"All of them?"

"All of them."

Tony pointed at the file cabinet, and all four drawers flew open. The papers within burst into the air like a thousand fat snowflakes. Tony waved his hands and the flying papers aged, browning and curling, two hundred years in a moment. Then they all crumbled to dust, leaving nothing but a smell like dead leaves.

Tears ran down Ailes' cheeks. Gino muttered one prayer after another.

"Now I can go," Tony said, and the world went black.

When he came to, he was outside the plant and Gino was leaning over him. "Are you awake?"

"I think so . . ."

"Do you remember what happened in there?"

"There were dead men. I saw Marco. Lots of others."

"Yeah. Hundreds. I think it was every man who's ever died in a Pennsylvania steel mill."

"Kensington."

Gino snorted. "Yeah, but he doesn't count."

"Are they still in there?"

"No. I think they all vanished when you passed out. There's nobody in there right now but a half dozen dead finks."

"Ailes?"

"He's talking with Mike Kelley. I think they're coming to an agreement."

"That's good." He closed his eyes.

Gus Collina was born on an autumn day, when the cool light streamed in through the windows of the new house his mother shared with his Uncle Tony and Aunt Sofia. The first face he saw in this life was Tony's.

He met Tony's eye and winked. And then he had a good long cry.

DIE, CHRISTMAS, DIE!

by David Bischoff

David Bischoff lives in Eugene, Oregon, after stays in Los Angeles, New York City, Baltimore, London, and Cambridge, England—and of course, his birthplace, the Washington DC area. He's just gotten married and has a son now, Bernie—starting a new family at the half century mark! His latest novel is H.P. Lovecraft Institute and he's just sold his very first mystery novel.

MARLEY WAS DEAD, a stake of mistletoe jammed through his belly.

My best friend was lying in his skivvies and T-shirt, on the floor, wrapped in a curl of ivy, mid-crawl to a table where a bottle of whiskey and a shot glass stood waiting. The holly berries mixed with blood that were wrapped around his throat were far from decorative.

The man in the black coat and black reflective glasses looked up from the body to me. "Sorry to have to make you see this, but we thought you could help us find your friend's killer."

"Yeah. I'll find him." I choked back a tear. "But Jake Marley's big mistake was keeping on working with you MetaBlacks."

"We understand your sorrow, Mr. Sledge. We respect your position. If you'd like to help us one more time, we'd like to bring the murderer of Jake Marley to justice."

"Yeah, sure. Just no fruitcake, okay?"

I went over and got Jake that last gulp of hooch. Then I drank one, too, and got down to business.

December was turning the New York starline into upside-down icicles. I was in my third-floor grav-up in the East Village, trying to sleep. I couldn't. My best friend was still dead, and we hadn't found any other clues to the killer in his apartment. The bowl of gruel I'd choked down for dinner was turning into cement shoes straight off the bottom of the East River, and the whiskey I'd drunk was broiling my pancreas. It was the twenty-first century: the rivers still stank, Manhattan still creaked, and the subway trains still screamed deep in the guts of Gotham.

My name is Joe Sledge. I'm a private op. I used to work for the Black Ops, and that's when Jake Marley saved my soul. My life, too, come to think of it, more than once in the manured field of duty. Now I was mourning him with straight-edged whiskey and some old Miles Davis from his bebop years hovering in my speakers. I passed out somewhere between a horn improv and a drum solo. I came awake when chains rattled from the omni-speaks of my compu-slice. The drunk was still crowding out a hangover, but I was conscious and sober enough to notice that there was a ghost in my room.

The ghost haunted my computer-holo, drifting and staring at me. I call it a ghost, and I say haunt because those are the words that come up.

It was Jake Marley.

"Sledge," he said.

From the transparent pixellated body of Jake Marley hung cords. Ever throw some electronics into a closet—tube cubes, PCees, electric frodos, what-have-yous—and just let them sit? Notice the electrical cords and connections, the printer cables and the leads, the antennae and the twisters—they all tangle up like a nest of snakes? From the transparent body of Jake Marley hung coils of these cords, coppery and silicon-gleaming. Tied around his head was a rainbow-colored ribbon cable. His eyes were ultra-diamond megachips. The mistletoe through his heart had blossomed out into a full-fledged Christmas.

"Jesus, Marley. Not so merry friggin' Christmas."

"Beware, Sledge. I come from Below to tell you to Beware!"

"Hell exists, Marley?"

"Hell, no. The CultureScape. The FedDreads were right. And there's a war going on down here. For control. And there's an evil force trying to take over the whole shebang."

"What? Who? Tell me what you're talking about, Jake!"

"Sledge! You must come down and stop—"

Jake Marley's head twisted sideways. The ribbon cable popped off his head. His jaw fell down to his chest. A fountain of bloody figgy pudding spewed from his mouth.

"The ghosts of Christmas! Arrgh!"

A scythe decorated with Christmas ornaments swung through the screen lopping off Jake Marley's head.

The holo-screen frizzed and a splash of energy crisped out at me. I ducked and rolled and it singed my bed. When I came up, all was peaceful again. I crawled to the kitchen to pour myself enough Christmas spirit to keep that hangover away for at least another day.

The MetaBlacks office was smooth and sharp and antiseptic. I sat in a hover-chair and watched Chief MacDaniel sit back in his stygian-dark fan-chair and tent his fingers. He had a long chin and a hawk nose, and hair and a mustache and black clothing carefully groomed every day. There were years of frustration and disgust in his look as he swept it my way. But he didn't give his emotions vent for long.

"Ghosts, Sledge," he said.

"Yeah. Ghosts. So Noir 'R Us goes *Weird Tales*."

"Not exactly."

"Gimme exactly."

"We're still dealing with the quantitative and qualitative. That is—the realms of science have expanded."

"Yeah. Right. Quarks, charms, and thingamajigs. Quantum mechanics and all that."

"More. We're talking realms of the psychic. We're talking a state of existence that undergirds our reality. Before, we influenced it. Now there's a backlash. It's the land where your Mr. Marley came from, Sledge. It's a land of what we used to call ghosts. Semibioenergies reflecting flesh and blood but not subject to all the laws."

"Having worked for ten years for you MetaBlacks, I think I know what you mean there."

CIA? NSA? Secret government operations? Add Illuminati, Freemasons, and Rosicrucian, shake a bit, add an olive. Garnish with a trillion bucks and you've got the MetaBlacks, the Global Secret UN of the late twenty-first century.

"Your position on our procedures was made clear

when you quit, Sledge. You continue in your romantic notions of an individual value system. Well and
good. It augments the Collective Unconscious."

"You want to explain some more?"

"In a moment. First I want to be sure that you're
sincere in your desire to help us."

"I want to find out who killed my friend."

"You'll go for a mission for us?"

"Sure But why me?"

"Because you're a throwback, Sledge. You may not
make much of a dent in the economy on this reality
level—but what you do affects Elsewhere. And that's
just where we're going to send you. Elsewhere. I've
got a feeling you can help us find out what the hell
is going on."

"Wait a minute. It's coming back to me. Jake Marley would talk about trips he took. He was involved
in this—Elsewhere. Wasn't he?"

"That's right. That's why he died. You'll do it?"

"Yeah."

"Good. You won't be alone. We have an agent already there. I understand that you know her. You've—
fraternized with her before."

"Who's that?"

"Jilly Satin."

I smiled. "I don't know about 'fraternize,' but the
action verb there starts with an 'f.' "

"Good. We've got a copter waiting for you. Can
you leave immediately?"

"I can. As immediately as you give me more
details."

"I can and will." Chief MacDaniel leaned forward,
frowning. "Sledge. Someone down in the bowels of
ultimate human consciousness is trying to kill
Christmas."

*   *   *

The black helicopter touched down on the tarmac. I clamped my left hand onto my porkpie hat. I stuck my right hand in the pocket holding my .44 Magnum as I stepped out into the blade winds. I stared off into the dark forms moiling in the CultureScape and my teeth clenched with anger.

Some bastard out there was trying to kill Christmas.

I had a forty-four–caliber chunk of lead in my heater to tell him what I thought about that.

A hand touched my arm.

"Sledge! This way!"

The voice barely reached above the sound of the rotors. I allowed myself to be guiding into the murk and the mist of unconscious dreams, lurking fears, and undersocietal backwash. My guts felt like wet cement and the harsh smell of the garbage of grief and repression reminded me again about how much I hated coming to any areas of this dimension. But Jilly knew this sector, she said, knew it well. And I knew Jilly, just about the sweetest bit of femininity ever to wrap herself around a civil servant.

She guided me over to a bleak outbuilding with a stark overhang that looked like a demon's pout. "Stand still just a moment," she said. "Decompress."

Her comforting hand slipped under my arm and we huddled in our trench coats, watching the black helicopter whisk off to its next destination. I think it had to smoke out some tax evader in Idaho. I kinda wished now I worked for a nonsecret supragovernmental group other than the MetaBlacks. But I was doing more than my duty. I was following my conscience. If I didn't remove this new growth from the underside of culture, and avenge Jake's death, a lot of kids wouldn't get their stockings stuffed next year. I'd had a few empty stockings in my life. That bites bad, buddy.

I closed my eyes. I took a deep breath.

I opened them and I could feel myself adjusting to the spectral energies of this part of the Underworld. Facing me now were a pair of gorgeous baby blues and a mass of blonde curls above a pair of the nicest gams that ever poked out of a trench coat.

She pulled out two cigarettes, fired up both, and handed me one.

"Well, sweetheart," I said. "Your move."

"Let's sit tight a moment and enjoy a Lucky Strike moment." She smiled at me. When I didn't immediately put the cancer stick in my maw, she frowned. "You do know how to smoke, don't you, Joe? You put your lips together and you suck."

She put a cigarette in her mouth and showed me. I got a shiver. I knew what that bogie felt like. Still, having worked for Big American Tobacco, I wasn't exactly in love with nicotine.

"C'mon, big guy," she said, when she saw that I was still hesitating. She nodded out toward the shifting 'Scape beyond. "It helps you acclimate."

I shrugged. "Whatever you say, babe." I pulled in some smoke, blew it out. "If it helps save Christmas, I'd smoke Grandma's panties." I looked out toward the 'Scape. "What a muck. You sure you know where we're going?"

"Yes. Like I said, I've been in this sector before and I've got informants. I pulled some of the local tails, paid off the right people. Got the combination for Boss Tweed's back door. We sneak in, do the deed, be back at dawn. Black helicopter comes and we swoop back to my hot tub." She winked at me. "Easy."

Some of that cement hardened south of my belly button. "Dunno about that. We'll just do our best, though."

"You always do your best, pal."

"I do my duty," I said.

I had a bad feeling now about duty, though. It felt like Uncle Sam's pet poodle was doing his duty on my grave. But then, I never feel right in the Underworld. You get the feeling down here that if you step on a crack, you'll break the universe's back.

When Dr. Carl Jung talked about the collective unconscious of mankind, he was just speaking in metaphor. What he didn't know was that bunches of secret organizations in the twenty-first century took him literally. And they *found* the damned placed. Then they did what all secret organizations do when they find dangling strings. They pulled them.

So now some Mob guy down here was putting the collar on the elves in charge of Christmas. That was what MacDaniel had told me anyway. That was why Jake Marley had died. He was onto the truth down here, and was about to stop them from their work, which would result, MacDaniel said, in a fading away of the Christmas holiday by the next century. This would undermine social conventions and tear at the fabric that kept society clothed. Gets damned cold in winter without Christmas, I'd think.

So the babe and I, we were here to take out this field. The babe's been here before. Me, I'm good at the less delicate aspect of these kind of operations. I shoot first and write reports later.

I finished my smoke. She handed me a pack of them and a lighter.

"You might need them later. C'mon. Geronimo

time, Chief. My people are meeting us at Twelfth and Eternity."

The tic at the end of my mouth quirked up. "Yeah, Babe. But does Forever have a bar?"

"You're in luck, Chief."

She plucked out a nice hefty flask from the inside of her jacket and tossed it back to me.

You'd need a jolt of Old Grandpop yourself if you were on the lip of this particular sector of the Underworld. Senses better adjusted, I could see why I needed more than one kind of spirit guide in this particular burg. Shreds of particularly greasy ectoplasm hung around this New York tilting like willynilly avant-garde. Picasso's dentist graveyard of a downtherescape. Multicolored nervestrands stretched out in a not-quite biological connecting mass from this Frank Lloyd Wright writhing-in-hellfire place.

All the sectors I'd visited during my Underworld work were pretty weird, but this boil was particularly rococo in the strange department, seeing as it was somehow even lower in the murk and muck of human unconsciousness than the rest. It was the place where belief and faith met the sewers of human need and, man, it stank of fear and drugs and booze and chocolate. Talk about wetwork. No wonder the Jilly called this a plumbing operation.

My gorgeous sidekick ducked into a back alley past a wiggle of gossamer spirit. I kept close, shivering with the occasional scram and moan that slid up from the grates on the side of the asphalt-and-cement sidewalks. Along the sides of the street blinking with neon were bars that beckoned with promise of burial and oblivion. The shot of Old Grandad in my gut sang a song of harmony and I regretted letting it inside me now. But duty kept my feet on the path behind my assistant.

"This way," she said, ducking down an even narrower alley.

The darkness was fuller here, the shadows grimmer. It smelled of the raw desperation of a seedy old porno-movie theater.

"Why did they choose this place to meet us?" I asked. There was some sort of gunk in the air that damped down my usually hypersenses. I could feel my usually keen trigger finger tilting toward impotence, but somehow the shot of stuff the Babe had given me and the jolt of paint remover made it seem less alarming than usual.

"Dunno," she said. "I'm just following orders." She stopped at a corner where a pile of empty trash cans was stacked. "Come here, Joe."

"Man, there's something foul in the air . . . Something . . . poison."

"Come here, kiddo. This is the spot. We just have to wait. Gee . . . gettin' kinda hot, huh?"

She had unlashed the belt of her coat, and I got an eyeful of decolletage and a whiff of some Paris perfume that was a hell of a lot nicer than the other smells down here. "Maybe we're a little bit early, Joe. How about a little instant replay from last night, huh?"

"Sure, sweetheart," I said. In the land of raw nightmares and drives, I was glad for a sweet-smelling dream to keep me company. I put my arms around her slender waist and pulled those moist lips up to mine—

And then a sockful of heavy night smacked into the back of my neck.

As I fell down to the gritty street and I drained into nothingness, I saw her smiling down at me.

"So long, sucker," she said.

And I remember thinking, as some kind of scuffle went on to the right of nowhere, she wasn't talking about candy canes.

When I came to, it felt as though my brain had been used for a piñata by Rudolph and his reindeer pals and then stuffed back into my head through my left nostril.

"Eggnog?" said a voice.

I looked up blearily. There was a guy in nineteenth-century duds, big blowsy guy with a big nose and dark, feral eyes, staring down at me.

"No, thanks. I think I'm keeping kosher from now on," I said, the memories coming back. The pain of the betrayal was greater than my headache. I swallowed it back and concentrated on the task of survival.

I recognized the bozo in front of me from the official sketches. They were collages from some old nineteenth-century rag, and they fit the joker to a T . . . or maybe just to an S, because there wasn't the avarice and greed in this black-and-white three-dimensional cartoon's eyes. Just a kind of cynical amusement.

"Joe Sledge. Private operative," he pronounced. "It's a great pleasure to make your acquaintance." His voice had a rolling Irish broque, a pleasant, almost comforting sound. "Your work for the Meta-Blacks is known in my quarter, yes. You do a fine job for them. You have—shall we say for want of a better word, an antiquated knightlike valor, an odd streetwise chivalry and integrity behind your hard-boiled facade. I respect that."

"Is that why you're trying to kill Christmas, Boss Tweed?"

"Kill Christmas? That's what the Metas told you?" Boss Tweed's eyes glittered with a kind of fairy mischief. "Now hold your tongue there. Kill the story of the birth of our Lord, Prince of Princes, King of Kings? Kill a relic of the faith that kept barbarism from engulfing the flickering taper of intelligent, rational thought? I swear upon St. Patrick's name, that's not the truth. No, I've none of that. We just run a few rackets down here. Squeeze a mere squirt of juice from the massy, messy place to have a pleasant interesting living. And that from a force so corrupt it would boggle the mind. I'm small-time, lad. Simply small-time."

"But why did you hire Jilly to turn on me?"

"Nothing of the sort, lad. Quite the contrary. We down here in this sector of the Underworld heard you'd been set up. We've got a little bit of power here and we simply used it to save your life and put a little stick in the wheels and cogs we dance around."

I shook my head and looked around. The place had a pleasant Victorian clutter of bric-a-brac. A fire breathed warmth from a hearth. On the wall was a crucifix. A rosary dangled from a Bible.

"It doesn't figure. Why'd they want to deep-six me?"

Boss Tweed raised an eyebrow. "You ask too many questions, Sledge. You dig a little too deep. Maybe you know a little bit too much more than what's comfortable to them." He leaned forward, steepling his fingers. "And then, there's the little matter of this chapel you've been visiting."

I blinked. "What? My cat died. I felt bad. I went and sat there a few days and put some money in the poor box. I felt better. I figured, hell, why not. Probably do it again."

Boss Tweed nodded cagily. "Ah, yes, and then you'll be gettin' religious, won't you?" He tsked.

"Look, bud. What are you telling me?"

He leaned forward and poured out some tea for me into a cup. He added some milk and a lump of sugar. Just the way I like it.

"Let me tell you, lad, about a fellow by the name of Thomas Nast."

She got up when I opened the door. She was sitting in a deep, high-backed chair, smoking a cigarette.

The room was cold, but her hair was a spray of warmth and light around the darkness of her eyes.

"Sledge. You've come to save me!" she said in a breathy whisper.

"Things kind of backfired, huh, baby?"

"Oh, Joe, I don't know, I'm so confused." She ran to me and threw that warmth and sexiness around me. I stayed cold and stiff . . . stiff in a way she didn't want me to be. She backed away. "Why are you looking at me that way?"

"I sure was a sucker, baby. I was a patsy. And you played me real fine. Only now I got a little visit to make. A visit to your real boss."

"My real . . . I don't understand. Who . . . ?"

"Come clean, baby. There's a secret part of the secret part of the secret part of the MetaBlacks. And it's run by this hoodlum . . . And he's the guy whose dime you lick . . ." I raised an eye. "I'm talking about Santa, baby. Santa Claus."

She frowned. "Don't go there, Joe. You'll be making a big mistake. Get me out of here. We'll go somewhere. Hide from this madness. Just you and me." She ran up to me and mashed her soft self against me. "Kiss me, Joe."

I pushed her back and put a bullet where someone had forgotten to put a heart.

The jury left the room, tucking its .44 back into its trench coat.

"Ho ho ho! Merry Christmas," said Santa. "Ho ho ho!"

The three hos were in garter belts and black bras and they sat on Santa's bare legs, dangling. I stepped into the room, my gun trained on his huge red nose.

"Merry Christmas to you, too, you bastard," I said.

Santa's mouth dropped. "Sledge! You're supposed to be dead."

I waggled my gun at the hos. "Okay, ladies. Go deck some halls somewhere."

The women flounced away, leaving the smell of mistletoe in the air.

Santa made his move. Behind his chair was a hatchet. Grinning evilly, he grabbed it and started running toward me. "And Merry Ax-mas to you, Sledge."

He'd forgotten to pull up his pants. He tripped and fell right on his gin-blossomed face, shaking like a tub of rotten jelly. The hatchet thunked to one side. I kicked it away into the corner and stuck my gun into his ear.

"Damn it!" he said. "How'd you get past the home-elves!"

"We had a little elf-help group, Nick," I said. "They surrendered to a higher power." I stuck that hot higher power farther into his ear. "Now I want names, Claus!"

"Names? I don't know what you're talking about." He smelled like last decade's fruitcake doused in cheap brandy.

"The hoods in your conspiracy. And the guys that set me up to come down here and get picked off."

The bells on his toes jingled. Sweat plopped past a nervous grin. "Conspiracy! I don't know what you're talking about, dear boy! I, sir, am Santa Claus. Every year I pack presents for all good little children, put them on my sleigh and visit good little boys and girls around the world and bestow them with gifts. I am all that is generous and righteous about this most glorious season."

"Cut the crap, Claus. You're a sack of sin wrapped in red. A corrupt spider in a web of ultimate moral larceny. I know where you come from, Claus."

"Come from? Why, Joe, I am the emanation of all that is good and right about the pinnacle of political systems, democracy!"

"Wrong, bozo. I shoulda done my homework a long time ago. You're the shill for a proto-Nazi political artist by the name of Thomas Nast. He created you for the *Harper's Weekly* during the American Civil War as fodder for the Union propaganda machine. You're a pagan Kraut fairy-tale parasite on the Christian story of Saint Nicholas. While Thomas Nast pointed his pen at a minor racketeer named Boss Tweed in New York City, he successfully mastermasterminded a cultural conspiracy to launch the most corrupt American presidency in history run by former Union general Ulysses S. Grant. Grant loosed the hounds of capitalistic hell upon the American nation, the robber barons—and together with you, Santa, dangled the carrot of endless economic riches before Joe Public while you exploited their labor. You've always been in the vanguard of illusions of plenty, Santa. A doll or tin soldier for the kids? Why bother? Mr. and Mrs. American Fool of the lumpen proletariat signed your name to a bunch of presents . . . and thus your pagan spirit was worshiped all around the world and your soul grew bigger and more powerful. You're all that's rotten about American Capitalism, pal. And I want to know the names of your henchmen in the Metas."

"Who do you think you are? Karl Marx?"

"No, Harpo. But I'm going to start talking. I suggest you do the same."

He waggled his fleecy white brows and he looked like he was on the edge of a coronary. "I know what this is about, Joe. This is about that Acme Private Eye Set you didn't get for Christmas. I'm sorry, Joe, I had you down for one, but I ran out. I swear."

"Names, Claus. Names." But that was one below the belt. The memory burned bad. I remember that year well, tearing through my presents and getting cowboy stuff and pirate stuff aplenty. I might as well have gotten lumps of coal for all it mattered.

I didn't notice Santa's hand sneaking under the big fat plate of Christmas cookies, but I did notice it coming out with a derringer.

He got off a shot that ripped through the top of the coat and grazed my shoulder. I sprang back to avoid any others and pulled my trigger.

The Magnum pounded into his midsection. Once, twice, three times it went off, each of the slugs burying themselves in lots of roly-poly.

"Ouch!" he said.

Gases began to spew. Little winged demons with the faces of Richard M. Nixon and Ronald Reagan started flapping out. Santa spluttered and spasmed as cheap fireworks speckled out from the holes, bursting upward. "The Star Spangled Banner" played off-key, miniature police and marines trooped out, hauling pork barrels. Elves and fairies in Wal-Mart bondage outfits tap-danced away. Elvis Presley dressed in an American flag stumbled out of the stomach, staggered over to the corner and then died on the toilet there. A naked Bill Clinton jumped out, and started chasing women dressed in McDonald's cheeseburger wrappers.

I saw America disgorge garishly from the gut-shot Santa, and it smelled like crisp hundred bills in someone else's pocket.

"I think I got those names, Santa," I said. "Thanks."

I spun around and left the parade early.

She was waiting for me by the landing pad in a chiffon number with her hair and nails done and a fresh coat of shellac on her face.

"I thought you were dead." I said.

"You don't die here. Just like some people don't really live up there."

"So you're stuck down here with Jake Marley."

"Jake says hi. He appreciates what you've done. He's sorry he was forced to lure you down here. But it all came out well, though, right?" Jilly pulled the cigarette from her mouth and blew smoke and words at me. "So, hero. Have fun?

Snow was starting to sprinkle down like sawdust from some invisible lumber mill behind the black curtain.

"I guess."

She snorted. "Why'd you bother plugging the guy? It does about as much good as shooting me!"

"It felt nice."

"Well, you're on your own now, Joe. I've got a limo coming to pick me up, and I'm outta the Black, I guess." She raised an eyebrow. "But maybe I've got bigger fish to fry."

"No black helicopter for me, baby. I'm staying solo."

"Solo? What . . . Geez, that's dumb. How's that gonna affect anything? What are you going to do that's going to make a hill-of-beans difference? Huh, Joe Sledge? You're just a cliché with good fashion sense."

I pulled out the pack of cigarettes she'd given me and tossed them at her feet.

"I'm gonna clean up Christmas. I'm gonna make it a decent place again, with ideals and hope, not the lapdog of greed and corruption."

"Oh, I'm so scared. But like I said, Joe— How are you going to hurt me? That big gun of yours sure couldn't."

"No Christmas present for you *this* year, baby."

I turned my back on her and walked away into the dark and the pulpy snow.

NEW WORLD'S BRAVE

by Daniel M. Hoyt

When not working as a rocket scientist, Daniel M. Hoyt writes fiction, poetry, and music. His short stories have sold to markets as diverse as Analog Science Fiction & Fact and Dreams of Decadence. He currently lives in Colorado Springs, Colorado, with his wife, author Sarah A. Hoyt, two rambunctious boys, and a pride of cats. Catch up with him at http://www.danielmhoyt.com.

"RECON SAYS it's a fifteenth-century sailing ship."

Impossible, Henry Cloudrunner Waite reminded himself, as he replayed the conversation in his head for what seemed like the fiftieth time. He curled his bare toes in the fine San Salvadoran beach sand and squinted at the rising sun as it boiled blood-red on the ocean horizon, slowly coaxing the black predawn to life. He took a deep, warm breath of the salty air and searched again for the telltale square sails of the *Santa Maria*, which by all rights, should have been half a millennium rotted below trillions of gallons of seawater. A thousand voices whispered in his mind, urging him to stop and enjoy the cool, tranquil sunrise—as his Ute ancestors had for generations, when

his native Colorado was still unknown to Europeans—
but he was too anxious to focus very long on anything but the ghost ship.

Cloudrunner's shoulder-length ponytail slapped
and scratched against his bare back in a slight breeze,
which brought with it the sting of the Caribbean
spray on his tender, sunburned chest.

Grandpa Bear Paw would be ashamed. From a distance, in his Speedos in the half-lit dawn, Cloudrunner probably looked like a classic loincloth-clad
Native American, proudly facing the morning, full of
promise and future glory. But after nearly twenty
years in the computer field, hidden away from the
sun, Cloudrunner's skin was almost as white as Eu-
ropean Americans, and he burned in minutes on the
rare occasions he ventured outside. He reached into
a ratty leather bag by his feet and donned a dingy,
once-white cotton polo shirt and stained beige pants
to keep from aggravating his itching sunburn.

Despite his discomfort, Cloudrunner was glad to
be here. Only the week before, he had been working
under tons of red rock, making modifications to
radar analysis software for a government subcontrac-
tor at NORAD, North America's Aerospace Defense
command installation dug out of Cheyenne Mountain, towering next to Colorado Springs, Colorado. It
was nice to get a break from the stale, pumped-in air
now and then.

"What's this, Waite?" Colonel Traggett had asked
when Cloudrunner demonstrated the new software
in a dimly lit staff meeting filled with dull stares and
gloomy faces. "What are those blips doing there in
the middle of the ocean?"

Traggett was career military, tall and muscled with
a slight middle-aged paunch below his square, straight

shoulders. Gray temples distinguished his otherwise unremarkable brown hair, cut close to his scalp. He moved with precision, never wasting a step, and held himself to the highest standards. Naturally, he expected the same from others.

"Blips? Right," Cloudrunner said quickly, without even looking at the computer screen, hoping the colonel would mistake his speedy response as confidence. "The demo script only *starts* in the middle of the ocean, after checking real-time for current vessels and choosing an empty area. But after *that*, it moves to a populated area. The script must have gotten ahead of itself. Nothing to worry about."

"Uh-huh," the colonel said, apparently satisfied. "Okay, then, team. We've got some new wrinkles to learn with our old software. Waite here is going to explain it all to you."

The demo went perfectly, except for the minor glitch with the blips, but once Cloudrunner had taken a look at the screen, he couldn't wait for the demo to be over, so that he had some time to talk to the colonel alone.

There was no glitch.

There were three ships, out in the middle of the Atlantic, where they weren't supposed to be.

His heart racing, Cloudrunner bounded up the service stairs to Colonel Traggett's office, only to be stopped by the colonel's ultra-efficient secretary.

"I've got to see the old man," Cloudrunner said breathlessly. "Is he in?"

"He's busy," Traggett's secretary said, without looking up. "And I'm at lunch." She smoothed down her knee-length black skirt and leafed absently through the latest *People* magazine. A half-eaten salad lay exposed in its open container on her desk to the side of her computer monitor. Judging by the wilted lettuce and soft cherry tomatoes, Cloudrunner didn't expect she was all that anxious to return to her lunch.

He couldn't blame her for her curt response. It was her job, after all, to deflect as much additional work as possible from the overworked colonel. And consultants asking to see the colonel usually meant more work.

"Come on, it's a military issue. I really need to see him. National security."

She rolled her eyes. "Yeah, right. Look around, Einstein. *Everything's* national security around here." She spun away in her chair, turning her back on him.

"Listen, could you just tell him the blips are real?" Cloudrunner said to the back of her dark blonde bouffant. "Let him decide. I'll wait." Cloudrunner plopped down in an uncomfortable-looking guest chair a few feet from the secretary's desk and waited. She disappeared into the colonel's office.

Five torturous minutes passed. Every move Cloudrunner made, no matter how slight, elicited a high-pitched shriek from the bowels of the chair, as if it were scolding him for his brazenness. Cloudrunner was just about to stand (so that he'd get some relief from the chair's incessant complaints), when Traggett's secretary finally reappeared.

"Go on in," she said dryly, and held the door open for him. She glared at him as he passed by.

"Okay, Waite," the colonel said gruffly from behind his polished cherry desk, "you're on to something. We've got visual on satellite. There's something out there where it doesn't belong."

Cloudrunner's heart skipped a beat. He'd worked in the mountain for two years without anything interesting happening. Maybe this new development would break up the monotony.

"You have top secret clearance, right, Waite?" The colonel's sharp, black eyes bored into Cloudrunner.

"Yes, sir."

"Good. We don't want to involve any more people than we have to on this, and we're going to need some specialized tracking code for this one. For some reason, it's only *your* program that sees the blips on radar. We've got visuals, of course, but nothing else."

Cloudrunner had leaped at the chance to go, and now he was here on a beach in the Bahamas, waiting for a *Nao* class sailing ship that hadn't existed for five hundred years.

"Aerial recon says there's three of them—one larger than the others—surface only and—get this—with sails and rigging straight out of the discoveries."

Impossible, Cloudrunner reminded himself again, then shook the thought from his head.

Cloudrunner himself had identified the course of the three blips and tied in the strange retro appearance of the sailing ships. If there was one thing any self-respecting Native American knew, it was the discovery and settling of the Americas, and Cloudrunner had put the pieces of this puzzle together immediately:

The ships exactly followed the path of Christopher Columbus.

And that meant that the strange ship out would be the *Santa Maria*. Rather, a reproduction of the ship. Undoubtedly, it would turn out to be some crackpots merrily sailing Columbus' original path in reproductions of his three ships, completely disregarding modern maritime rules and regulations.

On October 12, 1492, at around two in the morning, Columbus unwittingly found himself a new world, *somewhere* in the Bahamas—nobody really knew where exactly, but San Salvador, or Watlings Island, had been the accepted location for centuries.

Now, on the morning of October 11th, Cloudrunner watched and waited. The ship should be visible today sometime, if the history buffs were as meticulous as Cloudrunner expected. He raised powerful binoculars to his eyes, hoping the retro sailors opted only for period instruments. Advancements in optics over the centuries should help him locate the ships long before the sailors would be able to see him.

By dusk, Cloudrunner was discouraged. He'd spent the entire day on the beach, as it filled and emptied with tourists and their trash—most of that time beneath an umbrella he'd rented midmorning, in a desperate gambit to save his skin from peeling off entirely—searching, searching. His eyes were tired and sore now, and he wondered if his sun-cracked face, pinched from squinting through the bright sun, would ever feel normal again.

His tracking software was correct, Cloudrunner knew it was. The path was unmistakable; the little flotilla definitely was headed for San Salvador. But he couldn't predict exactly how fast the ships would go. Depending on the winds, they could make five miles or fifty in a day. There was no telling exactly when the ships would be visible, just where—*if* they followed the same course.

Sighing deeply to himself, the thought of a completely wasted day hanging over him, Cloudrunner decided to try one last time before turning in for the night. He raised the heavy binoculars and searched the blackening horizon.

There. Could it be? A light, flickering in the distance, out on the water?

Was it the ship, chasing the sunset? Or something else? A trick of the eye, perhaps? Just wishful thinking, so that Cloudrunner could go home—at least, back to his hotel—without feeling guilty.

Cloudrunner watched the light for a while as it danced on the waves, brightening suddenly and dimming without warning, sometimes blinking out entirely, only to blaze again in a few seconds.

The binoculars still pressed to his eyes, he snatched his cell phone from a pocket and thumbed it open, pinching himself as the cover snapped open.

"Who would you like to call?" a pleasant, recorded female voice announced.

"Traggett," Cloudrunner said into the microphone, engaging the voice-dial feature.

After a few rings, Traggett's displeased voice barked from the phone.

"Waite here, sir. There's a light on the horizon. About fifteen degrees off due east, to the north. It might be our target. Just thought you'd want to know."

"Thanks, Waite." The colonel paused for several seconds. "Are you and Sergeant St. Claire handling it?"

"Yes, sir. St. Claire's tracking by software back at the hotel; I'm on visual today. I'm heading back now to compare notes."

"Good job, Waite. Keep me posted."

Cloudrunner hung up and replaced the cell phone in his pocket before lowering his binoculars. Silently, he gathered his sand-encrusted belongings, shaking the loose sand off before carefully stowing each in his scratched, leather bag.

Once back at the hotel—although the term hotel was charitable, given the grimy bathroom and stained, threadbare carpet that greeted him at check-in— Cloudrunner paused outside his room, tense fingers pressing the outdated metal key's impression into his thumb.

The door was ajar.

As Cloudrunner shakily reached for the door handle, somewhere in the pit of his mind a thousand Ute ancestors sent up alerts. Smoke signals, warrior yells, suicide charge screams—all of them went off at once. Cloudrunner's heart stopped, and time seemed to slow considerably, as his blood rushed to his tensed muscles, preparing for battle against the unseen enemy.

Nothing happened as Cloudrunner cautiously pushed open the door. He let the door swing into the wall with a small thud.

Sergeant Simon "Ain't-no" St. Claire looked up and scowled from a wobbly chair by an open laptop, screen blazing, sitting atop the unmade bed. A tall, lean muscular man with piercing black eyes and sharp features, Ain't-no had earned a well-deserved reputation among his subordinates as a tough, take-no-shit badass. Yet someone had managed to tie the sergeant to his chair securely enough that the sergeant couldn't move.

Ain't-no kept scowling, and Cloudrunner realized that his expression had been frozen into place by a wide strip of clear packing tape. Stunned, Cloudrunner stood in the doorway and stared dumbly.

Cloudrunner didn't want to meet the someone

who had managed to subdue the formidable Ain't-no, but he suspected he had no choice. By an instinct he didn't know he had (perhaps a gift from his ancestors to aid him now), he struck out without looking, his fist clenched into an iron ball. The crunch of a jaw against his knuckles and a searing pain that shot up his arm convinced him of the validity of his decision.

Before he could turn to look at his foe, a sharp pain split his head and Cloudrunner's world went black.

Cloudrunner awakened with a hard slap across his face, only to find his head still throbbing. The acrid smell of salt water assaulted him—not the mild salt of the shoreline, but the full-bodied brine of the open ocean. Splintery wood beneath him bucked slightly, driving shards into his back with each wave. Seagulls squawked overhead, heralding nearby land.

Squinting into the sun, Cloudrunner could just make out the large head of an ugly, young black man grinning down at him. The man wore a dirty burlap tunic tied over once-white pants, now filthy, torn and frayed so badly they could pass for beachcomber shorts. His few remaining teeth were almost as black as his skin, and the hot, rotting-fish stench of his breath washed over Cloudrunner like a deadly fire. Cloudrunner's nostrils closed involuntarily, and his stomach spasmed.

He tested his hands, only to find them bound securely behind his back. Added to that, his ankles were tied together; Cloudrunner knew he wasn't going anywhere soon.

"*Quem e ele?*" A deep, male voice came from behind Cloudrunner, but he didn't dare twist around to see the speaker's face without risking another slap from the grinning black man.

"Quem e ele?"

The ugly black man nodded to the speaker behind Cloudrunner, then stared at Cloudrunner again.

Cloudrunner thought the phrase sounded somewhat Spanish, but he couldn't quite connect it with his now-forgotten high school Spanish.

The black man spoke finally, in what Cloudrunner thought was French. The black man tried a couple of other languages that Cloudrunner didn't recognize at all, until eventually he spoke in English.

"Who are you?" the black man asked, with an upper-class British accent that clashed sharply with his appearance.

"Cloudrunner." His dry throat made Cloudrunner's voice crack. "Cloudrunner Waite."

"A strange name, this," the black man said, but repeated it to the other man behind Cloudrunner, amid a long string of what sounded vaguely like the surf. After a short exchange, the black man addressed Cloudrunner again. "I am Black Henry. You are the prisoner of my master, the great sea captain Magalhães."

Magal-who? "Where's Ain't-no?" Cloudrunner croaked. "My friend?"

Black Henry raised his eyebrows and nodded his head to the side. "More strange names, yes? He is safe, over there."

Cloudrunner twisted his head. Ain't-no was laying on the deck, up against the side of the ship. He was trussed up similarly, but was still unconscious. Ain't-no probably put up more of a fight than Cloudrunner had; it was one of the reasons they got along so well, actually. Despite his heritage, Cloudrunner was about as far from a warrior as could be; Ain't-no was the fighter Cloudrunner imagined Grandpa Bear Paw hoped his poor excuse for a descendant would have been.

"You call him . . . Ayno?" Black Henry looked puzzled.

"Ain't-no," Cloudrunner said impatiently, specifically articulating the *t*. "Ain't-no St. Claire. *Sergeant* St. Claire to you."

Black Henry shook his head, grinned and muttered something in the surflike language. He stood, towering over Cloudrunner. "Well, you'll be well cared for on the *Trinidad*, I promise. Just look at me." He laughed, a full-throated bellow that echoed across the deck, then bounded out of sight.

Cloudrunner lay there for an hour or two while the crew bustled around him (talking in the funny language that sounded like waves crashing on the shore), the ship rocking on the waves as the merciless sun burned his already-tender skin. He stayed quiet and listened for clues that would reveal his whereabouts and the reason he was a captive.

At last, Ain't-no woke up, without the rude benefit of a slap. He struggled against his bonds for a minute before flipping himself around and discovering Cloudrunner there, patiently watching.

"Guess you aren't going to help, then," Ain't-no said.

Cloudrunner shrugged. "Can't. I'm tied up, too. Sorry."

"It's all right." Ain't-no looked around, but didn't seem to register any surprise at all at finding himself on the deck of a ship. Perhaps it was his military background: be ready for anything. Or maybe he'd been knocked unconscious *after* being brought to the ship. "But maybe we can help each other with these ropes. Try to get closer." He rolled over again, ending up only a few feet away from Cloudrunner. "By the way, where are we?"

"Ship called *Trinidad*," Cloudrunner said between grunts as he tried to raise himself to a sitting position. He glanced at the position of the sun and watched the seagulls for a few moments. "I think we're just off the coast of San Salvador, waiting." Something about the ship's name seemed familiar, but Cloudrunner couldn't put his finger on it just then.

"What are we waiting for?"

"I don't know. I don't understand their language. Spanishlike, but not Spanish."

Ain't-no rolled up next to Cloudrunner, back to back. "Let me at your wrist binds, okay? Maybe I can loosen them or something."

Cloudrunner felt rough fingers scratching at his wrists.

A deafening explosion boomed nearby and a cloud of acrid smoke choked Cloudrunner and stung his eyes. He struggled to see over the edge of the ship as it bobbed, new explosions punctuating the waves and rocking the ship even more. A couple of times he thought he caught a glimpse of another sailing vessel. "Help me up!" he yelled, and smashed against Ain't-no's rock-hard body, trying to get a better look. Ain't-no pushed back sufficiently that Cloudrunner raised his head higher for a few seconds, enough for him to get a clearer view, despite his smoke-filled eyes.

Nearby, there was a *Nao* class sailing ship, circa late fifteenth century, complete with square sails—on fire. Two more, smaller ships, lay beyond it unscathed, but four others, close to the *Trinidad*, were

launched in their direction, seemingly bent on inter-
cept. In the distance, an explosion rang out, a plume
of smoke trailing one of the distant ships.

"Holy shit!" Ain't-no yelled in Cloudrunner's ear.
Cloudrunner twisted carefully and glanced behind
him to see that Ain't-no had propped himself up as
well. "That's the *Santa Maria* there, burning! You
were right, Chief—it's the discoveries!"

"Yeah," Cloudrunner said calmly. "But, if that's
Columbus, who are we with?"

"Columbus!" The bellow was so close that it deafened Cloudrunner and made his ears ring. He
flinched away from the sound instinctively, losing
the precarious balance he and Ain't-no had achieved,
which sent them both sprawling to the deck. Black
Henry towered over them, fury pinching up his face.
"What do you know of Columbus? Are you a spy?"
He kicked Cloudrunner in the side.

Most of the crew nearby stopped what they were
doing and stared at Cloudrunner, writhing on the
smoky deck. "*Espiao?*" one of them said tentatively,
and then the word spread like wildfire across the
deck. Several of them abandoned their work and
came at Cloudrunner. Black Henry squatted down
close to Cloudrunner, murder in his eyes, balled a
fist and cocked it.

"Black Henry," Cloudrunner whispered and shut
his eyes, anticipating the blow.

"Oh, shit," Cloudrunner heard Ain't-no say, just
before Black Henry punched him unconscious.

"Chief! Chief! Wake up!"

Cloudrunner tried to open his eyes, but one of them
refused and the other was hazy. He shut them again.

His head throbbed as from a hangover, and he could feel something wet and sticky—blood?—running down one cheek. "I'm awake," he whispered.

"You've got to wake up and pay attention, Chief. There's a damn war going on out there. Open your eyes."

Cloudrunner fought the sleep and opened his good eye. "Fine," he said drowsily. "What is it?"

"We've got to figure out what's going on here, and fast."

Cloudrunner nodded and propped himself up, butting his head on the low, wooden ceiling. A layer of dirt and straw that stank of livestock cushioned him underneath, but stray, hard pieces poked and scratched him at the same time. The lighting was poor, but manageable after his eyes got used to the blinding darkness. Cloudrunner guessed they were belowdecks, in some kind of shallow, primitive holding cell.

"You said we were on the *Trinidad*, right?" asked Ain't-no. "And that big, black guy is Black Henry?"

"Yeah. The bitch of it is, *Trinidad* sounds awfully familiar; I just can't place it."

Ain't-no stared into space for a moment, then smiled widely. "Magellan, Chief, Magellan. I remember now, it makes sense. Listen up. Just before you came back, I spotted five more ships on your radar. Magellan sailed with five; the *Trinidad* was his."

Magellan? "And we saw four other ships attack the rest of Columbus' fleet. And Black Henry was Magellan's slave. *That's* why his name sounded so familiar." Cloudrunner frowned. "But, no, it can't be. Black Henry said his name was something else. Maga . . . Magaleinge, I think."

"Magalhães," said Ain't-no, shaking his head violently. "It's Portuguese. The British bastardized it to Magellan."

"Portuguese?" Cloudrunner eyed Ain't-no doubtfully.

"Trust me," Ain't-no said. "I dated a girl from Porto once. Got all hot under the collar when I called him *Magellan*. Turns out he was a local boy and they take great pride in that."

Cloudrunner sighed. "But it's still impossible. Columbus, Magellan, none of this makes any sense. Columbus came here in 1492, on the path we tracked those ships; Magellan's Spanish Expedition sailed in 1519. Besides, Magellan never came here."

A woman cleared her throat nearby. Cloudrunner twisted his neck, painfully, to see her. She was young and blonde, hair past her waist, with a ring of flowers around the crown of her head. She was dressed in a halter top tied around her breasts (no bra) and a miniskirt so short it exposed most of her pubic hair, growing wild inside her thighs. Her legs sprouted little blonde hairs, and little blonde mounds peeked out from her armpits. Her blue eyes were glazed over, and her head bobbled a little, as if she couldn't keep it on her neck without effort.

"He's right, man," she said. "But it don't matter now, 'cause they're, like, ghosts. And ghosts can do whatever they, like, want to."

Cloudrunner stared at the young woman. She could have walked right out of the late nineteensixties or early seventies, looking like that. A classic flower child. "I don't thi—"

"Hey, man," the woman said abruptly, her eyes flashing momentarily before glazing over again. "It's *my* trip, and I think ghosts are groovy, man. So, like, be cool."

"Just suppose," Ain't-no said after a while, breaking the silent tension, "that they really are ghost ships."

Cloudrunner was glad to have a reason to look away from the flower girl. He stared at Ain't-no. "Okay, I'm game. In the afterlife, Magellan decides to head off Columbus and take the glory for himself. He couldn't do it while they were alive, because he was too young. But now . . ."

"Now he can, in this bizarre ghost world. So he heads for the Bahamas, figuring he'll take out Columbus?"

"Yeah. I heard some of the islanders say that they see Columbus' ships out on the water, at two in the morning, every Columbus Day. It's probably these ghost shops, rediscovering the New World every year." Cloudrunner blinked some blood from his good eye.

"So Magellan finds out and decides to show up and attacks? Just like that?"

"Just like that." Cloudrunner shook his head slowly. "I don't know; it all sounds so crazy. But how else can you explain this. . . ."

Cloudrunner looked around slowly, and saw for the first time that there were a couple of dozen people sitting in the muddy straw around him. They sported attire from several time periods, ranging from a couple in swimsuits (the woman in a thong bikini, the man in a Speedo) to a gentleman with an uncomfortable-looking Elizabethan ruff, his body covered head to toe, but with the sleeves and thighs slashed and brightly-colored silk pulled through.

The Elizabethan in particular looked completely out of place, his crisp clothing in stark contrast to the earthy mess beneath him. Cloudrunner squinted in the darkness to see what the dandy sat upon—it appeared to be a rather large red silk handkerchief.

Cloudrunner realized with a start that all of the prisoners were tied up.

"They were all captured like us," Ain't-no said, as if he were reading Cloudrunner's mind. "I talked to them while you were still out. Every one of us saw the ghost ships just before we were taken. I hate to admit it, but it fits your theory perfectly."

Cloudrunner surveyed the faces around him, and several people nodded as Ain't-no spoke, as if they knew Cloudrunner needed their validation.

"Miss," Cloudrunner said abruptly, addressing the flower girl after a crazy thought struck him, "how long have you been here?"

"Like, a couple of hours, man," she said, her head swaying a bit.

"And what *year* do you think it is?"

"What?"

"What year is it? 1492? 1519?"

The flower girl giggled. "Wow, man, that's some pretty good shit you've got, if you think it's, like, 1492. You have any more?"

"No," Cloudrunner said quickly. "But what year is it?"

"It's, like, '69, right?"

The Elizabethan gentleman harrumphed. "Preposterous. It's the year of our Lord 1550. The *lady* is mistaken." He rolled his eyes as he said *lady*.

A shocked-looking farmer wearing well-worn coveralls said, "No, it ain't. It's 1877."

The swimsuited beach couple glanced at each other before saying, in unison, "1998?"

Cloudrunner watched in silence as others chimed in with different years. After a while, nobody else spoke and the holding cell went silent.

"Hey, Chief," Ain't-no said. "I think it's time to get out of here."

"Yeah."

"Chief?" the Elizabethan gentleman said softly. "Are you an Indian, my good man?"

Cloudrunner grimaced as a thousand Ute ancestors whooped and yelled angry war cries in his head. "Native American," he said indignantly, pointedly ignoring the Elizabethan.

The gentleman pressed on, undaunted. "One of those chaps the colonials are having all those problems with?"

Cloudrunner bit his lip until he tasted warm, salty blood in his mouth. His tense arms shook so much with anger he could feel his binds loosen under his burning wrists. The thought of escape calmed him, so he concentrated on working the bindings.

"Yeah," Ain't-no said, "he is, a few generations back."

"My Lord," the gentleman said, "you lot are supposed to be deadly warriors. Impossible to capture."

Cloudrunner closed his eyes and tried to ignore him. Work the binds. Get free.

The blonde hippie girl gasped. "You're an Indian? Wow, man, you can, like, just talk to the sea spirits and have them rescue us, right?"

Cloudrunner opened his eyes and stared at her in disbelief. Couldn't *anyone* see he wasn't what they thought he was? It was bad enough that his mind-ancestors tormented him with their steadfast belief in his courage; now, total strangers were counting on it.

"We're saved," the Elizabethan said.

Work the binds, work the binds, Cloudrunner thought desperately. They're looser already. Just work the binds and ignore the idiots.

The flower girl said glibly, "Hey, man, Mr. Indian, have you got any *peyote*?"

The Elizabethan took this for agreement and gushed on. "We'll wait for nightfall, and the savage will sneak out and take care of the crew in their sleep! Silent killers, those Indians are."

The voices in Cloudrunner's head screamed even louder, fueling his rage, so that he forgot about the binds, which were now slick with blood, but close to coming off. The Englishman's pronunciation of *Indian* sounded too much like *Injun* for Cloudrunner's resolve. He opened his mouth to yell at the insensitive bastard—

—and light spilled in directly above, blinding Cloudrunner. All at once, one hand came free and he reached up swiftly, grabbing at a nearby sailor. His bloody hand closed around grimy, rough fabric, and Cloudrunner used the handhold to haul himself to his feet, his weight smashing the surprised sailor down onto the deck in the process. Adrenaline fueling his muscles with power he didn't know he had, Cloudrunner scrambled from the hole onto the deck. Ankles still bound, he leaped up and vaulted over the sailor, only to lose his balance and flop to the weathered wood deck. Enraged, he kicked the stunned sailor into the hole with the other prisoners. In a flash, Cloudrunner rolled on his stomach and pushed up from the deck with his free arms, scraping his hands on the deck in the process. He made it to his knees before muscular hands grabbed him roughly about the chest and shoulders and slammed his face back down onto the deck with a sickening crunch. Cloudrunner's head exploded with pain. Someone kicked him hard in the ribs and rolled him over on his back. Black Henry slowly knelt beside him and stared at Cloudrunner's smashed, bloodied face.

"What are you, spy?" Black Henry said after studying him for a while, his face within inches of Cloudrunner's.

Cloudrunner glared with his one good eye, but said nothing. Blood from his broken nose trickled into his ear, but he didn't care anymore. His Ute ancestors raged in his head, urging him to kill, kill, kill, and that's all he wanted now. He could see the murderous intent in his own eyes, reflected in Black Henry's cool, unconcerned eyes.

"*What* are you?" Black Henry repeated, then pulled away to arm's length. "I've not seen one like you before. Your skin is red. Why? Are all spies red?"

Cloudrunner's blood boiled. He *knew* Black Henry didn't mean his sunburn; he *knew* it in his gut, even though his rational mind told him he was overreacting. But his instinct won. "I am Native American, and proud of it," Cloudrunner said through clenched teeth, his voice rising with every word. "*You* didn't discover this land; not you *or* Columbus."

Black Henry flinched at the mention of Columbus, and glanced out at the sea. Murmurs of "Columbus" and "*espiao*" swept the crew again, as nearby sailors overhearing Cloudrunner's outburst instantly judged and condemned Cloudrunner.

"Columbus," Black Henry said with contempt, and spit on the deck before standing, towering once again to yell at Cloudrunner. "He's not half the man my master is! Columbus was lucky, nothing more. Of *course* he did not discover this land—only a fool would think he had."

Cloudrunner snorted. "But he *did* open up trade in these parts, which is more than *Magellan* did around here."

Black Henry nodded curtly. "Aye, he did. And for that, he is revered. While my deserving master is disgraced in his own land." Black Henry's face darkened and he spun around violently to face the sea. Throwing both arms out wide, he screamed, "Columbus must die!"

His words echoed over the deck. "Die, die, die."

The crew, already whipped up with battle fever, took up the cry and screamed along with Black Henry, gesturing wildly and yelling obscenities. After a few minutes, the din died down, but they still stared out to sea.

Trying to act undaunted by Black Henry's diversion, Cloudrunner struggled to his knees and pressed on with his own deflated tirade. "I don't care about your stupid beef with Columbus. The point is, this land was *ours* for generations before any of you came. You had no right to take it from us. I demand you release me and the others immediately."

Black Henry shook his head sadly, still staring out to sea.

"Then what are you going to do with us?" Cloudrunner asked.

Black Henry spun around to face Cloudrunner and grinned. "The others? They will be sold." His grin vanished. "You? You are clearly a spy. You know much of Columbus, my sworn enemy. Even tied, you attack us to escape to him—though it would do him no good." He pointed out to sea, where the crew seemed to be looking. "What say you now, spy?"

Black Henry made a motion with his hand. Two muscular men dragged Cloudrunner to his feet. While they tied his hands behind his back again, Cloudrunner stared out at the sea and saw all three of Columbus' ships engulfed in flames. Magellan had lost a ship, too, but he was clearly the victor with four intact ships.

As if on cue, the mast of the *Santa Maria* fell over into the water.

Cloudrunner's Ute ancestors screamed at him, ordering him to face his enemy with courage and dignity. Ute warriors never feared death, they said. The battle wasn't over until the last Ute fell, they said. Cloudrunner was a Ute, and a warrior, was he not? He was bound by honor.

Cloudrunner squared his shoulders and fixed his good eye on Black Henry. "I say nothing. I'm just a computer programmer who came here to see the ships."

The ships, Cloudrunner reflected, that would never discover America now. His mind raced as the implications flooded his thoughts. What had happened here? If Magellan indeed won this battle, did it change history? What was the impact of this upset victory? Would Magellan be the one to discover America? What did that mean?

"What is this . . . com-pu-ter, spy?" Black Henry seemed genuinely interested, yet wary.

Cloudrunner paused, partly because he was lost in his own head, trying to puzzle out the ramifications of Magellan killing Columbus before the discovery of the New World, and partly because he was wondering how to explain a computer to a sixteenth-century seaman.

But Cloudrunner waited too long to answer.

Black Henry grinned. "So be it. A trick to confuse me. Now, spy, you die." He motioned to the muscular men and turned away. "Throw him overboard."

"You can't kill me," shouted Cloudrunner. "You're a damn ghost."

Black Henry threw back his head and laughed, full and deep. He stopped, but didn't turn around. "That I am. And I am free at last." Black Henry walked away, leaving Cloudrunner to the hired muscle.

Struggling as best he could, screaming for help, Cloudrunner was hoisted like a sack of rotten potatoes. He sailed through the air and hit the water with a hard splat. Without the mobility of his hands or his feet to help him attain buoyancy, he sank into the clear water, swallowing brine as he thrashed about for air.

Passing by the hull of the *Trinidad* as it sped away, Cloudrunner spun down with the current, deeper and deeper underwater. He struggled against it for a few moments, his lungs bursting in his chest, but the current sucked him under nonetheless. It struck him at once how futile his struggle was, and he stopped resisting. He sank more slowly, but he still sank.

Cloudrunner watched the shimmering hull disappear in the distance. It didn't really matter who won, Columbus or Magellan, Cloudrunner thought as he blew out the remaining air in his lungs. It would always be the red man who lost.

SEASON FINALE

by Bradley H. Sinor

Not too long ago a friend of Brad's commented that Brad wrote family stories. "Yeah," Brad told him, "if you're related to the Addams Family or one of Dracula's relatives." Brad has seen his fiction appear in such anthologies as Warrior Fantastic, Knight Fantastic, Dracula in London, Bubbas of the Apocalypse, Merlin, Lord of The Fantastic, *and others. He will have several more coming out in 2005. Two collections of his short fiction are* Dark And Stormy Nights *and* In the Shadows.

I HADN'T WALKED more than a half dozen steps into the convenience store before the clerk noticed me. Of course noticing customers was part of her job, but this time it was something special, watching her head turn around quickly, her eyes large with surprise.

To be perfectly honest, I would have been a little bit disappointed if she hadn't been startled. After all, how often, even in a university town the size of Norman, Oklahoma, do you see a guy dressed in medieval garb: hooded cape, fur-lined leather vest and chain mail, come walking out of a cold January night?

Not that the girl, who looked to be about twenty and was wearing a blue smock with the store's name on it, had anything to say about looking unusual. The pink-and-green dyed hair and nose ring were probably not listed in the store's employee manual. If this little mom-and-pop place had one.

"Something I can help you with?" she asked.

"No, thanks," I said.

The store wasn't that big. I could find what I needed without a problem. I mean, how difficult is it to hide the chips and the French bread? I grabbed what I needed, along with a six-pack of Pepsi. There would probably be plenty of the things I liked to drink at the party, but I didn't want to take a chance.

As I turned to head toward the counter, I heard the buzz that announced the front door opening. That sound could easily get very annoying, though I imagined that you learned to screen it out after a while. The new customer was a lean man, dressed in an overcoat, a scarf wrapped around his neck, and a pipe emitting smoke from cherry tobacco, held between tightly clenched teeth.

"Be anything else for you?" the girl asked when I set my stuff down. Before I could answer, she began picking things up and running them in front of the bar code scanner attached to the cash register.

"So, aren't you a little late or are you just really, really getting a jump on things?" she asked.

"No, I don't think I'm late," I said, with a quick glance at the big Coors clock behind the counter. My watch was in the belt pouch hanging around my waist and a bit hard to get to. It was only a quarter past nine. The party would just be getting started.

"Well, if you're dressed like that for Halloween, then I would say that you're about a couple of months late. If it's for that Medieval Fair, its not supposed to roll around until April, and the last time I looked it was still January," she said.

"January sixth, to be precise," said the man with the pipe, putting a loaf of bread down in front of him and gathering up a newspaper from the nearby rack.

I waited until he was heading out the door, to the accompaniment of the same annoying buzzing that had announced his entrance, before I said, "Who was that masked man?"

"Was he really here at all? Or did we just imagine him," the girl chimed in. "So what's so special about January sixth?"

"It's called Twelfth Night. Have you ever heard that old song "The Twelve Days of Christmas"?

"Yeah, my grandmother used to love to sing it at the holidays. All about turtledoves, peacocks, and a bunch of dorky lords a leaping and stuff like that, isn't it?"

"Sort of," I said. "In medieval times they actually stretched out the celebration of Christmas over twelve days, starting on December twenty-fifth and ending on January sixth. That's where the name Twelfth Night came from. It was the night of the biggest celebration.

"I belong to a local medieval reenactment group. Every year we hold a big blowout party on or as close as we can get to the sixth of January. This year it's on a weekend so we actually get to celebrate it on the right day."

"Wild, man. So do all the women come and run around like tavern wenches or damsels in distress?" asked the girl. She began putting my purchases into a big brown paper sack. "That'll be eight fifty."

I laid a twenty dollar bill on the counter. "As for

the women in our group, they come as whatever they want, and party with the best of them. By the way, my name is Conner, Conner McMannus. What's your name?"

She arched her head slightly, as if giving me the once over. "Nikita. Before you ask, no, I'm not Russian. I just like the name, and yes, I picked it."

"Works for me," I said. In the medieval group we all picked out medieval sounding names and went by them. "Think maybe you would like to go to the Twelfth Night party with me? I can come get you when you get off. It'll be going on all night."

"Don't bother coming back to get me," said Nikita, a note of finality in her voice. I had expected her to say no. This girl didn't strike me as being too interested in things medieval. Hey, it wasn't the first time I had been turned down for a date and it certainly wouldn't be the last. "Well, maybe another time."

Nikita pulled her smock off and tossed it on the floor. She twisted the key in the lock of the register, then pulled it out and dropped it down a small slot in the back of the counter. Grabbing an army surplus field jacket from a peg on the wall, she slipped it on.

"Why come back later? I'm going with you now."

"I didn't really like that place anyway," Nikita said. "I'd been planning on quitting on Monday. It was boring. The guy who owns the place was such a grouch; besides, I think he wanted to fuck me."

Nikita spat on the floor as she talked about the store owner, which didn't bother me a bit. I knew that guy, and her description pretty well summed things up. Besides, it was her floor, in her apartment, and she could do anything she wanted.

The Twelfth Night party was set in a converted church a few blocks from the convenience store. I knew from past experience that there was virtually no parking in front of the place, so I had left my van in a lot behind one of the administration buildings just a couple of blocks away.

Nikita had been insistent that we stop by her apartment so she could change clothes. Since it was only a block or so out of the way I didn't see any need to retrieve my van.

"It won't take that long. Not to mention that you said yourself the party was going to go on all night."

"Well, m'lady," I said, "far be it from me to deny you the chance to get all gussied up."

"Look, if you're going to start sounding like Lord Billy-Bob Clampett I may just have to kick you where the chain mail don't shine," she said.

"Actually," I mused, "the place you're talking about probably gets pretty shiny. You know, all that rubbing against a saddle and what not."

Nikita didn't say a word, just produced a key and opened the door. Her apartment was the top half of a two-story house. From the mailboxes it looked like the bottom floor had been cut up into two apartments.

Not that the three rooms—kitchen, living room and bathroom—were all that big. A large mattress filled up one end of the living room. The only other furniture was a table, some scrounged kitchen chairs and a bookcase made from bricks and boards.

Nikita murmured something before she disappeared into the bathroom, which apparently doubled as a closet, since I could see some clothes hanging from the wall.

I walked over to her bookcase and scanned the

titles. Most were fantasy, Tolkien, Howard, de Camp, and Drake, with a few horror titles thrown in, as well. I felt a sense of relief when it occurred to me that there wasn't a romance title in the bunch. Not that I had a problem with a girl who read romances, mind you.

Peeking out from a small nitch between the bricks and the wall was another book. It crossed my mind that this might be her diary. I considered for a moment just leaving it and respecting her privacy, but prurient curiosity won and I pulled the slim volume out where I could see it.

It was the size of a paperback book and was bound in worn leather. I flipped through a couple of pages. The paper felt like old, old parchment. There was neat precise writing inside, broken up every couple of pages by drawings done in such fine detail that it was scary to think they had come from a human hand.

I'm not sure when it occurred to me that it wasn't written in English but rather Latin. It had been half a dozen years since my last Latin class, the result of an attempt at Catholic education by my parents, so I had forgotten most of it. But here and there I did recognize a few words. There was something about hounds, and it looked like the word hunt reoccurred a number of times.

"Curious and curiouser," I muttered.

"So is there more to this Twelfth Night thing than just a last night of Christmas party?" asked Nikita.

I shoved the book back into its hiding place.

"Yes, as a matter of fact. There are some cultures that considered the time between Samhain, that's Halloween, and the end of Christmas to be a Season of misrule, where everything got flipped on its head.

The peasants could be kings and the rich act as servants. That sort of thing."

"Cool," she said, stepping out of the bathroom. Nikita had replaced her jeans and T-shirt with a long black sheath dress, a chain mail belt and dagger riding on her hip.

"So, will I fit in with your medieval crowd?" she asked.

Okay, so the pink-and-green hair wasn't exactly what you would have seen on the dance floor in the halls of Richard the Lionhearted, but everything else worked for me. She walked up to the edge of the bed, just in front of me. "Well?" she asked.

I bowed, took her hand, and kissed the back of it.

"I ought to let you know that there are a few of the people I usually hang with who would say that gesture alone would suggest you were gay and would want to beat the crap out of you."

"That's their problem." Three years army special forces and ten years of martial arts training were enough to let me know I could handle most anything. "As for my sexual orientation, that's none of their business either."

"We can discuss that part, in more detail, later." She touched the edge of the bed with her foot. "But right now, m'lord, I believe you promised to take me to a party."

"Indeed I did."

The roar of a motorcycle just below the apartment window seemed to shake the very foundations of the building. A moment later the sound was gone and replaced by the baying of a dog.

Nikita went stiff, the color draining out of her face, her grip on my arm tightening to the point of cutting off circulation.

"What's the matter?" I said.

"That, that, dog. I don't like dogs. I never have."

I went over to the window looked around. There was nothing there, just a couple of trash cans, an empty packing crate and signs left over from a garage sale the previous week. I wasn't sure just what I had been expecting, the vicious glowing specter of the Hound of the Baskervilles or what.

"It's okay," I said, gently. "If you want, we don't have to walk to the party. I can go get my van and come get you here."

"No, no. It . . . it was nothing," she said. "Just put it down to my being frightened by a Chihuahua with an attitude when I was a little girl."

"If you're sure."

"Trust me, the last place I want to be tonight is by myself."

Anyone who happened to drive past the old church that night, or any other night, for that matter, would not have paid much attention to it. All they would have seen would have been a red-brick building, bracketed by heavy bushes, with a huge round stained-glass window above the door.

The place hadn't actually been a church for over ten years. Five years ago friends of mine, Al and Kathy Jennings, had bought it and begun to convert it into their dream home. The results had been spectacular enough to merit an appearance on a national television series devoted to unusual homes.

As we walked in, I recognized most of the people who were already there and had a pretty good idea of who would come drifting in over the next few hours. Some were friends of long standing, other people I knew by name but had barely even spoken to.

The place was not huge, but it felt like it. There was a single downstairs room with kitchen in the back, while an upstairs balcony wrapped around the second floor, hiding the family's private quarters. Everywhere there hung banners carrying household and personal badges, flowers that wrapped around the stained-glass windows, and an assortment of weapons and musical instruments on the walls.

Nikita and I deposited the items I had bought on the buffet table near the kitchen door. There was food of all sorts, from what passed for traditional medieval dishes to things that had the distinct look of having come from local fast food places.

"Your friends here sure know how to lay out a spread," said Nikita.

"Oh, yes. There are some very, very good cooks here tonight. You will not go home hungry," I said. "But just be glad that one cook didn't bring anything."

"Just who would that be?"

"Me."

"And just why is that a good thing, then, that you didn't cook?" she asked.

"Less chance of fatalities," I laughed. "I'm honest enough to admit that I'm not a very good cook."

I filled up two pewter mugs with hot apple cider and passed one to Nikita. She sniffed it, and then took a hesitant swallow.

"Don't worry, I didn't spike it with anything. Although there is a whole selection of much stronger drinks available, should you desire them."

"Don't worry, m'lord, you don't have to get me

drunk to have your way with me. *If* I choose to let you," Nikita said.

"I'll remember that."

Just then two men with lutes, a woman with a harp, and a couple of drummers who had set up in one corner of the room began to play.

It occurred to me that if two hours ago someone had told Nikita she would be listening to Celtic music, and hopefully enjoying it, she would have likely not believed it. After three songs I noticed her mouthing the words, almost in sync with the musicians.

Several couples had moved out into the center of the room, clearing away a couch and a couple of chairs, and begun to organize a group dance. I touched Nikita on the shoulder.

"Would you care to dance?"

"I'm not sure," she hesitated. "This is a bit far from a rave or a mosh pit. I think I can pick up the steps if I watch for a few minutes. Then, if you're still interested . . ."

"I stand ready for you, m'lady."

I heard my name called from the back of the room. Standing in the door to the kitchen was the owner of the house, Al Jennings, or, as he was known in the group, Jon de Vitte. I knew him for three years by that name and when I learned his real name it just never seemed to fit him, at least in my mind.

"Jon! How come you let them keep conning you into hosting this little shindig year after year."

"Hey, you know me, I'm an easy mark. Kathy just smiles sweetly and I give in, despite my best intentions. Look, can you give me a hand? I need some help to bring in a table from the garage. I'm seriously thinking that we are going to need it."

The garage was a separate building, about thirty feet from the main house, as solidly built out of heavy red brick as the church itself. The whole backyard was wrapped in the same sort of bushes that wound around the front. There were several leafless trees whose bare limbs hung like specters in the moonlight, marking the path to the garage.

Normally, the porch and backyard would have been full of people indulging in a tribute to the nicotine demon. This time there were just Jon and me, along with the cold and the full moon.

We had just swung the garage door closed when the sound of dogs howling filled the night, echoing off the building and the trees. It seemed to come from everywhere and nowhere at once. I had an eerie feeling of déjà vu, times a hundred.

The same way it had happened at Nikita's apartment, the sound was suddenly gone, leaving a loud silence in its wake. Jon and I just looked at each other, neither of us seeming to want to say anything.

Finally a grin rolled across his face and Jon said, "So who let the dogs out?"

"Or who chased them back in?" I asked. "I think the technical term for that little bit was . . . just plain weird."

"I love it when you talk dirty," laughed Jon.

I was about to grab my end of the table when I looked back toward the alley gate. Someone stood there, a tall man, dressed in leather jacket and black leather riding chaps. I thought I caught a glimpse of a motorcycle behind him. I couldn't see his face; it was too dark.

I assumed it was just someone arriving late and coming in the back way. No doubt he had his change of clothing in saddlebags on the cycle. I couldn't have turned my head for more than a second, but when I looked back, he was gone.

The roaring of motorcycles filled the backyard for a few seconds and then faded in the distance.

"What was that term you used earlier? Just plain weird?" said Jon. "I don't know if that qualifies, but it's close."

"Yeah," I grabbed up my end of the table and we headed back inside.

Finding Nikita wasn't too hard. The house wasn't that big, no matter what it felt like. She had moved away from the area where the dancing was going on to talk to another woman it took me a second or two to recognize. This was an old friend, Lady Serina de Lyman, who in the real world answered to the name Serina Smith. She wore a long crimson Italian Renaissance dress that looked like it had been designed for her.

"Lady Serina? I might have known. It looks like I came back just in time. I suspect that you two ladies have been plotting and planning."

"Of course we have, Conner," laughed Serina. "And you are to be the victim of all our plans. I would suggest that you be on your best behavior. I've been telling Nikita all about you, every nasty little detail."

"Oh, boy, I'm in deep trouble," I said. Actually Serina could tell her a lot about me; things I would prefer didn't get around. Our families had been friends for years and we had known each other since sixth grade. "As I suspected, Lady Serina, you are being a very bad influence on this innocent newcomer to our gathering."

"M'lord," she said with a sly smile. "I do my best

to be a bad influence, wherever I can. Now, if you will excuse me. I must go forth to spread chaos and terror in my path."

"It was nice meeting you, Serina," said Nikita. Turning to me she said, "Serina told me that I was a very lucky girl. That you are one of the nicest, most considerate men she has ever known."

"Well, Serina doesn't get around much," I laughed.

"No. I'm beginning to get the idea, Conner Ryan McMannus, and she told me that that is your real name, that you are a man of many facets. I wish I had the time to explore them all. I have a feeling that your walking into the store tonight was one of the better things to happen to me lately."

"We'll see." I leaned forward and put my hands on Nikita's shoulders, drawing her closer to me. I could feel a moment's resistance, as if she were unsure. Then, as our lips met, it was as if she were trying to push herself closer and closer, her arms wrapping tight around me. I've been kissed before, but nothing like that.

In the back of my mind a little voice was saying, "Man, hold onto this woman."

For a long time the only thing I could feel was the pressure of her lips against mine, and every inch of her body, breasts, legs, hips pressing hard against mine, our hands digging into each other. I could imagine the sort of show that we were putting on for everyone around us. Frankly, right then I didn't give a rat's ass.

Naturally, that's when everything went wrong; very, very wrong.

The front door to the church blew open, slamming so hard against the wall that it nearly ripped itself free from the metal hinges that were anchored in the brick. There was no way a natural wind would do that. A couple that were standing close to the door barely got out of the way in time.

Two of the largest dogs that I had ever seen, like some mutated crossbreed of a wolfhound and an elephant, stood just inside the doorway. Other dogs surged around them into the church, growling as they went, herding the people back.

Out of the corner of my eye I saw Jon come out of the kitchen, a very large battle-ax in his hand. Around the room I didn't have to see to know that swords were being unsheathed and daggers drawn, weapons appearing in the hands of not only men, but women as well. I had a hunch that more than one person in this room was weighing their chances of reaching their cars where more lethal weapons might be found.

I still had my arm around Nikita. I could feel her muscles tightening with every passing second. "Just wait," I whispered, trying to give her a reassuring squeeze. "There may be a way out of here without anyone getting hurt."

"There isn't," her voice was husky and far away.

The dogs had cleared a corridor into the center of the room. From outside walked a man; dressed in the same black motorcycle leathers as the man I had seen standing in the garden gate. Another half dozen figures followed behind; clad in leather, their faces masked by scarves, goggles, and protective helmets. Behind them I caught a glimpse of a line of motorcycles, silently awaiting their riders' return.

The man came into the center of the room and turned toward Nikita and me. He raised his arm and pointed at her.

"No!" I said pushing her behind me. From all sides armed people took a step forward, ready to fight at my side.

"Conner!" I looked toward the balcony. Someone threw a sword to me. I have no memory of catching it or unsheathing the blade. I just knew that it was in my hand, ready to use.

"Now, I admit that was quite an entrance," I told the man. "But somehow I don't think that you and your friends are welcome at this party."

The stranger stood, unmoving. Then, with slow, precise movements, he slipped off the helmet, holding it under his arm, and took off the scarf and goggles. I knew that face, it was the man we had seen earlier in the convenience store.

"A brave man," he said. "Willing to fight, to defend this woman, even though he doesn't know what he might be fighting for."

"I suppose you're prepared to tell me."

The man's gaze shifted to Nikita. That same sad smile I had seen earlier was on her face now. "I am not the one who should do the telling."

"I think, I would prefer to hear it from you," I said. "Are you suggesting you have a claim on her?"

One of the dogs picked that moment to growl and charge me. I swung at it, intended to put my sword as deep into its body as I could. But the dog was just a bit too fast. Instead of connecting with the blade, I had to slam my hand, wrapped around the sword hilt, into the side of the dog's head to keep it from sinking its fangs into me. To say this was like hitting solid steel, and freezing cold steel athat would be a pretty good description of how much it hurt.

The dog yowled and was about to wrap his teeth

around my arm when the man in front of me spoke a single word. The sound was soft and direct, literally pulling the animal back.

"You are brave," he said. "Through the years few have been willing to raise a blade to one of our hounds. Usually, they simply throw their arms up and hope to die quickly. Yet you fight."

"A man fights when he has to," I said.

"Indeed."

"Perhaps you will understand more about us, and the woman, if you see my brethren and myself in our traditional forms," he said.

With that he made a gesture with his hand and everything changed. Neither he nor his companions wore the motorcycle leathers that they had a moment before. Now all were dressed in various forms of medieval clothing, breeches, boots, and capes, their helmets adorned with stag horns, with swords and other weapons hanging at their sides. They pretty well seemed to fit in with the rest of us. Where there had been motorcycles now stood horses.

"Do you know me?" he asked.

"No, but that's one hell of a trick," I said. "I'd say The Force is definitely with you."

"I am . . ."

"Prince Wilhelm Vladimir Dagget-Eletsky," said Nikita. "Once the ruler of a providence in the Balkans. Now, cursed to ride forth as the Hunt Master for the Wild Hunt."

I had a bad feeling in the pit of my stomach, remembering that book I had found in her apartment. I looked over at Nikita, knowing that I would find her changed. Her black dress was gone, replaced by leather breeches, a tunic, vest, and cape. All adorned with chain mail so fine that it was hard to tell the individual links. The green-and-pink hair was gone, replaced by a whitish-blonde braid that hung down her back.

"This night the Hunt rides forth for one reason alone," he intoned. "We have come to reclaim one of our own."

Nikita placed her hand on my cheek. "Conner, each of the Huntsmen are cursed to ride with the Hunt, instead of moving onto wherever souls go to find peace. I have been a part of this group for more than five hundred years.

"Do you remember how you said earlier that Twelfth Night was the last night of the season of misrule, where the peasants could be kings and everything was reversed? Also during this season the barrier between the worlds is stretched thin and one of the Hunt can walk among humans again, to be reminded of all that we have lost to this curse that damns us!"

"This year it was Nikita's turn," said the Hunt Master.

"No," I said. "Take me instead. Let her live out the time that would have been mine. I will ride at your side for however many eternities is the price to free her soul."

The Hunt Master chuckled. "That cannot be."

Tears rolled down Nikita's cheeks. "Conner, soon not even you will remember me. It will be as if I was never here. No one at the convenience store, even the grumpy owner, will recall I worked there. If you go to my apartment, you will find a couple living there who know nothing of me. That is the price each of the Hunt pay for these few brief days where we walk as human again, the knowledge that no one will remember our time among them. I knew this was the last night of the season that I was free, I did not want to hurt you, but I did not want to recall what was going to happen."

I kissed her again, pulling her to me as tightly as before. When she finally stepped away I felt like part of my heart had been ripped out.

"If I recall the legends of the Hunt correctly, within limits your magic is strong." I said to the Hunt Master.

"Within limits."

"Then grant me a simple request. Let my memories of Nikita remain mine. Let her ride with you, but know that someone remembers her," I said.

"You are a brave man," he said. He drew his sword, the hounds growling around him, and then touched it against my blade. Very gently he laid a gloved finger against my forehead. "It shall be as you wish. I hope in the years to come you will not regret your choice. Remember Nikita, remember us all, my friend."

I watched as the Hunt left our hall and mounted their horses. One had been brought for Nikita. Then they all disappeared into the night, the hounds running beside them.

I stood on the porch for a long time after they were gone, not really sure what to do.

"There you are," said Serina, handing me a glass of wine. "Don't look so long-faced. This is a party. You're supposed to be having fun."

"I'm doing my best. I guess I'm not in a party mood right now."

"Maybe I can get you in a better mood, later," she said. "Come on back inside."

"Okay."

"Can I ask you something, Conner?"

"Sure."

"Did something weird happen tonight?"

"No weirder than normal, I would say," I laughed.

"That's a relief."

VOICES IN AN EMPTY ROOM

by Richard Parks

Richard Parks' first short story collection, The Ogre's Wife: Fairy Tales for Grownups, *is now available everywhere. His short fiction has appeared in* Isaac Asimov's Science Fiction Magazine, Black Gate, The Year's Best Fantasy #1 & #2, *and has made the* Locus *Recommended Reading List. He lives with a wife and three cats who don't believe a word he says, except on his birthday and certain designated major holidays.*

ELI CHECKED his sensic as the seconds ticked down. His latest projected time was displayed in the upper left corner of the screen. The dented and blackened pocket watch propped up on his table between the salt and pepper shakers wasn't much help—its spring was broken and its gears and hands frozen.

Until, all on their own, they began to move.

As soon as the second hand ticked off one discrete, impossible second, Eli checked the time index. 9:27:42 AM.

Damn. I'm still three seconds off. . . .

"Mr. Mothersbaugh? I'm Jessie Nichols."

Eli's first impression was of a rather severe blue suit on a trim female figure, but his attention was elsewhere. "Give me a moment," Eli said. He turned away from the time display to the sensic data, but it was already too late; the glow that would have shown an active energy signature was already fading.

Missed again.

It had all been captured digitally, of course, but Eli found there was no substitute for seeing the sensic visuals in real-time; he tended to pick up things that the recorders often missed. Still, no help for it now; he'd review it later. Eli looked up to where Jessie Nichols was not so patiently waiting and took a good look at her. His first impression of form and attire was correct, but the face didn't quite match what he'd expected. Jessie Nichols was a thirty-something redhead; she wore her thick, curly hair pulled back in a simple ponytail and she looked like someone who knew how to smile, even if she wasn't doing so at that moment.

"Imperfect social skills," she said. "I'd heard that about you."

Chagrined, Eli didn't bother to ask from whom. The information could have come from any one of dozens of reliable sources. He rose then and extended his hand, which she accepted. "My apologies, Ms. Nichols. You caught me in the middle of logging a reading."

"You've already started?"

"I was a little early for our appointment. I thought I'd use the time."

Jessie Nichols sat down across from him. Eli's table was on the sidewalk outside La Parisian, the decent if pretentious French café on the ground floor of the

Walthor Hotel. It was the oldest of several buildings, mostly offices, surrounding Armfield Park. Eli looked across the large expanse of green where several dozen office workers were juggling comcells and lunch, young mothers pushed strollers, and a group of students from nearby Armfield University sat in a circle under the warm spring sun. Jessie noticed his eyes wandering.

"Lovely day, isn't it? Looking at it now it's hard to imagine such a thing happening here," she said.

Eli didn't have to ask what she was talking about; the bombing of July 4, 2015, was still fresh on everyone's mind even ten years after the fact. Just over a hundred killed on the grand opening of the new Brian T. Armfield Municipal Park, timed to coincide with the Independence Day celebration. Despite the tensions in the world, no one had expected such a thing in the middle of the crowd at an obscure Fourth of July ceremony in the even more obscure city of Canemill, Mississippi. Not so obscure now, and so to remain as long as the nation lasted.

"Hard to imagine such a thing happening anywhere. Yet, somehow, they managed to happen anyway. Memory is short, Ms. Nichols," Eli said, "History is long."

"You can call me Jessie. I assume you were briefed before you arrived?"

"I'm Eli. A haunting, with apparent ties to the events of July Fourth ten years ago?"

She nodded. "So it seems. The phenomenon was apparently gradual, so no one picked up on it right away. Yet it's more than noticeable now, and people are talking. Apparitions have been sighted, noises heard where no one is visible, the usual. As deputy mayor, I'd like to get this resolved as soon as possible, yet obviously this is no common situation and must be handled with some delicacy."

"Obviously," Eli said, but that was all.

Jessie looked at him. "Is there something you're not telling me?"

"Jessie, with all due respect I could ask the same of you, but never mind that for the moment. Do you have any idea yet how many victims we're dealing with?"

She met his gaze squarely. "I assume several, considering how many people died."

Eli shook his head. "Nasty as the death-event was, it would be very unusual for more than a handful to manifest postmortem after such an extended period. There would have to be special circumstances."

"You're the expert. Do *you* know how many victims are present?"

"I've detected only one so far," Eli said. "But he's not a victim as such."

Jessie just stared at him for a moment. "But . . . that makes no sense! In ten years no one else has died here! Who else would be haunting Armfield Park?"

"Who else? Think about it, Jessie."

Jessie did think about it and turned a little pale. Eli nodded. "I'm afraid so. Ahmed Ali. The bomber."

Eli spent most of the rest of that day taking readings at various points around the park. He got a few curious stares but not much more than that. The sensic resembled an old-fashioned laptop closely enough so that most people just assumed he was a retro-hardware fancier. Mostly what Eli saw was life going on, as it usually did among the living.

As he was looking over his notes that afternoon, a

visitor arrived from the mayor's office. A clean-cut, handsome young man in the standard business suit uniform. "My name is John Black, Jessie Nichols' executive assistant. I was sent to inform you that the mayor's Office has decided that the investigation is unnecessary."

Eli didn't look up from his monitor. "It doesn't work like that."

The young man blinked. "Pardon?"

"Once an investigation is initiated, the Field Operator—that's me—decides when it's closed. I have not so decided. I can be overruled by the director of the Bureau, but he's not so inclined. Ms. Nichols is welcome to try and persuade him, of course."

"You've spoken to your director?"

"Right after my appointment with Ms. Nichols this morning. I suspected she'd try this."

"The mayor strongly feels—"

"Bull. The mayor is in Aruba, has been for the last two weeks, will be until next Friday, and, I'm willing to bet my sensic to your Armani, is *not* thinking about dead terrorists. If anyone has decided anything, it's Ms. Nichols herself. If Ms. Nichols wants the investigation ended, I'm perfectly willing to discuss it; she knows where to find me."

There were times when Eli was grateful for his lack of social skills, and he proceeded to ignore the young man. After a very short time, John Black went away. Eli barely noticed. He did notice that Jessie didn't attempt to contact him right away. He assumed she was checking the statutes and calling in favors in an attempt to circumvent him. He wondered how long it would take her to find out that, in this special case, there was no back door. It was only after he'd eaten dinner that evening and was resting in his rooms at the Walthor that he got the answer.

The phone rang. It was Jessie Nichols. "Meet me out front in ten minutes."

Eli considered her tone. "Should I bring an escort?"

"Bring the goddam Mississippi National Guard for all I care! Just be there."

Eli sighed and put his shoes back on. In eight minutes he reached the park. Jessie was waiting for him, leaning on the edge of the basin of the central fountain; she was carrying a small notebook. She'd also traded her suit for a pair of jeans and a plain white blouse. "Eli, don't you have anything better to do?" she asked.

"That depends. What's the real reason you want me to quit?"

She stared at him for several long moments. "Aren't you getting ahead of yourself? I haven't given you *any* reason yet!"

Eli sighed. "Did you have to? These aren't ordinary circumstances, as you said yourself. The victims have all been designated 'Martyrs of Freedom' by Presidential fiat, for one thing. I assume the press release was already written, something about the mayor's office seeing that peace was given to some poor victim of July Fourth?"

Jessie had the decency to blush then, but she didn't look away. "Only it didn't turn out that way, did it?"

"I'll say. It's not a poor victim at all. It's the guy who created all those 'Martyrs of Freedom'' in the first place. Politically, how does it look to do a damn thing for him?"

She sighed. "Isn't that reason enough to forget the whole thing?"

"It's not a reason at all, Jessie. Bureau matters are confidential; it's in the charter. All you have to do is keep quiet, whatever happens. No political fallout at all."

"That's not the point!"

Eli shrugged. "Then what is? What if I do free Ali's tortured soul or whatever the bioremnant energies are? No one's going to know except you and me, and I'm enjoined from talking about it. You say whatever you want to say, including nothing at all. Now, if I leave this unresolved, the incidents continue. People ask questions. People go looking for answers anywhere they can get them. Do you want someone *else* to bring the Bureau in? Someone less concerned with discretion and the politics of the matter?"

"To hell with the politics! It's just not right, doing anything to help that son of a—"

Eli stopped her. "All right, that's a reason I believe, even if I don't agree with it. But you misunderstand—it's not Ahmed Ali I'm trying to help."

"But you said he was the only one here!"

"He is. That's the problem. See this?" Eli held the item up for her inspection.

"It's a beat-up old pocket watch. So?"

"It's Ahmed Ali's watch. It was his great grandfather's and he always carried it, including the day he died."

Jessie took a closer look at it. "How did you get that?"

"Through legal channels. It goes back in the evidence files when I'm done. So. Notice anything unusual about it?"

She shrugged. "Other than the fact that it survived the blast? No."

"It didn't come through unscathed; the mechanism is pretty much frozen. Except when it runs."

She blinked. "Runs? When?"

"When Ahmed Ali makes his rounds. That's around 9:27 AM, though I haven't got the time index for each phase of his journey yet. That's what I was working on this morning. I should have made our appointment for later."

"So what does this prove? You still haven't explained what you meant. Who are you trying to help?"

"I'm not good at explanations, and, since you've already made up your mind, I don't think you'd believe me. I need to show you. Will you meet me tomorrow morning at, say, 9:15? Here by the fountain would be fine."

"I've wasted enough time on this," she said.

"Waste a little more. Let me show you what I've seen, and if you honestly think there's no point after my demonstration, I'll mark the investigation file 'inconclusive' and leave. Deal?"

Jessie's look was pure suspicion. "You're serious? My sole discretion?"

Eli nodded affably. "Entirely up to you."

"All right, but I'd advise you to pack."

Eli already had the sensic in place on the edge of the fountain and set before Jessie arrived at 9:15 on the dot.

"So what now?" she asked, "We wait?"

"Not for long. You see, 9:27 is when the main event occurred; there will be some preliminaries."

The "preliminaries" didn't take long to start. The sensic was the latest model, with full holo capabilities. Eli had created a miniature version of Armfield Park that floated in the air about a foot over the instrument, with all the energy signatures represented in faint glowing miniature. There were Jessie and himself standing by the fountain. Here and there were the benches, and here and again there were people sitting on them. Several students waiting for classes at the university Arts Center adjoining the park. Two fiftyish men in business attire sitting and talking. A few early morning joggers, walkers, and strollers.

A new glow appeared on the far side of the park. It seemed no different from the others, except this one changed every other one it came in contact with. Two young mothers chatted on the sidewalk, their baby strollers parked beside them. When the glow passed them, they became suddenly agitated, and in another moment the conversation was over as they stalked off in opposite directions. As it happened in the projection, so it mirrored what was happening out in the park. Eli watched the two women walk away from each other. Jessie did, too, frowning, but she said nothing.

"You'll see it again, here."

Eli didn't say what "it" was, but Jessie seemed to understand. The glow approached the two sitting businessmen, passed them. In another moment they became agitated, almost on cue. They didn't walk away as the two women had done. They argued. Loudly. It wasn't until the glow was well past them that the argument tapered off and quieted down, but it didn't end. Eli held up the pocket watch, and in a moment the hands started to move.

"Almost here," Eli said. "Wait for it."

Jessie glared at him, but she didn't move, even as the human-shaped glow headed straight for them, through them, past them.

Eli shivered. "Nasty."

"And what the hell is all this supposed to prove?"

"Why are you shouting?" Eli asked.

"I'm shouting because this is stupid! You're wasting my time!"

"You're angry, Jessie. Why?"

"I just told you . . ." She stopped. "Well, okay. I'm annoyed. I should be annoyed."

Eli smiled. "Perhaps, but you weren't annoyed. You were enraged."

Jessie took a deep breath, let it out. "What just happened?"

"The same thing I noticed yesterday when Ali appeared; the same thing that's only going to get worse the longer this goes on. Whatever you want to call it—hate, rage, madness that Ahmed Ali was carrying that day ten years ago. He's still carrying it. What's more, he's sharing it."

Jessie's voice was much more subdued now. "Oh."

"Oh, indeed. I've seen this a couple of times before: once in Memphis, another in New York, but nothing on this scale. The reason there have been 'incidents' is that the living are picking up this aspect of Ali's energy signature, even those who can't see or otherwise sense him."

"Then why weren't you affected?"

Eli glanced at the sensic display. "Because I know how to shield. You don't. As it was, my blood pressure probably went up a few points. But the show's not over. Watch."

They both watched as the revenant that had been international terrorist Ahmed Ali approached the front of the Walthor Hotel, the epicenter of the blast. Eli forced himself to take slow breaths, mostly so he would remember to breathe. Jessie's eyes were fixed on the display, her face a blank mask.

Ali reached the front of the hotel.

Ali kept going.

Absolutely nothing happened. In another moment the revenant was outside of the sensic's range and disappeared from the display.

Jessie just stared. "That doesn't make any sense!"

Eli switched the display from mapping to charting, then back again. Sometimes there was just no substitute for raw data, but it told him exactly what the holo projection had.

"It must make sense somehow, because it did happen. Ahmed Ali didn't stop. Proves one thing, at least: the manifestation may be periodic, but he's definitely not a repeater."

Jessie laughed harshly. "Hardly. Blowing yourself and a hundred innocent people up is not the sort of thing you can do more than once."

"Not 'repeat offender.' A *repeater*. It's a ghost that simply repeats a past action, endlessly. There's nothing left of the 'self' or the 'soul' or the 'coherent memory construct' or whatever we're calling it this year; it's an energy signature and nothing more. It's like a recording. If Ahmed Ali had been a repeater, he would have walked to the middle of where the crowd had been ten years ago and then winked out at precisely 09:27:45 AM. He didn't. He kept walking."

"I'm still having trouble with the idea that scum *had* a soul."

Eli nodded. "I think that bit of anger is all yours. Ali didn't give it to you."

She didn't look at him. "Oh, yes, he did."

"You're referring to your late husband, yes?"

Jessie took a deep breath. "Well. No one can say you didn't do your homework."

"I find it makes the job easier . . . or rather, possible. For what it's worth, I'm sorry about your husband."

"Me, too," she said bitterly. "We were barely back from our honeymoon. I still had a semester to go, but Hugh already had a job on Mayor Hemmings' staff. He as assisting with the ceremony; the police placed him maybe three feet away from Ahmed Ali when the bomb exploded; they never found all the pieces. Yes, Eli, I'm angry. Go back to Washington now, like you promised. Whatever passes for Ahmed Ali's soul can walk the Earth for eternity for all I give a shit."

"Do you like feeling that way?" Eli asked quietly.

Jessie stared at him. "What are you talking about?"

"You hate Ahmed Ali. You have reason; I didn't say you shouldn't. I'm asking if you enjoy it."

"What kind of stupid question is that??"

"It's a very simple question, Jessie, and I'm asking because I need to know. Think about what it feels like to hate these last ten years. Think about it being no different for the rest of your life."

"I can't change what happened," Jessie said softly.

"I'm not asking you to. I'm asking you to think about what's going to happen next, and change *that*. You saw the effect Ali's having on everyone here. That's going to continue. It's going to get worse."

Jessie smiled unexpectedly. "Rubbish. I've been doing my homework, too, Eli. Ghosts tend to fade over time, not get stronger."

"Usually, yes, though it can take hundreds of

years," Eli said, "but these aren't usual circumstances. Whatever Ali was raging against is still there. He's as mad as he ever was. I'll admit two samples aren't enough, but there's a very slight differential between them. Today he was slightly stronger. I'm betting if I read him tomorrow it'll show another change for the worse."

"And I say again, it doesn't make sense! He did what he set out to do; it was one of the most spectacularly successful terrorist attacks on US soil since 2001! Not to mention the added symbolic significance of pulling it off on July Fourth. The son of a bitch should be thrilled!"

"So why is he still here? Why is he still angry?"

"I don't know! Do you?"

"No. But I think it would be a very good idea to find out."

She smiled grimly. "My decision, remember? That was the deal."

Eli sighed. He hadn't wanted to play his last card, but Jessie wasn't going to back down. If this didn't work, maybe giving Ahmed Ali free run for another ten years might be the only solution, though Eli shuddered to think what might be left of Jessie Nichols' humanity by then. Not to mention anyone regularly in the vicinity of Armfield Park.

"*After* the demonstration was the deal," Eli said. "I'm not quite done yet." Eli bent over the sensic and made a few adjustments, then gave the instrument a voice command. "Replay from time index 09:24:00," he said.

"Eli, we already saw—oh."

Eli nodded. "Right. You didn't see this."

"This" was a series of figures that were not in the original display. They appeared as very faint traces, like will-o'-the-wisps compared to the bright miniature sun that was Ahmed Ali. And whenever he came close to them, they disappeared entirely, lost in the glow. Most of them were clustered by the entrance to the hotel, and when Ali passed through them, they all went away.

Poof.

Jessie looked a little pale. "If this is a trick . . ."

"I don't do tricks, Jessie. Do I have to tell you who those people are?"

She shook her head, slowly. "No . . . Hugh?"

"As it is, it's impossible to say who's here and who isn't. Ali's energy signature is like a high wind blowing away anything else. They're trying to manifest and they can't."

"Why are they trying? What do they want, Eli?"

"Maybe to finish the ceremony or just to enjoy the day. It was supposed to be a *celebration*, Jessie. *These* are the kind of spirits who fade, Jessie, and it doesn't take hundreds of years. Usually because after a while there's no longer any reason to stay. As it is, they'll never get the chance to do what they've come to do. Ali has them trapped."

Jessie sat down hard on the bench by the fountain. She didn't say anything for several long moments. Then, "Why didn't you just show me this to start with?"

"With you within a whisker of sending me packing, not sure how you'd react? I played it close to the vest, Jessie, that's all."

"And whose fault was that?" Jessie demanded. "You didn't have to make the deal in the first place."

Eli smiled. "No, I could try to finish what might be a very long and difficult investigation with the mayor's office in the person of *you* snagging me at every opportunity. I took a chance."

Jessie smiled, too, but hers was a weak, tentative thing. "Fair enough. All right, Eli—Ahmed Ali deserves an eternity of rage, but his victims don't. I want this settled. I . . . I want *them* settled. If that means bringing peace to Ahmed Ali's spirit . . . if that's the price, so be it. I'll stay out of your way."

"Thanks, but I may need a little more than that. There are some personnel files that even *I* can't get to without the cooperation of the city. I need to know I can call you when I have a question."

Jessie nodded, looking weary. "Sure, but the mayor will be back next week and I can't guarantee he'll see things the same way. Any idea when you'll see that answer?

"Just as soon as I know what the question is."

When Ahmed Ali's spirit passed through the location where the bomb had exploded and kept right on going, Jessie had drawn the obvious inference: "It doesn't make sense." Eli was reluctantly coming to the same conclusion.

There was so much about the events of July Fourth that didn't quite make sense. If Ahmed Ali was really a deeply placed terrorist agent as the FBI had said, why pick an obscure target like Canemill, Mississippi? After the fact, naturally, there had been claims of responsibility by various obscure terrorist organizations, one or two credible, but the investigations had failed to prove a connection to any of them. Still, the US had taken the terrorists at their word and acted accordingly.

After Ali's round the next morning, Eli was no

closer to reconciling the revenant's actions to what was known to have happened on Saturday, July 4, 2015. Ali had crossed the park, past the admittedly lax security, and blown up nearly everyone present: The mayor, Jessie's husband, picnickers, lovers, children waving small red, white, and blue flags. Those were the facts and the event was history. So why wasn't Ahmed playing his part?

Eli had been standing, sensic primed and ready, when the revenant arrived the next morning, punctual as an atomic clock. Eli followed the energy signature that had been Ahmed Ali as it passed through the middle of what had been the opening ceremonies to Armfield Park and passed through the doors of the Walthor Hotel, up the carpeted stairs—the thing could at least have taken the elevator, Eli thought grimly as he hurried in pursuit—to the third floor. It passed through the door to room 303 at the end of the hall. The door was locked, of course. Eli read the signature's disappearance with his sensic but couldn't actually see what, if anything, had happened in there. After a few moments the signature, surprisingly, reappeared. Yet the readings became a little diffuse at that time, less focused.

As if someone else was there. . . .

Before the third day, Eli made arrangements with the front desk and there was a rather grumpy-looking young assistant manager waiting with the keycard when Eli arrived, again on the trail, at the same room the following morning. The manager got the door open quickly and Eli had full view of the inside of room 303 before the signature again vanished and he saw . . . nothing.

It was just an empty hotel room. Eli thanked the manager, who left Eli alone on the condition that he not make a mess for the maid. Eli swept the room with his sensic several times, but there was nothing, no residual traces, no persistent bio-remnant spoor, nothing. The open door had told him no more than the closed door had: Ahmed Ali walked across the park, past the blast's epicenter, into the hotel and into room 303.

But why? Nothing happened here. He never got here— Eli stopped. And then he smiled.

"Well, Ali, 'ol son," he said aloud, "I *am* quite the idiot, aren't I?"

Eli checked the time index and waited a little longer. When the new ghost appeared, Eli wasn't even surprised. He used the sensic to read the image's lips, but she didn't say more than a word or two, a silent voice in an empty room; then she walked into the bathroom and disappeared.

When Eli came down the stairs and out in the park again, Jessie was already there. She was sitting on a bench by the fountain. There was a PDA in her lap and the same notebook Eli had noticed before beside her, but neither was in use. She just stared back toward the hotel as he approached.

"Is my time running out?" Eli asked mildly.

She sighed. "Not everything is about you, Eli. I come here fairly often."

He sat down on the opposite end of the bench. "Jessie, I hope you don't mind a personal question, but you never remarried, did you?"

Her face was as expressionless as a statue's. "I hope you don't mind a personal question, such as 'why are you asking me something I know is already in that database of yours?' "

He smiled ruefully. "Fair enough. I couldn't think of a better way to broach the subject."

She shrugged. "Not that it's any of your business, but I'm not living in the past, Eli, if that's what you're getting at. Nor am I playing the bereaved widow of a 'martyr of freedom' for political gain. I'm doing what I do because I believe I can make a difference. Hugh believed the same, and that's why he was here on July Fourth. I accept what happened."

"Then why do you come here?"

"It's a nice place to spend a day . . ." Jessie apparently saw the dubious expression on Eli's face and sighed. "Oh, all right. I said I accepted what happened. I didn't say I understood it or could reconcile it with my idea of a sane world. So I still think about what happened to Hugh and the others, and this is the best place to do that."

"What's the notebook for?"

She shrugged. "This? I was in therapy for a while . . . you know, after. It was my therapist's idea: write down what I thought, my anger, my grief. This is the notebook I bought to do that ten years ago."

"So what's in it?"

"Nothing," Jessie said. "Not one damn thing. I keep coming here hoping that maybe one day I'll know what to write."

Eli didn't say anything for a while. Then, "I think I've finally got a question for you. There's some information I need."

"A personnel file?"

"Some of what I'm looking for is public record, but I also need billing records from the Walthor Hotel for two separate dates, and those aren't. It'll require a court order, I'm afraid. Can you help?"

She smiled grimly. "Give me the dates and stand back. Is that all?"

"I wish it was. I've got some more digging to do

on my end, but, barring a total misread of the situation, I can finish the investigation tomorrow if you get those records."

"The judge is Hugh's father, Eli; we're still close. That shouldn't be a problem."

"Thanks," Eli said, and that was all.

She hesitated. "Eli, you look worried, and that worries *me*. What do you think you're going to find?"

"The truth," Eli said simply.

She frowned. "Wasn't that the whole point?"

"No, getting enough facts to figure out how to free Ahmed Ali from his endless anger was the point. The truth was something I didn't expect at all."

"Explain that, please," Jessie said.

"It's about what people believe. What we know to be true . . . rather, what we accept as true. Not quite the same as facts. Sometimes the one doesn't affect the other. Sometimes facts change the truth completely. Sometimes that's a good thing and sometimes not, but it's always scary."

Jessie just stared at him. "You'd think a politician would be better at seeing through bullshit. Eli, but I didn't understand one word of that."

Eli shrugged. "Jessie, if you come to the park tomorrow morning, usual time, you'll know as much as I do."

The day was overcast and windy. Eli thought perhaps rain was coming; he could practically smell it on the breeze. He set the corner of the sensic on top of the facsimile edition newspaper he'd brought with him. Jessie arrived a few moments later, glanced at the paper.

"I haven't seen a paper edition in five years," she said. "Where'd you get that?"

"A lovely lady named Mrs. Lee at the Department of Archives and History was kind enough to make a facsimile for me. *Canemill Reporter,* July 9, 2018. Turn to the obituaries; I've marked the one you're looking for."

"Stacy Prentice, aged twenty-six,' " Jessie said and then frowned. "That name sounds familiar."

"I imagine," Eli said. "Read it."

Jessie scanned the neat columns. "Oh . . ."

Eli nodded. "Exactly. Ms. Prentice was Ahmed Ali's wife. His soon to be ex-wife; they had separated and she'd filed for divorce. She was using her maiden name at the time."

"I actually remember a little about this. She committed suicide, poor woman, three years after the attack. Apparently, she couldn't live with what Ahmed Ali had done."

"Why?" Eli asked.

Jessie blinked. "I don't understand."

"It's a simple question. Why? She was questioned at the time, but there was nothing to link her to the attack; according to the FBI investigation, she hadn't even been living with Ali during the 'planning phase' and was publicly cleared of any involvement. The mayor's widow was seen hugging her on national television, for pity's sake. So why kill herself?"

"So when is guilt logical? Are you saying she *did* know about the attack?"

"No, I'm saying that there's something she knew that we didn't."

"Clear as day-old mud, Eli. And why bother making a paper copy? Couldn't you just download the text?"

"I need a physical copy for the sensic to scan and model for the simulation."

Jessie shook her head. "You're right—you don't explain very well."

"Sorry. I tend to get worse when I'm on the trail. All will become clear . . . maybe. Put this on." He handed Jessie a wireless headset with video-enabled lenses. "Nice, huh? Last year I was still using a VR helmet." He settled his own headset into place, and a three-dimensional simulation of the park came up. It mapped directly to the physical objects already there; the resolution was so fine that it was difficult to tell one from the other.

"We already have the park, Eli," Jessie said, looking around. "Why simulate it?"

"This isn't just a simulation as you know it, and these aren't avatars of us you're seeing; they are mapped projections using an energy signature congruent with bio-remnant signatures."

"You mean . . . he can see us?"

"That's exactly what I mean. If you'll blink down your menu, you'll see the 'hide' function. When Ahmed Ali appears, I want you to vanish. You'll still be able to see what happens."

"Like hell."

Eli blinked. "Pardon?"

"If you think I'm going to pass up the chance to confront the scum that killed Hugh, you're crazy!"

"Do you want this ended or not?"

Jessie didn't say anything for a moment. "There are a lot of things I want ended, Eli, and they all start with Ahmed Ali. You show me this and then ask me to give it up? I can't!" she said, then looked him directly in the eyes. "I won't."

"Look, there's no time to argue—"

"You're right. He's coming," Jessie said.

Eli sighed. No help for it now. He'd just have to see what happened.

What happened was that Ahmed Ali appeared right on time on the far side of the park. This was full scale, not the miniature holo display he'd been looking at earlier. Ahmed Ali was a very large and angry young man striding purposefully across Armfield Park. The dark eyes, the flowing black beard, all were as the news photos had shown; only the faint bluish glow that surrounded him marked him as something no longer human. There was no sign of the explosives he'd hidden under his long coat on that fine summer day.

You'd think someone would have noticed the coat.

Eli stood his ground on the sidewalk, but the ersatz-ghost that was Jessie marched forward with full purpose and anger that could match Ahmed Ali blow for blow.

He's not a repeater. He should be able to see us.

There it was. Hesitation. Puzzlement. The reaction that Eli had expected but not quite. There had already been a hesitation logged; the time index on the sensic from the previous three days of readings showed the same thing.

Is it because of us?

In a moment Eli got his answer; Jessie stood in front of Ahmed Ali, master terrorist, and let him have it with a string of invective that would have blistered chrome and cracked titanium. The few choice words she'd used to Eli before now were nothing compared to this, and for a moment Eli could only watch in awe at a master at work.

The revenant just frowned. The puzzlement was there, stronger, but then the hesitation was gone. He walked past Jessie as if she truly wasn't there.

"You will not ignore me, you worthless piece of shit!"

But he did, and nothing Jessie said or tried to do made one bit of difference. At one point she even tried to reach out and grab him. Eli wasn't sure what good Jessie thought that might do, but of course it didn't work. Her ghostly fingers closed on nothing, touched nothing. Eli waited. When Ahmed Ali was only a few steps away, he'd held up the paper. Another frown, another hesitation. This one wasn't in the sensic's data.

Eli nodded. "Yes. . . . There's a mind of sorts in there somewhere, isn't there? Use it."

Ahmed looked past Eli, started to walk past just as he'd done to Jessie. Eli moved the newspaper, shoved it right in front of Ali's nose, making him see it. He tapped the image of a column of type. Another hesitation.

"Curiosity. That's right, Ahmed. Look."

Ahmed looked. His right foot, already in motion, stopped. He stood still, and as Eli held the image of a seven-year-old paper in front of him, Ahmed Ali read. By the time Jessie reached them, the ghost was already fading.

"Eli, what have you done?"

"Ended it," Eli said, and in another moment Ahmed Ali was gone. The sensic told the same story.

Jessie looked around her. "He *is* gone," she said. "That's it? It's really over?"

"Not quite," said Eli. "There's something else we need to talk about, but it can wait. For right now just come on, if you don't want to miss this." He reached out, living flesh to living flesh, and took her hand.

"Miss what? Where are we going?"

"To the ribbon-cutting, of course," Eli said. "I

think it's finally getting under way. Remember the ghosts who were trying to manifest? Now they will. It's happening."

"You're serious? We can . . . oh. Hugh?'

"If he's there. I have a feeling he might be."

They hurried toward the Walthor Hotel where the long-delayed crowd was finally gathered.

Later they sat on the bench by the fountain. There was a long silence while Eli reviewed his data and Jessie just sat, staring into space.

"I can't believe it. Not a terrorist attack at all," Jessie said finally. "A fucking accident!"

"Not technically," Eli said without looking up from his data. "I believe the law says that there are no accidents in the commission of a crime, and Ahmed Ali definitely intended to commit a crime."

"But a domestic dispute? That's what all this was about?"

Eli shrugged. "There's no hate like a personal hate. Some of this may be conjecture, Jessie, but it all fits: Consensus at the time was that Ahmed Ali was a deep cover terrorist agent, but I believe that's wrong. The FBI didn't find his terrorist connections because there were none. He was a thug, not a fanatic. Stacy Prentice was divorcing him for violent abuse and a host of other good reasons. Without the marriage, odds are he would have been deported."

"Why?"

"Turns out he had a record of violence in his own country that family connections managed to quash long enough for him to emigrate. He was wanted for assault and attempted murder, among other things. He blamed Stacy when that all came out during the proceedings."

"I assume that she was the one in room 303."

Eli nodded. "Yes. Ali found out Stacy was staying in the Walthor and decided to make a rather loud and messy statement. We may never know if he intended to die from the start or simply meant to plant the bomb close enough to his wife to do the job. In either case I'm betting he didn't even *know* about the ribbon ceremony until he showed up; that explains the first recorded hesitation."

It was obvious that Jessie believed him, but her common sense had to make one more try. "I admit what you say does fit, and I guess it's possible, but it's all a bit far-fetched, Eli."

"Not as far-fetched as Ali being a terrorist. Ahmed Ali never fit the profile. Consider the bomb itself— an FBI reconstruction showed that the device may have been powerful, but it was also crude and unstable, not the work of a trained terrorist with all the time he needed to pick a target and prepare. All it took was one good jostle from someone in the crowd on his way through and that was that."

When Jessie spoke again, it was almost as if she were talking to herself. "The man was just a violent moron."

"Yes, but I will give him points for focus. With some ghosts you just have to prove to them that they're dead; all Ahmed Ali wanted was proof that his *wife* was dead. Her suicide—three years later in that same room—suggests she knew the attack had been intended for her all along. I think that's what she couldn't live with."

Jessie nodded, looking glum. "If it was me . . . yes, it makes sense. But Hugh, and all those people . . . The really sick thing is that, in some places, Ahmed Ali is a hero—" Jessie sat up then, as something new occurred to her. "Eli, we fought a *war* over this!"

Eli sighed. "I wondered when you'd remember that part. A very brief but nasty one, yes. Maybe it made sense at the time but it's history now. Legend. To this day there are people who believe that Ahmed Ali was a terrorist and people who believe he was a hero. They're both wrong, but that doesn't change what happened."

"We . . . oh, God, what will we do?"

Eli took a deep breath, let it out ."I'm sorry, Jessie, but it's what will *you* do. Bureau investigations are confidential; more to the point, they're *sealed*. That rule isn't always convenient, but it's one I don't break. Ever. I told you that when we first met, and nothing's changed: whether you tell this story or not is entirely up to you."

Jessie just looked at him in disbelief for several long moments. Then she said, "And here I thought Ahmed Ali was a son of a bitch."

"I wasn't joking when I said the truth was scary, Jessie."

She smiled then, wistfully. "Guess I should have been paying more attention. Funny thing though—I never wanted to be the widow of a 'Martyr of Freedom' in the first damn place. Good-bye, Eli."

She got up, started to leave. Eli glanced at the bench. "You left your notebook."

"I don't need it. All I really wanted to do all this time was say good-bye to my husband, and now I've done that. I've got no right to complain about the price."

"You may not believe it, but I am sorry about this, Jessie."

She smiled then. "I'm not."

Eli watched her go. He brought up the sensic one last time to confirm what he already knew. No ghosts in Armfield Park. Not even one. The ribbon-cutting ceremony and July Fourth celebration of 2015 was officially over, and only ten years late.

That just left the ghost in room 303.

Eli sighed. It wasn't part of the original investigation, strictly speaking. Yet there were things he couldn't fix, and then again there were things he could, as the saint used to say. Eli was far from a saint, but the things he understood, he understood very well indeed.

"Ms. Prentice," he said aloud, "I think it's time you and I had a chat."

MEMORIES UNDERFOOT

by Ruth Stuart

Ruth Stuart is a Canadian fantasy writer, with her first novel, Kin to Chaos, presently under consideration by a major US publisher. She has been very active in the Canadian SF/F community for many years. When she isn't playing with words in her work at a major insurance company, Ruth enjoys playing with words in her own worlds. She lives with her geriatric cat and more books than should be allowed in one place.

STRAIGHT ROWS of gravestones surrounded by neatly trimmed grass spread before Indra. The pathways to her left teemed with people leaving the Mother's Day church service. Their voices moved toward her on the spring air, tightened around her, chipped at her self-control. Jamming her hands into her jacket pockets, she walked along the right-hand gravel pathway. Past parents trying to keep their young children from playing tag among the graves. Past bored teenagers sneaking a cigarette behind a granite angel. Past a woman in tears beside a freshly filled grave. Past the discreet signs telling her she was exiting the Oak section and entering Pine.

So many people, she thought. *Why did I have to come today?*

A sharp pain below her ribs bent her nearly double. She leaned against the nearest gravestone, panting for breath. When she felt the familiar ache in her lungs, it was an almost welcome distraction. Straightening slowly, she thought, *I know why. I will not have another chance.*

She stumbled toward the sign announcing the beginning of the Maple section. Here the oddly warm mid-May sunlight gave way to shadow. The gravel slid into dirt beneath her feet. She stopped in a patch of light and pulled a folded scrap of paper from her pocket.

The gum-snapping cemetery office trainee had looked up the area and lot number for her, scribbling it on the paper. When Indra had asked if there were clearer directions, the girl had conferred with her older coworker. The woman had glanced up, her smile freezing and slipping from her face.

"Look for the horse," she had snapped.

Indra had bolted from the office but not before she heard the girl ask, "She's the one?"

She pushed the paper back into her pocket. *Why did I think no one would recognize me? Their minds may be small, but they have long memories.*

Stepping from the pathway to the weed-choked grass, she picked her way through leaning gravestones, some nearly on their sides exposing naked compressed soil to the air, toward the only horse she could see. Atop a pitted limestone plinth stood a mounted hunter. She crouched and ran a finger over the worn lettering. "Carter," she whispered as she stood. "Not hers."

Indra glanced at the closest gravestones. None held

the right name. A sudden gust of wind rattled the branches above her head. Something glinted a moment within a mound of tangled vines. She took several halting steps toward it and dropped to her knees. With a trembling hand, she tugged at the greenery pulling when it would not come free. She ignored the vines cutting into her fingers as she tore them away. Throwing the final vine beside her, she rocked back on her heels.

Angus Cameron. Mary R. Cameron.

Fighting angry tears, she stared at the names. "I'm sorry, Momma."

Her step-grandparents must have paid for the stone. One of the first families of the town, they had never accepted her or her mother. They had refused to call her Indra or her mother Rupa, demanding they answer to Cindy and Mary so the Camerons could speak of them without embarrassment.

At least I didn't have to see them again after—

She stopped the thought, swallowing hard against the bile creeping up her throat. *After what happened, I didn't deserve even that much happiness.*

As she shoved her hands into her pockets, her fingers found a hard object in the bottom corner of one. Indra pulled it out and stared at the heart-shaped stone resting on her palm.

Her mother had found and given it to her, telling Indra that as long as she had it, her mother would be with her. Indra worried the stone, then placed it on the gravestone.

Her deep breath turned into a racking cough that shattered the silence and left her weak. She rested her shoulder against the gravestone and closed her eyes. *How much longer?*

A child's voice echoed her thought. "How much longer do we have to stay?"

My voice must have sounded like that. Full of pain and confusion. The Fitzgeralds had brought her here after everyone else had left the graveyard. They had given her a home when no one else would, tried to give her the semblance of a normal childhood.

Indra sighed and used the gravestone for leverage to climb to her feet, thinking to leave those standing behind her to the peace of the cemetery. It wasn't the Fitzgeralds' fault she had had to endure the hostility of the town's adults and the bullying and torment of its children. They were the only reason she had stayed as long as she had.

"How much longer?" the small voice repeated.

"Soon, little one. Don't you want to say good-bye to your momma?"

Indra froze. *I know that voice. But it can't be.* She spun and staggered back.

Jack Fitzgerald stood near the horse monument, his camel coat open and flapping in the gusty wind. Jack Fitzgerald who had taken her in. Jack Fitzgerald who never accused her as the others had.

Jack Fitzgerald who had been dead for two years.

"Little one?"

Tearing her eyes away from him, she looked down to where his hand rested on the glossy black hair of—

She fell to her knees, panting. The child she had been twenty years before stared through her. "I want to leave," the little girl said as Indra mouthed the words.

"How? How is this possible?" Physical pain dropped her to her hands and knees, head bowed and heart pounding. *How can Jack be here?* She tried to catch her breath, fighting the dizziness that washed over her. *I know he's dead. None of this makes sense.*

A gentle touch on her shoulder seemed to remove the pain. Dashing away tears, she raised her head to see the hem of a black cloak. She pushed herself to her knees and looked up. The cloak billowed slightly, but all she could see within was darkness.

"Who are you?" she whispered. She strained to see the figure's face beneath the hood, but it was hidden from her. A bony-fingered hand appeared before her. As she took it and rose to her feet, the words *Be at ease, child* slipped through her mind.

Indra tried to step away, but the hand tightened on hers. "Who are you?" she repeated. "What do you want of me?"

To go home.

Her eyes grew wide. "Why?" When she received no answer, she whispered, "I can't."

When he released her hand, she reached back to touch her mother's gravestone, to reassure herself she was still in the cemetery. As her fingers brushed the stone, the familiar ache in her lungs returned and she gasped in shock.

She glanced toward the horse monument. Jack and her younger self were gone as mysteriously as they had appeared. Indra looked at the figure. He stretched out one hand, pointing toward the pathway. Shaking her head, she whispered, "No. I can't."

The figure stood before her, implacable, as if he would wait until the end of the world for her to agree. Indra closed her eyes. *Can it hurt any more than it already does to be here?*

When she opened her eyes, she saw he had not moved. Without looking back, she walked away from her mother's grave. The figure fell into step with her as she retraced her path toward the cemetery gates.

Indra clung to the car door a moment before slamming it shut. Main Street stretched toward the bridge, straight as an arrow, away from her. A few cars waited by the curb, their windows cracked open to catch the slight breeze. *It hasn't changed,* she thought. *After all this time, shouldn't it have changed?*

With an effort, she rounded the car and stepped to the sidewalk. The moment her feet touched the cement, she stopped. *Nothing else has changed,* she realized. *Why should this?* Leaning against the car, she closed her eyes and whispered, "This is a mistake."

Silence responded.

She opened her eyes and looked at her companion. He stood a foot away, attention focused on the street. Despite the warmth in the air, he kept his black cloak wrapped tightly around him, emphasizing his slight build.

Long denied anger toward this place and its people and the one who was making her face it all again threatened her control. Her hands clenched at her sides. Indra glanced at the almost empty street. She had come home. Returned to where everything had happened. All because of her companion.

She tried to see his face, but it was hidden within the dark shadows of the cloak's hood. Shivering, she hugged herself, her heart pounding an irregular beat. "Must I?" she whispered. When he remained silent, she closed her eyes. *I don't want to be here. I never wanted to be here.*

Indra opened her eyes to see him standing a few feet ahead of her, still facing the expanse of the street. Her nails bit into her palms. *Why do I have to do this?*

As if he could hear her thoughts, he reached a skeletal hand toward her. Letting out a shuddering breath, she bowed her head and walked past him. She concentrated on putting one foot firmly before the other and tried not to trip over those places where the cement had heaved and buckled. Her companion matched her pace easily, gliding at her side. From the corner of her eye, she saw his cloak fluttering like bat wings.

Many of the main street stores of her childhood and young adulthood stood empty, windows covered over with yellowed newspaper, the black print faded almost to white. A few restaurants and more video rental stores than she cared to count waited for customers, their doors propped open in the late afternoon sun. The only busy store was the flower shop, its display window covered with a Mother's Day sales banner.

Indra and her companion met only a handful of people as they walked. They all passed by quickly, stepping from shadow to shadow, barely looking at her. Those who recognized her glared and scowled.

"This may not have been the best idea," Indra said. She slammed her hands into her pockets, fingers tightening around the keys she found there.

She glanced at her companion, daring him to speak. He remained silent, hunched over as if bracing himself against a stiff wind. As they neared the bridge crossing the river, she slowed her pace, each step becoming increasingly difficult to take. Her feet stopped, frozen to the sidewalk before the papered windows of what had been the stationery store. Her gaze became fixed on the yellowed newspapers. "HOUSE FIRE UNDER INVESTIGATION," screamed one headline. "CHILD AT FAULT? ASKS INSPECTOR," read another.

Indra swallowed heavily. Her eyes flicked away from the headlines and met the reflection of her partner in the glass. His face might have been that of a man her age, but his skin stretched so tightly over his bones she could almost see his individual teeth behind his closed lips. Her breathing quickened painfully. When she tried to look way, black pupils so large she could not see the white surrounding them held her. One hand slipped form her pocket, reaching toward the glass. As her fingers touched the reflection of his face, his eyes released her.

Palm braced on the window, she closed her eyes, panting. Like a black hole, his eyes took in everything around them, reflecting back nothing, stretching time to its breaking point. There was a beauty in them, the answer to a yearning she had not known she had.

Indra took a slow breath, wincing at the pain. *I'd do anything to see the eternity in his eyes.* She opened her eyes. *I hope I can see that again.*

She realized with a start that he no longer stood beside her. Pushing herself away from the window, she looked hopefully the way they had come. The sidewalk was empty. She turned and saw him standing at the corner, head bent. He held out his hand to her. Hesitating, she leaned a shoulder against the window and licked suddenly dry lips. "Are you sure?" The words came out in a whisper but she knew he heard.

His hand stretched out further. With a shuddering breath, Indra took the six steps to the corner, turned and stopped.

She found herself facing the tree-lined street of her childhood. The path, no sidewalk here, was littered

knee-deep in memories. She stared down at her feet.
The layer was thin here but potent.

Her knee ached as she saw herself fall from her
first two-wheeler, scraping her elbows, blood running from the cut on her knee. To the left, the puppy
who had followed her home, rolled on its back, begging to have his stomach rubbed. A ghost hand fell
to her shoulder, ghostly lips met hers when she saw
the place where the old maple had stood. Under its
spreading limbs, away from the watchful eyes of her
mother and stepfather, she had received her first kiss.

She glanced at her partner. "Do I have to do this?"
Indra hated the pleading tone in her voice.

His hand moved to point down the road.

Carefully stepping forward, she picked her way
through the memories. She slipped her hands into
her pockets, not wanting to touch anything. The
closer she got to her old house, the thicker the memories lay. Her body ached from remembered accidents.
Her eyes burned with suppressed tears. She shuffled
her feet, thighs laboring to push through the layers.

"What is that smell?" She gagged as the smell of
rot grew stronger, filling her nostrils. Moaning, she
clasped a hand over her mouth when she saw the
dog's body lying alone in the yard. Angrily wiping
away her tears, her breath caught as her house came
into view.

It stood back from the street, a canopy of trees
hanging menacingly over the roof. Here, the memories were stacked like cordwood, piled high over her
head. She closed her eyes, taking great gulps of air
despite the pain in her lungs. As she opened her eyes
and fumbled for her keys, her companion moved to
the front walkway and opened the gate. She stared

at him, at the flood of memories that poured out onto the path.

She tried to force herself to step through the gate. Shaking her head, she gasped out, "I can't." She hugged herself, rubbing her upper arms, as shivers raced through her. Her companion remained at the walkway, one hand on the gate, waiting.

From behind her came the whir of bicycle tires on hot cement. As the sound grew louder, she heard the familiar squeaking of a chain in need of oil. Indra looked over her shoulder, heart racing.

Her younger self approached at breakneck speed. As she slowed to turn onto the walkway, Indra heard her mutter, "I can't be late. Can't be late."

Indra reached for her as the bicycle went by, her hands passing through the girl. "No. Don't go in there."

Brakes squealing, the girl slid to a stop. Leaving the bicycle on its side on the front lawn, she bolted for the front door. Indra found herself beside her companion, staring at the house, wishing she could change what was about to happen. As the girl reached for the knob, the door was flung open.

Angus Cameron stood framed by the open door. He was shorter than she remembered but, twenty years later, Indra was still intimidated by his presence. She winced as he grabbed the girl by the shoulder. She remembered the feel of his hand, how his strong fingers had compressed her muscle to the bone.

"You're late," he growled.

"I'm sorry," the girl whispered. "Mrs. Thomas asked me to stay after school."

"Mrs. Thomas isn't the one you answer to, is she?"

"No, sir."

Indra trembled as Angus dragged the girl inside the house and slammed the door. Swallowing hard, she waited, remembering what came next.

A voice, made muted and indistinct by the closed windows, rose and fell in anger. Then silence. A few moments later a second door slammed followed by a rhythmic pounding as Angus tried to break down her bedroom door.

She remembered huddling in the darkest corner of her closet, knees clutched close to her chest as she waited for him to succeed. It wasn't his anger that had frightened her. It was the look in his eye. A calculating, considering look.

She had refused to leave her room, even after her mother had returned. Rupa had talked to her, but she had not been able to explain to her mother why she was so scared.

Indra glanced at her companion. "How much longer must I watch this?"

As he raised his hand, the sky darkened around them, stars rushing in to fill the night. Indra looked where he pointed. The house had changed.

She saw cracked windows, broken panes, the wood surrounding them blackened. Smoke hung in the air and curled slowly up from the basement. "So many years ago," she whispered. Faintly, in the distance, she heard a scream and the sound of shattering glass. This, she knew, was part of her companion's magic, allowing her to see the past as it truly was, not blunted and changed by the passage of time and other people's stories.

She blinked away tears and focused on the house as a chair flew through an upper window. Thick smoke rolled out and up. Indra fell to her knees as a small figure was pushed out onto the porch roof.

"Momma? What's happening, Momma?"

Indra clamped her hands over her ears to keep the small, frightened voice out. An explosion from deep within the house shook the structure and the child on the roof lost her footing, sliding toward the edge. Indra dropped to her hands and knees, then to her side as the figure fell from the roof. When it landed in the bushes, Indra's scream mirrored the figure's. Pulling her knees to her chest, she squeezed her eyes shut. Whimpers, then a low keening escaped her. *I never wanted to go through this again. Why?* "Why did you make me see this again?"

The hand on her shoulder forced her to open her eyes. She saw a neighbor climb the fence, pull the child out of the bushes and carry her far away from the house. In the distance, sirens wailed, growing closer with each passing second.

"Please. Make it stop," she whispered.

The hand tightened, bony fingers digging into her muscle. His other hand pointed toward the house. Indra stared up at the second-floor window. A woman stood there, silhouetted by the flames.

"Momma?" Indra struggled to her knees. In the house, a man grabbed the woman's arm and tried to pull her aside. She fought back, shoving him away. Over the sound of the flames and the approaching sirens, Indra heard her mother scream, "At least my daughter will be safe from you." A wild punch connected, knocking the woman down. The man had one leg through the window when the roof collapsed, dropping him back into the house.

Indra barely felt the hands on her shoulders as she tried to see the house through her tears. "No one told me." She pounded her fists against her thighs. "They all said it was my fault. That I'd started the fire."

The hands moved down to her elbows, then her wrists. As her companion leaned over her, his cloak covered them both, blocking the house from her view. Slowly, she uncurled her fingers and laid her hands flat on her thighs. Quietly, she said. "No one told me my mother saved my life."

His hands moved back to her shoulders. The cloak pulled away from her face. Indra wiped the tears from her eyes and blinked in the afternoon sun. A brick ranch house stood where her home had been. In the distance she heard the shrieks of children at play.

"I understand," she said as she touched his hand. "It wasn't my fault."

The hands disappeared from her shoulder. One appeared in front of her. She placed her hand in his and climbed to her feet. The band of guilt around her heart loosened and, for the first time since that night, she felt free. His fingers tightened on hers, their touch releasing her from her physical pain. Suddenly, she knew who he was and why he was there. Still staring at the house, she asked, "Is there anything else I need to do before we can go?"

He stepped in front of her and held out his other hand. Without looking at him, she took it.

"Are you ready?"

His voice as surprisingly deep and startled her into glancing into his face. She dropped her eyes, then raised them again to meet his gaze.

"Yes. The past has no hold on me now."

Releasing her hands, he slipped one to her shoulder and used the other to raise her chin. Leaning in, he gave her a gentle kiss. With a sigh, Indra opened her eyes and took a step forward into the eternity of his.

JUDGMENT

by Kerrie Hughes

Confirmed Celtophile and former Goth girl Kerrie Hughes will tell you about the time she met a ghost if you ask. A working artist, she has recently turned to writing science fiction and fantasy in between projects, and finds it surprisingly satisfying.

FAR BENEATH the earth, or rather, existing within the earth, the Fast of Samhain reached its peak. The inhabitants of the kingdom of the dead ate and drank to excess, toasting those they had left behind. Jesters and dancers wove around the crowded tables partaking of a bite of food and a sip of wine whenever offered. The merriment was at its highest on this evening but not everyone was at the festivities; many had secreted themselves in their rooms and peered into scrying bowls to watch the living. The scrying was a nightly activity, but tonight was more of a temptation because the veil between the two worlds was at its thinnest on Samhain. Some tried to reach across the boundaries to communicate with departed loves ones, or to exact vengeance on their enemies. Most were mournful souls and longed to fill the void between life and death. The feast was to

distract those who might violate the boundaries on
this sacred night, but it was also a farewell dinner
for those who were preparing to return to the living,
if they were allowed.

At the head of the feast table sat the Dagda and
the Morrigan, the King and Queen of the Otherworld, toasting the people at the long table directly
in front of them. These were the dead who had successfully petitioned to leave. To the royal couple's
right sat the Cerridwen, the Servant of the Cauldron
of Life. She was the one who would be approached
when those who had won the right to leave decided
to exercise their privilege. On any other day their
duties consisted of allowing the petitions of the next
life to plead their cases. One by one they came before
the Royalty of the Otherworld and asked for passage
beyond. The script was always the same; Cerridwen
asked the petitioner their name and why they wished
to go back. The petitioner would answer respectfully
and wait while the Morrigan and the Dagda conferred with their advisers to each side of them . . .
and then the answer came.

Erin Smith stood in front of her latest painting,
Judgment, and answered questions from her classmates
on its execution and meaning. Erin wore paint-
spattered jeans and her usual long-sleeved black T-shirt
with the name of some band that was popular only
with the local Goth kids. She wore a clean one today
for her semester review at the London School of Art.
Her hair was dyed cherry red with black streaks and
was a shoulder-length blunt cut that she usually
pulled back into pigtails. Her brown eyes were heavily lined with kohl, and her lips were resplendent
with dark purple lipstick. Around her throat she

wore a wide black ribbon with a cat-headed dangle charm. As far as she was concerned, this would do for a Halloween costume, let everyone tell her that she dressed for Halloween every day. Small and pale, she looked like dozens of other Goth children in the clubs of London, except Erin was eighteen, an American, and struggling with her studies.

"Erin, why do you leave all of your paintings unfinished?" asked her painting professor, Mrs. Rollins. It seemed an absurd question coming from someone dressed in rabbit ears for the so-called holiday.

The students in the class murmured about the answer they expected to hear. Erin was known for her adamant views on everything and anything and the class expected to hear a firm answer. One they could either mock or admire based on their own narrow views of art and the world. They also wore a haphazard jumble of tacky costumes for the holiday, but no one seemed to notice that they were too old to go trick-or-treating.

Erin looked at the painting and brushed her fingers along the bare canvas at the bottom right corner. The rest of the painting was an abstract creation of angry faces and clenched hands done in dark, muddy reds and black. The only bright color was a spot of brilliant blue ethereal wings attached to an eye. Behind the faces and hands was a large gray tree with branches that contained green doors. This had become a theme in Erin's art and she could talk about the meaning for hours.

She sighed and pondered the question before her. Why couldn't she finish any painting she started? Erin felt it would be better to ask why she couldn't finish anything. She never finished food, finished a book, or completed a painting. She couldn't even plot her own suicide to its final end. The long sleeves she wore hid the cut marks of practice slices that she made when she felt particularly empty. Erin refused to drink or do drugs, she hated not being in control of all her actions, but she could not explain why she would cut her arms with a razor when she was alone and unoccupied with art. The night before last, she had toyed with the razor along her scars and thought about slicing deeper this time, but something stopped her. Something that felt like a hand on her shoulder and a whisper in her ear," *No, this is not the way. Go the other way.*"

But this was today and she stood there and scratched at her latest wounds, they were itchier than usual, and answered Mrs. Rollins' query.

"I don't know," was all she could say.

Later that evening, Erin watched an old man settle himself on the cold sidewalk outside the McDonald's at Piccadilly Square. He leaned against a light pole and busied himself with items he pulled out of his coat pockets. She sat uncomfortably on her stool inside the greasy smelling restaurant and ate her hamburger, too far away to identify what held his attention. Her meal distracted her for the moment; it tasted like any other assembly line burger from any other McDonald's in any place she'd lived. *It never ceases to amaze me*, she thought as she half enjoyed the salty ketchup and the chopped, reconstituted onions. *Everywhere I go, no matter how remote, there's a Mickey D's.*

She resumed her study of the elderly gentleman in his tattered overcoat, nondescript brown slacks, and a navy blue sweater that had seen better days. He was becoming as familiar as the pickles on her burger. One semester in London and she had counted ten sightings in as many places, and always he seemed to be searching for something. Erin felt no threat from him, she had lived in Chicago for ten years and was used to homeless people to the point of being able to assess someone's potential for danger within seconds.

This is England after all, she mused to herself. *No one here packs a gun and the fights all seem to be confined to sporting matches and pubs.*

The homeless were plentiful in this city known colorfully as "bloody, poxy, London." The only difference between these people and the street people of Chicago, other than an occasional weapon, was the eye contact. The panhandlers in London kept their heads down when they held out their begging cups to request change and did not heckle the colder hearts that had none to spare. Ironically, the receptacle of choice in both places was usually an empty McDonald's coffee cup.

Once again proving that fast food has become the religion of choice to subjugate and control the masses, Erin thought as she guiltily ate the last bite of her burger. Normally, she shunned the doors of what she considered to be a slave-wage market that ruined the environment and caused poor health, but she was sick of English food. *If I eat one more piece of fruit that tastes slightly of fish-meal or eat one more dinner that comes with minty-peas I'm going to become anorexic as an alternative,* she resolved.

Erin listened to the sounds of the restaurant and eavesdropped on the couple in the booth to the left of her. They were arguing in a manner that was uniquely American, loud and with drama, oblivious to others around them. She suspected him of hitting on her girlfriend while he accused the same of being a liar and a slut. *How boring,* she thought as she dunked, nay bathed, her fries in ketchup. *Who decides how much salt to put on fries, and why ketchup?* she mused. *The English like malt vinegar on their "chips" and the Dutch use mayo.* She smiled as she changed the subject in her head. *Such deep thoughts; perhaps I need to bring a book with me for times like this.*

Hoping to occupy her mind with something more interesting, she looked back out the window and wondered what kind of life the old man had, and how he had come to his current fate. He looked up from his task, whatever that was, and stared at her as if in answer. Erin did not avert her gaze, his eyes had a familiar warmth in them and she felt a strange kinship.

Do I know him? She thought to herself. Visions of relatives infrequently seen filed through her head but none matched those wizened eyes.

A touch on her shoulder asked for her attention, and she turned to see the man from the street at her elbow.

"I have been looking for you. It's nearly time to attend the judgment," he said with quiet concern.

Erin sat up quickly and almost fell off her stool. She looked back out the window to where the man had been moments before to see him shuffle past the crowded street, his profile toward her, munching on french fries. Erin's eyes went wide as she turned fully toward where the same man was standing beside her . . . and he wasn't there.

What the . . . Her head felt light and she braced herself against the table with both hands . . . *am I hallucinating; is the salt and boredom getting to me?*

She glanced back at the remnants of her meal and

found that her fries were missing. She looked on the floor, but they were not there either.

Did that old man . . . Maybe he? . . . I . . . think it's time for bed . . . and perhaps I won't eat junk anymore . . . my body . . . no . . . my brain can't handle it anymore. Erin puzzled over what had just happened as she gathered up her things and tossed her remaining food in the trash.

After a long shower and a cup of tea, Erin picked up a newspaper and began to read. The headlines were not as shocking as the ones in America, but every so often a horrendous story made the front page. *"Woman Kills Husband of 25 Years—Feeds Flesh to Children." I hope she hangs,* Erin thought to herself before continuing on to the less gory articles. She was suddenly too tired to care about the upcoming exhibits and openings around London and decided to lie down on her dorm-sized bed and read a book about Pre-Raphaelite Femme Fatales. *These chicks knew the score,* she thought as she leafed through the stories about women who lured men to their doom.

Her concentration kept drifting to the sounds of traffic outside and the noises of the building. Erin could hear a few dorm mates coming down the hall and chattering to each other.

"I'm going to get soooo drunk," said one voice.

"How's my costume? Is there enough cleavage?" asked another.

Morons, she thought with just a hint of jealousy. Her stomach gurgled, not settling well after the junk she had eaten. *My next answer to "Would you like fries with that?" will be a definite no and keep the burger, too.* Fortunately, sleep overrode the nausea in her belly and the book soon lay unread on her chest.

*   *   *

Erin felt herself drift through a green field toward a cottage. It had a thatched roof and stone walls but no window glass. The wooden shutters were thrown wide to welcome the summer sun and she drifted inside. Below, Erin saw a girl about twelve years old dressed in a clean peasant frock and long-sleeved shift. She was sitting on one side of a large wooden table peeling potatoes. Her long brown hair was pulled back in a single braid and a healthy glow was on her skin from laughing. Her brown eyes sparkled with glee while an older man with a face Erin could not see clearly, whittled a piece of wood while telling the young girl a story that must have been funny. Erin strained to see the old man's face, but her attention kept going to the figure of a cat that he was making. It was sleeping, curled up with its tail tucked under its chin. He added the eyes and the whiskers with few deft strokes, then inspected it one last time and gave it to the girl. Erin watched the old man reach across the table and she extended her hand to take it as though she were now in the young girl's body. Her eyes met his eyes, green with brown rings and gold flecks . . . just like the man at the restaurant.

Erin sat up in bed, her book falling off her chest and tumbling to the floor. Her reading light was still on and the bedside clock revealed that she had been asleep for only twenty minutes. Embarrassed by how easily this short REM journey had startled her, she leaned over the side of the bed to retrieve the fallen book. On the floor where the novel should have been was the whittled cat from her dream. Erin's chest clenched and her heart beat faster with surprise.

I have lost it! I have really, truly lost it! she thought

with alarm. Erin spent the rest of the night with every light in the room on.

Saturday morning found, Erin overtired and restless; everywhere she looked she saw reminders of something familiar but somehow unremembered. She found it unnerving to sit still, but the more she moved about the more restless she became. Finally she decided to go to the National Gallery for inspiration and meditation.

In the tube station Erin thought she glimpsed the old man, and was both disappointed and relieved when it turned out to be a different but definitely homeless man. She placed a quid in his cup and proceeded to her stop. *That could be me one of these days if I don't get my act together*, she thought.

On the train she saw two young men pretending not to look at her. The pair were not English, and when they saw she had noticed their attentions, they smiled. Erin felt a moment of panic; her mind told her they were harmless tourists from America who recognized a fellow American, but her eyes saw something else.

Two young scruffy faces smiled at her from the yard. She was inside the cottage again, but only saw the old man and not the young girl. He was outside speaking to the two men. They had approached the cottage on horseback, and led a line of three other horses behind them. Erin recognized two of the animals as belonging to neighbors. She wondered what these men were doing with the property of the Erskines and the Halorans. Both were young and dressed in slightly tattered clothes. One wore the jacket of a soldier and the other a thin coat that was once fashionable but now worn through at the elbows. Erin got the impression that the men were neither farmers nor employed . . . and probably trouble.

She did not hear them speaking but could guess what they were saying. The one in the soldier's coat was demanding her grandfather's horse for a paltry sum. The argument went back and forth, with the rude young man quoting the recently passed penal laws that forced Catholics to turn over any horse worth more than five pounds for the sum of five pounds. Her grandfather argued that he had heard of no such thing, and ordered the young men away before he lost his temper. Erin picked up the short carving knife and concealed it in her apron pocket before going to the door. When she appeared to the men's sight they first looked concerned and then amused. The one in the thin coat approached her with a leer on his face.

Erin snapped back to reality when one of the men spoke.

"Is something wrong?" he asked with genuine concern, "You look like your blood pressure just went through the roof."

The man next to him nodded in agreement, and Erin realized she was clutching her chest with one hand and was flushed with heat.

She took a deep breath and with great effort mumbled, "No, no . . . sorry . . . I'm okay."

Before the two men could say anything else, the next stop was called and she exited the train, leaving the concerned pair behind.

Erin climbed the steps of the underground to emerge at Trafalgar Square. The tourists were doing their usual bit with the bold pigeons of the square, and she quickened her pace to get to the National

Gallery. Her thoughts muddled over these recent events, and she worried that she might need Prozac or some other form of mind candy for the masses. *Screw that. I'm not letting the empire of pharmaceutical overlords take my brain!*

By the time she reached the museum and headed for one of her favorite paintings, Erin had decided that the old man and the grandfather in her dreams/ visions were one and the same, and perhaps she was subconsciously trying to tell herself something.

But what could the message be? she wondered.

As she gazed at a pastoral scene, Erin thought the cottage looked familiar. Even the old man driving the cart looked like . . . well, the old man.

Just as this thought passed through her head, she felt someone sit down beside her. She turned, knowing it would be the old man, and raised an eyebrow of silent inquiry. He smiled, and the space around them vibrated softly while a low buzz made her head feel thick and heavy. She closed her eyes but opened them again when he laid a gentle hand on her arm. The noise and sensation evaporated and she found herself still sitting on the museum bench but now surrounded by a green meadow. Directly in front of her was a water fountain of a simple design, round with a spiral design carved along the rim. It was made of obsidian and water bubbled down from the sky to fill it.

"I need . . . some . . . answers." Erin managed to stammer in a near whisper.

The old man patted her arm reassuringly before beginning, "These things are never easy to do in the short time we need to do them," he said, more to himself than to Erin. "I was your grandfather in your first life on Earth and I have been asked to be your Guide to a judgment before I myself walk through the passage of rebirth."

Erin blinked twice and asked, "I am being judged?"

"No," he quickly answered. "You are to be the judge."

"The judge of who?" she asked.

The old man looked back at the well but did not take his hand off her arm. He seemed not to be look-ing at the water but beyond it, and after a minute of reflection finally spoke. "You will judge the man that killed you."

His words hit Erin in the forehead where her spirit, or nether-eye would be. Her mind flooded back to the memory of her last minutes on Earth when she was a young girl in 1705 Ireland. She saw the two young men grab her grandfather, one punching him across the temple hard enough that he crumpled to the grass. She took the knife out of her pocket and ran at the man who was about to kick her grandfa-ther in the chest. His companion moved to catch her and took a cut across his face for his trouble. Scream-ing, he clapped his hand to his cheek and let her go. The assailant of the old man looked up just as Erin stabbed him in the stomach with all her strength. It had all happened within seconds, and before she could scream or run, the man she had cut first put a knife to her throat and slashed her through.

In real time, Erin sobbed into her hands until her grandfather placed his arm around her. "There now, girl, it's been a long time ago, and you have much time ahead of you."

Erin gained control of herself and pulled a wad of tissues out of her coat pocket to blow her nose. Wiping her tears, she composed herself before speaking. "Did you survive?"

"Ah, lass, you were always concerned with my health before yours," he said with a smile. "I lived only long enough to see you die and to see the one who slew me die as well. The one who killed you placed our bodies and his companion's inside our cottage and burned it down after ransacking it. He would not hang for stealing the horse of a Catholic, but he might for killing an old man and his granddaughter."

"So he got away with it?" Erin asked.

"In this world, the physical world, he went unpunished for your death, but in the Otherworld, where we all must pass before moving on to a new life, he is punished." He replied and then added, "Come with me."

They walked toward the well while he talked. "When you died, you passed to the Otherworld where you existed for several years." He took a cup from the edge of the well and filled it half full before handing it to Erin.

"This isn't going to trap me here forever, is it?" she asked.

The old man laughed. "No, you will not become Persephone in Hades. This is the Well of Memory. It is necessary for you to recall your life here and the ones you lived on Earth. We want to do the Judgment quickly and without distressing you unduly. The longer you are here in your current form, the more danger there is of remembering this place when you go back. I'm sure you realize that would not be right."

Erin thought it would be fine with her, but she accepted the cup and took a sip. Her grandfather added, "Do not worry if the memories do not come right away. Sometimes it is difficult."

But Erin did not feel distressed as thoughts flooded her head and embraced her mind. She knew the stone walls that were now forming around them. Trees of the Otherworld filled her peripheral vision and she smiled with the joy of knowing she had climbed every one of them. This world was like the inside of a castle and the outside in a park tumbled into a maze. The sky was nighttime dark, but the light felt like dawn to the east and sunset toward the west, and the effect was intoxicating.

"I remember now, I loved it here. I didn't want to leave." Erin acknowledged as she looked around. Ten yards in front of her was a spiral staircase carved from an impossibly large tree. The steps were two feet deep and five feet wide at their narrowest. Branches and roots seemed to reach out in all directions. Lights adorned ever appendage, dimly lit but in a large enough quantity to create a marvelous beacon against the endless sky and landscape. This was the tree she had sketched, doodled, and painted over and over again. Erin had spent nearly fifty years in the Otherworld climbing up and down the Tree of Knowledge, exploring the branches and the rooms they led to. Her own sleeping room had been located in a lower branch looking over an ethereal forest of Othertrees. These were the spirits of trees on Earth for it was only trees that could exist in both the Upper and Other world at the same time. They were immune to the process of death and rebirth of the soul. The ancient druids understood this fact and used the natural portal of a tree to try to commune and gain favor from Otherworlders. Sometimes they had succeeded. Erin shivered at the memory of watching an Otherworlder attempt to achieve power over the living druids by asking for sacrifice and sex-magic. But the ephemeral fairies were everywhere in the Otherworld and reported all activities to the council. They meant no harm but they were tattle-tales, she recalled. The Otherworlder had met a harsh fate, with penitence extracted for his victims before he was judged and declared unforgiven.

Grandfather spoke. "We must be hurrying to court, lass. Your case will be coming up soon." He gestured toward a tall clock to their left. It was a large and grand construction embedded in a stone wall. The timepiece made no noise as it marked off the minutes and hours from the Upperworld. It also displayed the day and year. A larger clock dial marked off Otherworld time, which was measured in larger, increments. Essentially, the time on each clock face was equal minute by minute, but the Otherworld clock was in literal alignment with the Sun and Moon. No months or leap year were displayed on this dial, only seasons and major events like Samhain and Solstice. Below the two great dials were scrolls in gilded frames lined up on the wall. They announced the events of the day in beautifully written calligraphy. Erin clearly saw her own announcement, **Liam Healey: to be judged by Mary McLean of 1705.** Below the title were details of the event and then a ticker counting the minutes down till the appearance.

The two walked past the Tree of Knowledge and entered a clearing where a large stone wall held a closed pair of ornate giant doors. Metalwork in the shape of a large spiral covered the wooden doors. Two guards were posted, one at each door, each holding a long spear and wearing a dagger at the waists. They were dressed in violet pants that were fitted but well made of leather for fighting. Their shirts were white and their vests had the emblem of the spiral the same as the door. Erin followed her grandfather as he approached the guards.

"Good day. Do you have business with the council?" the taller guard asked.

Grandfather answered. "My once granddaughter, Mary McLean, now Erin Smith of the Upperworld, is to judge Liam Healey."

The second guard consulted a scroll on the wall behind him and turned back before stating, "Yes, we have been expecting you."

The taller guard bowed slightly to Erin and spoke. "Welcome back. If you have any questions while inside the court, address them to your guide first and he will direct you."

"Thank you," answered Erin as she walked in behind her grandfather and lost herself in memories. *Mary McLean, that was my name for twelve years above and fifty-five below.* She recalled that, amid her wanderings of the endless and beautiful Otherworld, she also longed to see the Judgment of the one who slew her. She harbored a hatred for Liam Healey that worried the fairies and the council until they asked her to appear before them during a Beltane meeting. In the Otherworld, Samhain was a feast before judgment and Solstice the time of rebirth, but Beltane was a time of reflection and planning. At this time the council concerned themselves with citizens of the Otherworld who were unhappy and festering in pain or regret of their past lives. A common theme in the Otherworld was "Renew and move forward." It was a farewell saying that was the equivalent of "Have a nice day" in the Upperworld.

Erin had chosen not to go through the rebirth during her fifty-five years in the Otherworld. Instead, she had delighted in exploring the realm and had marveled at the endless feasting, games, and conversations that, when alive, she had not been able to afford, but she had also dwelled on the past. She had dwelled on the murder and the tragedy of her first life and that of her grandfather. She had even taken to haunting the area where she was murdered, hoping to hear news of when Liam would die and be forced before her for Judgment. Sometimes she would sit over a scrying bowl for days and try to communicate her hatred to him. This was a violation of Otherworld rules, but she no longer cared. She knew she would deny him the luxury of a day's rest in this peaceful realm and call for his Judgment the moment he died. It was her right to call Judgment if she existed in the Otherworld when Healey died, but it was his right to call for his own Judgment once his penance was served. When Erin had existed here as Mary, she had seen at least 250 Judgments, but she had been perplexed when the council had summoned her during the Beltane time, when Judgments were not done. They had questioned her about her activities in this realm and when she intended to proceed to the rebirth ceremony. Erin pronounced that she would not go until she had condemned Healey to the Afterdeath.

The Dagda himself reminded her that a verdict before a trial was not the way things were done.

Erin recklessly answered, "Even if I have to go to hell with him, I will condemn him, no matter what, no matter when."

It was these words that brought redness to her

cheeks now as she realized she was only moments
away from going before the court, and the Dagda.
Please let him not remember me, she thought.

As they entered the courtroom, Erin and her
grandfather were greeted by a female clerk who quietly asked their names before checking her roster.
Once she was sure they were participants and not
observers, she led them away from the visitor area
to a line of oversized chairs built into the wall. The
architecture in the Otherworld was reminiscent of
Celtic design and natural bloom. Trees grew at regu-
lar intervals, pruned to look identical, yet each one
was still unique. Fireplaces were positioned to cast a
warm glow throughout the courtroom and to prevent
dark corners where conspirators might gossip. Even
the vines that grew around the rafters of the tall ceilings and the posts that supported the walls tangled
in an orderly and balanced fashion. It was as if disorder were in bad taste once anything entered the
court. The clerks also wore uniforms that featured a
symmetrical leaf design, appearing as a natural ex-
tension of the nature around them.

Erin sat down next to her grandfather and noticed
there was room for a third person on each bench.
She had never sat in this area before and had only
observed from the raised gallery at the back of the
court. The seats were cushioned in green velvet and
their comfort relaxed her for the moment. Her grandfather leaned over and whispered, "Do you have any
questions, my dear? Do you remember how the proceedings go?"

Erin whispered back with just a hint of her old
malice, "I remember enough and I already know
what my decision will be."

"Granddaughter, please do not prejudge the ac-

cused. The Morrigan does not look kindly on those
who do not listen before they speak."

"I am sure I will be attentive and she will not look
upon me as disrespectful, Grandfather, but I do not
now nor have I ever understood why you forgave
the man who killed you and allowed him to go
through the rebirth without penalty," she nearly
hissed in her effort to be quiet.

Her grandfather looked a little hurt and somewhat
disheartened. He turned away for the moment and
missed the instant regret that crossed her face. He
turned back and before he could speak, she said
softly, "I'm sorry. I don't mean to hurt you." Then
she took his hand in hers and squeezed it lightly.

He squeezed her hand back and spoke, "You have
a right to your anger, and some of it is the pain of
having lived only four times, and short lives each
time.

Erin felt immense shame. She could recall all of
her past lives and was well aware of her suicides in
the last two. The torment she felt in her current life
was the same torment she'd felt in the lives she had
lived since the first one when she was murdered.
Each time she had come back to the Otherworld, she
had tormented Liam Healey as he carried out his
tasks as a servant. The penance for most murderers
was a life as a servant for the ones who did not take
life. Liam had been sentenced to clean the floors of
the court and to repair the endless walls on the land-
scapes of the Otherworld. Those who were to be
judged took turns at cleaning the court floors as a
reminder of their own coming Judgment. Erin knew
it was bad manners for a victim to torment her accused while he was serving penance, but each time
she saw him, she called his name and sneered at him.

She sought him out just to make sure he knew she was still waiting for him, but he had borne it with good humor and continued his chores in silence. It infuriated her, but she could not judge him till he served his full term of penance.

Her grandfather's voice interrupted her train of thought. "I have done seven lives now, and my happiest was with you as my beloved grandchild." He paused for a moment, then continued before she could answer his declaration of affection. "My dear, I have the advantage of six lives that were well lived, but I also hold the memory of my second life when I was not a kind or innocent man."

Erin was stunned for a moment. It had never occurred to her that her grandfather had lived a life that was not . . . her grandfather. Thoughts swam in her head. *Why did I never ask? Am I so young that I cannot see beyond myself?* . . . and finally, *What did he do?*

The old man sensed her last question and began to speak in a low, quietly guilty voice. "I killed many people, and burned too many villages as a Viking long before they knew the shores of Ireland. I was a raider and a . . . He stopped here and looked aggrieved but did not continue this line of thought. Instead he continued in a different direction. ". . . if it had not been for the mercy of the Morrigan and the Dagda, who are the only ones who can judge a man who has killed in times of war and famine, I would have been condemned by my victims to go to the unknown, the After death." Tears ran down his face now and he reached for a kerchief in his pocket.

Erin rubbed his back and felt both guilty and foolish. "I'm sorry," she said again.

"No, no, lass . . . I am the one who is sorry, I

should have told you this when we were together here in this world. But I was afraid. You were so angry and upset over your own loss of life and mine that I could not face you." He sat up a bit and wiped his face before continuing, "I went through the rebirth ceremony to avoid telling you and spent my last life regretful and depressed." He turned and looked at Erin with full attention. "My dear, dear granddaughter, do not allow yourself to carry bitterness from one life to the next. I know that the life you live now is sad, but it is sad because you feel unfinished. It drives your . . . suicidal . . . well, it controls you."

Erin was stunned. She knew ever word he said was true and while it felt difficult, she became aware of a deep calm pushing away the rise of panic that came at his word . . . unfinished.

At that moment another court clerk, this one male, walked up to the pair and said quietly, "It is time . . . please come with me."

Before the court, Erin stood in her dirty jeans and T-shirt. Her grandfather was a few feet behind her in case she needed support. Erin did not feel she needed any help at this point. She was well acquainted with the process but understood why someone might want a guide to stand with them. She could not imagine the bewilderment a newcomer might feel at these proceedings. Her lack of balanced and Otherworldly attire made her feel very shabby in front of the spectacularly dressed court and attendants, but her lack of fine clothing was secondary to the embarrassment that grew as the Dagda and the Morrigan looked her over.

The Cerridwen approached, wearing robes of light green with the pattern of the trees stitched throughout them. She held a large scroll and unrolled it gracefully, then announced, "Mary McLean versus Liam Healey," to the Royal Court in a voice that sounded like life itself. The Cerridwen spanned the world between life and death more closely than any other soul dwelling in the Otherworld. It was the Cauldron of Renewal that lent her this advantage over death. Hers was a position, like all Royal positions in the Otherworld, which was bestowed by the reigning monarchy to the next holder of the title. To be the Cerridwen was to be declared the holder of life itself. Her Cauldron was under constant protection by her own personal guards, two of whom watched over it now. One male and one female, they would send those who would drink from it without permission to the Afterdeath before they had a chance to let its elixir allow them to cross back to the Upperworld.

After announcing the case to the Royal Court, the Cerridwen handed the scroll to the male clerk who now read the charges, "Mary McLean, now Erin Smith, stands before us. She has been summoned by her assailant Liam Healey to judge him."

At this cue, Liam was led into the room to stand off to one side but in full view of both court and Erin. He wore gray robes with a swirl of patterns resembling birds and dogs, symbols of his violence on Earth. Erin felt a quick shiver run through her shoulders as sweat beaded her brow. She worried she might faint. Sensing her discomfort, her grandfather stepped forward to touch her shoulder. She turned and patted his hand before speaking. "I'm okay. I'll be all right."

When Erin turned back, the Morrigan was smiling at her. Erin was overwhelmed by the woman's

beauty. Even as a child she had stared at her, afraid
to meet those emerald eyes that danced with knowledge and concentrating instead on her heavy curls of
dark brown and robes that were stitched with thread
that sparkled like diamonds. Her pattern was that of
the Triskelion, representing the three phases of
women: Maiden, Matron, and Crone.

The Morrigan addressed her, "As you are in the
middle of your fourth life, I shall address you by
your current name . . . if you don't mind?"

This was less a question than a command, and Erin
bowed in agreement while murmuring, "Thank
you."

The Morrigan smiled slightly. Erin loved that smile
as did all, or most, of the inhabitants of the Otherworld. It was the knitted brows and frown that everyone dreaded. The Morrigan was loved but feared.
She suffered no fools and looked upon everyone as
her children, as was her right. It was rumored that
she had lived a hundred lives before earning her
term as the Morrigan from the previous one.

"Erin," she began, "it is unusual for someone to
be summoned from their current life to judge someone from their past but not unheard of. Liam has
been a servant here for two centuries in penitence
and has spent this time atoning for what he feels was
a horrendous mistake. He now has the right to wait
for your death in relaxation and if you deem it, to
be Judged."

The Dagda gestured that he wished to speak, and
the Morrigan nodded her relinquishment. He had
silver-gray hair pulled back in a long braid and a
tightly cropped beard. His eyes were blue and mirrored in them was a great deal of pain and woe.
Crow's-feet creased the edges and revealed his con-

stant worry. He had confessed to 135 lives lived and had patience, but could be very distant. His robes were dark blue and patterned with the symbol of the Stag. His was a position as consort and protector of the Morrigan though his position was equal to hers.

"Young lady," he started, "I remember your determination to convict this man and as I wish to get you back to your current life as quickly as possible, I will be blunt."

Erin felt her heart beat hard in her chest; she was uncertain at a time she thought she would be brave and determined.

The Dagda leaned forward and continued, "Liam has violated a basic law . . . the requirement that the dead not interfere with the living."

Erin knew this law and was not surprised by his lack of conformity. She looked over at Liam, but he did not return the glance; instead, he was looking twice as nervous as she felt. *Good, you should be shaking.* The thought gave her courage.

The Dagda continued, "He sought to influence your life so you would not cut it short by your own hand a third time."

Erin felt intensely aware of her heart in the back of her throat now as the Dagda continued. "He has prevented you from cutting your own wrists on several occasions, and while his intentions were good, he has still broken the law. . . ."

The Morrigan interrupted at this point, sounding like a scolding mother, "My dear child, you have thrown away the precious gift of life twice and without thought of those you left behind. The grief you have caused is selfish and unforgivable."

Erin suddenly felt as though she were the one on

trial now, and her eyes watered at the thought of her past failures.

The Dagd placed his hand on the Morrigan's arm. She quieted noticeably, and he continued for her, "Erin, Liam has decided that if he cannot 'stay your hand,' he will give up his right to wait for your natural death and allow you to judge him now. He knows the consequence could be your condemnation, but he hopes it will allow you to take this weight off your soul and move forward . . . to live this life to a natural end."

Erin felt her head spin, it was all too much to take in. *Liam* had been the presence that kept her from making that final cut. She looked at him directly. Maybe, he was the one she had felt each time she was alone and distressed, loathing everything she could not finish and herself. He met her gaze and smiled weakly.

"May I address my accused?" he asked the court timidly.

Both the Morrigan and the Dagda nodded their consent, with the Dagda commanding, "Just be brief and mind your words. We cannot keep her here much longer."

Liam bowed while murmuring his thanks, then turnd to Erin. "I have no excuse for what I did beyond greed and fear. I knew this for all sixty years of my life. Then for the next two centuries I watched you on Earth as a child and sometimes here when you returned as well. I felt horrible shame when you took your life the first time. I knew it was your subconscious hatred of me and your fear of life that kept you from living fully.

"The next time you returned to the living I secretly

delighted in your every word and action. It was as if you were my own child and . . . and my shame . . . my guilt was immense. I had no right . . . to harm you the first time. I'm sorry, I sound like a doddering fool. All these years I've practiced what to say to you and it isn't enough. But I need you to know that when you took your life again . . ." he stammered and tears filled his eyes. "I knew I needed to make sure . . . I mean, I've watched you as I've watched my own children. When you died . . . I'm . . . I'm horribly sorry . . . I know it's not enough, but I am deeply and truly sorry. Please, judge me, for better or worse, please judge me and live." He was sobbing now and no one comforted him. Both the Dagda and the Morrigan looked at Erin, avoiding his shame.

Erin looked at him; she felt conflicted over what her grandfather had told her about his own past, but she also felt the knot of hatred that she had fostered for this man. This hatred burned in her now and she did not see the pathetic plea before her. She saw a vicious youth with a knife. *He's like half the people in prison, more sorry they got caught than sorry for what they did. Why should I believe him?*

Erin spoke her thoughts out loud. "Why should I forgive you? You didn't kill in self-defense or by order of your King in time of war. You preyed on an old man and his granddaughter!" Erin paused as she realized she yelled her last question. *I need to be calm*, she thought before continuing. "How do I know you aren't lying to me, to the court? How do I know you won't go back and commit worse crimes? How do I know it was you who stopped me from killing myself?"

Liam looked stunned and was about to say something but the Dagda spoke. "Young lady, I can assure you that the Watchers," he gestured to the myriad of glimmering blue lights that were actually small fairies who reported the activities in the Otherworld to the council, "observed this man stop you from suicide on two occasions in the last six months. That fact is not open to question," he stated firmly.

Erin felt humbled and continued in a less defiant voice, "I'm sorry. I have to believe the Watchers, of course, but how do I know he is sorry? How do I accept the apology of a man I have hated for so long?" Much to her own dismay, her eyes began to water and she turned to look at her grandfather. He stepped forward with a nod to the court and spoke quietly to Erin.

"My dear, you are becoming hysterical." He embraced her and whispered in her ear, "Remember, this is for you. You can forgive him and move on with your life, or you can condemn him and still move on with your life." He then released her and spoke normally. "Do what you feel is right."

Erin felt better and her thoughts became more coherent, *I was wrong to take my own life. I know that. I know I need help and I know it was Liam who stopped me from suicide. But I also know he had no right to take my life in the first place. My God, I sound like a whiny child. People die every single day from hundreds of diseases and wars. Famine takes the life of thousands ever year, but who gets judged on that? Government? I can't keep letting my own tragedy run my life.*

As her grandfather moved back to his position, she looked back to where the prisoner was standing and knew what to do. Liam seemed scared but resigned to whatever would happen next. He was avoiding her gaze.

How dare you not look me in the eye, she thought.

Erin walked over to where Liam stood. At her small height she looked into his face and he could not avoid her. The guards did not move forward as they did not perceive Erin as a threat. The court, however, took great interest in her movement and everyone became quiet.

"Liam Healey," Erin started calmly. "You look me in the eye and tell me you were wrong."

Liam seemed stunned by what she asked but quickly met her gaze and answered, "I was wrong and I am sorry." The answer sounded sincere and he did not drop the gaze until he was done.

"Fine, then I know my verdict," she said out loud without taking her eyes off his face. Then she slapped him, hard.

Liam reeled from the slap; he had not expected one and was not braced for it. He fell to the floor as the spectators of the proceedings gasped.

"What did you think of that?" she asked him.

"I think I deserved it," he answered as he rubbed his offended cheek without moving to get up.

"Good," she replied as she held out her hand to help him get up. "I forgive you."

Liam rose with her aid and looked surprised, "Thank you."

The Dagda smiled, suppressed a chuckle, and spoke, "I believe we have a verdict."

The clerks announced the verdict and Liam was led away to prepare for his renewal ceremony with the Cerridwen. He looked back at Erin before leaving and smiled, then bowed to her. She did not respond.

Her attention was then commanded by the words of the Morrigan. "Erin Smith, thank you for your time, but Samhain is about to end and you need to return while it is still easy for you to pass through.

Please hasten as we don't want you to be stuck here until next year's Samhain. Farewell. Renew and move forward, my dear."

Erin followed her grandfather back outside but by a side door so they did not have to walk back through the gallery of spectators. *I have to go back to my life now.*

As they approached the Well of Memory, her grandfather spoke, "I wish we had more time, but we have only a minute to get you safely through the veil."

Erin hugged her grandfather and told him, "Thank you, I'm not sure what to say other than I loved you very much." Tears again welled in her eyes.

Her grandfather smiled and agreed. "I know, lass, I know. I loved you more than anyone I knew in the past."

Erin was about to say more, but he stopped her. "No, no. There is no more time for words now. Walk past the well and through the shimmer you see behind it and hurry. There are only seconds left," he said urgently.

Erin didn't waste any time. She remembered the stories of those who became stuck in the veil. They rarely survived with their sanity. She did not hesitate at the veil but stepped quickly through, then felt herself walking down a city street in London.

She could remember what had just happened, but it was fading fast. *I want to remember; maybe if I try to hang on to the images in my head.* Erin struggled, but her body felt as light as her head and she wasn't sure if her feet were really on the ground. She stopped walking and thought she might faint till she saw the old man from McDonald's next to her.

He placed a comforting hand on her arm and said, "Are you all right my dear?"

"Yes, yes. I think I'm just hungry," she answered and looked at her wristwatch to see that it was quite late, a minute past midnight to be exact.

Erin heard him mutter, "Well, good night, then. You'd best be off home."

She looked up to see him walk away, but he was gone, and by the time she realized it was dark and she was definitely hungry, she had forgotten all of it.

Across the street was a fish-n-chip shop with a small sign stating it was the best in town and open late for pub hours. Erin walked across the street and decided to judge for herself. She ordered a large helping and sat herself at one of the small tables inside. The shop was noisy and people were talking to one another about nothing in general. She looked at the malt vinegar when she saw no ketchup on her table and, much to her own surprise, tried it on her chips.

Pretty good. I would say this is the best meal I've eaten in a long time. Then, while she munched on the last of her fish and chips, she thought of her next painting and it was complete in her mind. Erin sketched it quickly on a napkin and headed toward her studio to start it.

COVER ME

by Nancy Holder

Nancy Holder has written over sixty novels and two hundred short stories, essays, and articles, including many projects for Buffy the Vampire Slayer, Angel, and High-lander: The TV Series. Her books have appeared on The Los Angeles Times bestseller list, and she has received four Bram Stoker Awards for fiction from the Horror Writers Association. Her work has appeared on the lists of recommended works for the American Library Association, American Reading Association, The New York Times Library Association, and others. She lives in San Diego with her daughter, Belle, two cats, and a dog.

IT WAS FEBRUARY FIRST, and the House of Caffeine was shattering at the highest of octane. Yo, mama, the coffeehouse worked the fun zone—triple espresso and driving music, everybody shakin' just stayin' alive, stayin' alive.

The vibes zinged, winged arrows set for kill; watch out, these kids have death rays!—mirrors were cracking. Windows really, really wanted to split in two, right down the center so that they splayed open like Georgia O'Keefe karma camellias. You come and go, grrrrrl!

Any second now, the floor was going to rumble asunder and form a new techno-tectonic continent.

Jackers, the manager, who was tall and thin and from England, was anxious because there were so many kids jammed inside that the walls were actually bulging . . . okay, hyperbole, if you took the right drugs. If one was unaltered like Lilith, everyone was spilling onto the street in chalkface laughter, black lipstick, spiced cigarettes, spiked coffee, not a single damn beret in sight. The poetry geeks had retreated for the night. They were far too cool to consider doing something containing an actual component of extroversion-based fun. So the boisterous kids had taken over the streets as well as the house.

Lilith had moved to San Diego with her shields up; it was tough being a PK—Preacher's Kid. But this crowd had adopted her at first sight. She wondered if it was her swagger or her incredible wardrobe of jet-beaded blackery. At any rate, sure of a home here, Lilith was loving the night; loving the buttery full moon; loving Fils Maurice, who had finally noticed that she took up space on the planet.

Mmm, he smelled of home-mixed oils. He was wearing a black T-shirt, black jeans, and black boots. "You staying?" His name, Fils, was pronounced "Feece" and it meant "son" in French. She figured it wasn't his birth name. Her actual name at home was Mary Elizabeth, which was also not bad. The Christianity of it didn't bother her. It was just . . . it was her old name. Yes, she knew that Lilith was Adam's first companion, but that she had been "disobedient" and cast away for the meeker Eve. Why else would Sarah MacLaughlin call her all-women tours Lilith Fairs?

Fils was honey brown, with spiky bleached hair and eyes of kohl. Though incredibly eye-catching, he was an exercise in neutrals wishing aloud for some color. But as he sidled up to her, he flipped open a little kit complete with an absolutely beautiful Art Nouveau damascene lighter.

"Come down the hall?" he asked her.

She glanced at his works, surprised. She didn't do drugs. She wondered about the state of his health, and she thought about the awesome tatt at the base of his long, straight spine. She had seen it during team basketball practice, when she had gone back to fetch her gym clothes out of her locker. A mental picture formed—tattoo studio, some guy looking like a cross between Colin Farrell in *Daredevil* and Ray Bradbury's Illustrated Man; and Fils not asking the right questions about autoclaves, not asking to see the needles popped open in front of him. There was no way to know if he had been careful.

Maybe I shouldn't make any impetuous plans about his crotch . . . she thought, but he really was awfully fetching.

The coffeehouse dollied around them. San Diego, even in February, glistened and glistered. There were a lot of yuppie Republican parents in their neighborhood, who billed too many hours at their law firms and mortgage brokerage houses, socking it away for private schools, surf camps, and high-ticket universities. That left their children with lots of freedom and discretionary income but little parental oversight. San Diego kids spent their days in the sun, moving and doing and having adventures, and a lot of time on their appearances. They looked like movie extras in glossy high-budget films about growing up. They were beautiful. In San Diego, if you didn't manage to look at last basically stylish, you were not managing the career of being you very well.

"Yes?" he asked leadingly, and she stirred herself from the many moods of Lilith. She was used to being a loner. A PK gig was hard, but what had happened up the coast in Santa Barbara to her family was even harder.

"I'll go with you," she said to Fils. He gestured to the kit, and she shook her head. "Not into it. And you should be careful with that," she admonished him. "There's been an increase in the number of people dying from AIDS."

He flashed her an insouciant grin, as if to say *Not me, never me.* A light dusting of anger flared inside her; she wanted to pluck that grin right off his face and feed it to the ravens. She had gone with her father on a number of hospital calls, sitting in a corridor while he went in to comfort the afflicted, to comfort the dying, to remind his parishioners that Christ Himself had risen from the grave to life eternal.

In private, her father used to discuss the mythos of Christ ology and the need for concrete images to describe an impersonal but very real tendency for good in the universe. In private, he also had sex with four male members of the choir—all at the same time—and got caught with his pants down—literally—on the job.

Despite the assurances given by Christ that no one was supposed to throw any stones, there were such things as church laws and criminal penalties, talk of rape, talk of forced sodomy. So only mythological stones thrown through the miracle of jail time. Lilith's mother had secured a position at San Diego State so she could haul her family out of Santo Bizarro and pray her husband back to mental, spiritual, and emotional health without people staring at her in the grocery store, the bank, and the welfare office.

Dad had some more months on his sentence. And thus it was that Lilith's mom didn't really have the capacity to police her daughter with the same rigor as before the debacle. So it was the same for her as it was for the kids whose parents neglected them simply because they were amassing vast amounts of mammon.

Lilith knew that when her mother said, "Where are you going?" and Lilith said vaguely, "Out with my new friends," that her mother just crossed her fingers and hoped for something not too horrible. It was as deeply as Mom could drink in the well of good fortune. Her God had flown out the window with Dad's heterosexuality and his lack of Christian morals.

Lilith would never admit it, not to their marriage and family therapist, nor to her mother, nor any of her friends, but she had been exhilarated by her father's actions. She had read a lot about religions and religious cults, and she figured her father was a follower of the great god Pan, father of appetite and lust. He was no dry husk in a clerical collar droning on about salvation. He was a full-blooded man unable to curb his sexual aggression; he was a primitive; he was a satyr.

He was human.

She looked up at Fils and said, in case he hadn't understood, "I don't do drugs. But can I watch?"

He smiled at her. "This drug feels good, J."

"And the first one's free," she shot back at him. "Let me watch."

He shrugged. She saw color in his dark cheeks,

and she wondered if he was embarrassed that she
had rejected his offer; or if he was excited that she
wanted to watch.

He moved his head for her to follow him. She did.
He smelled so good. He looked so good. She was a
virgin, but she had decided she wanted to give it up
this year. Her father had inspired her.

If he was a careful guy with his needles, maybe
she would sleep with Fils for her first experience.

His back was broad and muscular as she followed
him down the hall; the narrow corridor smelled of
cigarettes, sweat, cinnamon, and coffee. They were
heavy odors, the incense of youth on the prowl. Faces
glanced her way, slightly apprehensive at first; then
they would tick to Fils and read something there that
reassured them; *she's cool. She's with me.*

She liked that he was her ticket into the inner
sanctum.

Then, thoughtfully smiling at her as if to reassure
her, he pushed aside a hanging curtain of purple silk
and silver stars across the hall from the bathroom.
She had never noticed it before.

The space was illuminated by the warm yellow
glow of two or three candles, and furnished with
couches pushed cheek by jowl, and a couple of overstuffed chairs. The smell of marijuana rolled over the
five or six people in the room. One guy's head had
fallen back against a burgundy couch, and the smile
on his face tempted Lilith to try whatever had sent
him into bliss.

Fils took her hand—*yes!*—and led her to a couch.
He plopped into the center of it—no springs
attached—and gestured invitingly for her to join him.
As she did so, he accepted a joint from the guy beside him and inhaled deeply. His chest expanded as

he took in the smoke and held it. Then he exhaled, contracting like a balloon.

Lilith watched him. His head dipped toward his chest, he looked up at her through his lashes and grinned.

"It's good stuff," he said.

"That's nice," she replied, sounding prim to herself.

He moved one large, handsome shoulder. "Too bad."

"Not so much."

They sat for a while in companionable silence. Lilith was content to smell him, savor the warmth of his body against hers. She wondered if this night would end up with her first sexual experience.

"It's almost midnight," Fils observed after a time. "Groundhog Day."

"Yes." She didn't add that in the Christian lectionary, it was Candlemas. The Catholics recognized the day as the Feast of the Purification of the Blessed Virgin, when Christ's mother, following Mosaic law, offered herself to the temple priests for ritual cleansing. Pagans celebrated Imbolc, the feast of fertility. And for more moderate Protestants, such as her family, Candlemas was the first time Jesus Christ was presented in the temple, to be oohed and aahed over by the prophets as the Word made flesh.

And as Fils had said, it was also known as Groundhog Day. She was vaguely aware that there was a little groundhog back in Pennsylvania who wobbled out of his burrow and looked for his shadow. If he saw it, winter would last six weeks longer. It all took place back east, and Bill Murray had been in a movie about it, but at her age those things held little interest. Still, Lilith appreciated the continuum of ancient belief to secular silliness. So much of her own life seemed silly at the moment.

Very silly. Floatingly silly.

I'm getting a contact high, she thought with a bit of alarm.

She leaned slowly back against the couch, aware that she was spinning.

They were quiet for another stretch of time, as the super-powerful pot seeped into her skin like fine oils. The warm yellow hoods of the candles burned softly, dimming as she drifted. Beside her Fils talked gently with the others, and she was aware that he was getting out his kit again.

She tried to lift her head, but it was too heavy. From the back of her head, a small thought stirred; she blinked with heavy lids and had the sense that the thought was attempting to move to the forefront of her brain. But there were so many convolutions, folds, and paths along its way. Inside her lay the vast field of the Great Labyrinth, and Diogenes with his lantern had had too much to smoke. . . .

"You okay?" Fils asked her, fingers grazing hers as he moved a little closer to her on the couch.

"Mmm." She grinned lazily at him, barely making out the outline of his silhouette as the candle glow smoothed to a sheen, diffusing detail, texture, and dimension. "I'm watching my mind. It wants to come out. It wants to see its shadow."

He chuckled. "Damn, you're easy, Lilith. You didn't even smoke anything."

The small thought scampered along the brain folds; each time it hit a dead end, it lit up like a tiny firefly, alternately anxious, alternately thrilled.

She heard someone whispering the old hymn, *"This little light of mine, I'm gonna make it shine."*

The room was papery with whispers as Fils got out his lighter and his spoon. Conversations unreeled

like threads; Lilith couldn't follow them; the purple
silken words tissued thin through her fingers, then
evaporated like so much sacred smoke. Birds ate the
bread crumbs; there was no path home.

"Does this scare you? Does this upset you?" he
asked her. "Watching me shoot up?"

The light in her brain danced and capered, no
stately groundhog this, but a tiny mouse raising up
on its hind legs to sniff the air, which was redolent
of incense and communion.

She didn't speak, only shook her head. And then
she said, "Don't you think it was odd, that after the
Virgin Mary gave birth to Jesus, she was considered unclean?"

Fils regarded her with a blank look, and then he
smiled. "Oh, I forgot. Your father is a minister."

Sex offender.

She closed her eyes as the light scampered on; she
could actually observe it making its way through her
neural pathways. She could see herself following it,
like Sleeping Beauty trailing after the spindle on the
spinning wheel that would plunge her into a
sleeplike death.

"We don't believe that," she managed to slur. "The
unclean part."

"Sure you do." He smoothed her hair away from
her forehead. "You can't be a Christian and believe
that women are equal to men."

"Not true." She grinned back, feeling languid and
safe. *This little light of mine, I'm gonna make it shine . . .*
"That's Mosaic law. Jewish. Christ came to replace
the law with love."

"Tired argument," he countered. "The Crusades,
the Inquisition . . ."

"Protestant Reformation," she riposted. But it was

a tired argument. Kids with pastors for fathers went through a lot of them, unless they refused to play.

"Put that in me," she said to him, indicating the needle.

"No way. You gotta come to the god yourself."

When Fils injected himself, he moaned, and she stared hard at the needle as it pierced his vein, delivering what appeared to be six more heartbeats of sunshine to his life. Fils draped his head on her shoulder and closed his eyes.

They stayed that way for a long time, Lilith somnolent but partially awake. Fils dreamed and soared; she had no idea where he went because she had never gone there.

The definition of hell was the knowledge that one was separated from God. Lilith was very comfortable with the notion that there were many ways to reach Him—or Her—and that at this moment, Fils might be visiting with the sublime.

Her little thought-light capered and danced, and Lilith smiled, liking the way this Candlemas Eve was turning out. It was far, far better than anything she could have hoped for, back in Santa Bizarro, when her father had been shamed.

For being a man, she reminded herself. *For doing nothing but being a man.*

In ancient Greece, the highest form of love was that of an older man for a younger man—women were vessels for giving birth, created for the expression of blood and filth as the ideal of man was made flesh and therefore, established as more limited and corrupt than the god's image of him. Man reminded woman that he was imperfect. And man hated woman for that.

Some of that hatred must spill like seed from one

generation of men to the next, the imperfect society
of men blaming women, not Satan, for original sin,
as wars and famines depleted their vigor and reminded them that heaven was not theirs. Lust for the
bodies of women was aggression, and aggression
built cities and space stations . . .

. . . lust for the male body brought poetry, and an
end to war.

"My father . . ." she began, then closed her mouth
as her little mind light jittered and skittered, seeking
the dusky warmth of the room.

"You kids okay in here?" That was Jackers, the
manager, from the doorway.

To her surprise, Fils gave the man a wave. He
seemed to have awakened a little. She wasn't sure
what to expect, never having run before with a
crowd who did indictable drugs.

Jackers said, "Do you think we'll need another
cup? Not sure we can catch it all in just the one."

Fils slurred, "She's pretty little." He put his arm
around Liliths' shoulders. "It's going to be easier
than we figured."

Lilith looked from Fils to Jackers and back again.
Jackers gave her a glance in turn, and for one giddy
moment, a dozen movie moments featuring Mexican
standoffs ripcorded through her brain.

The light inside her head had nearly walked the
labyrinth; there was supposed to be a revelation at
the end of such a journey. And here it was:

She tried to stand, said unsteadily. "I have to pee."

"I'll show you where it is," Jackers said.

"Let me help you up." Fils rose with fluid grace,
putting Lilith eye-level with his crotch. The heat surprised her, warmed her. She swallowed, tempted by
his nearness to do something audacious, plant her

mouth over that length and fan the flame with her warm breath. . . .

Fils took her hand and walked her across the room, which had grown silent as the other dark dreamers in the room dreamed. A guy was stretched out on the floor.

Midnight chimed, and it was the first time Lilith realized there had been a clock ticking the entire time she had been in the room. In the corner stood a large, old-fashioned grandfather clock.

Fils escorted her to the threshold, where the purple drape had eased aside again, and there Jackers stretched out his hand. His hand closed around hers, making a double fist.

His eyes twinkled, just like in the old Christmas poem, which was about a huge imp stealing into people's houses. It had been dressed up for popular consumption. Consumption had long been on the mind of the collective unconscious—ritual feasts; the bartering for favors with gifts; anything to keep death from devouring one's muscles, sinews, spirit, and soul . . . Satan ate the goodness right out of you. Tuberculosis settled for the scraps. Better to eat than to be eaten . . . hence, the Body and Blood of Christ . . . eat the god before the god swallows you down like a minnow in the belly of a whale.

Jackers tucked Lilith's arm through his. He was wearing a purple silk shirt. In the Christian lectionary, purple was the color of Candlemas.

"Come on, my little virgin queen."

He opened the door and flicked on the light, which was gentle on the eyes. Not a fluorescent, but a dim bulb. The floor was linoleum squares of black and white. On a black wooden table, sat a small purple-and-black Indian lacquer incense box, a cone burning in a metal dish atop it, accompanied by a couple of really beautiful purple candles.

Feeling rather unwell, Lilith pulled down her pants.

And the light in her mind finally found egress, and birth into her consciousness.

She began to shake.

My meds are wearing off, she thought anxiously. *What time is it? Did I forget to take one?*

Fighting down her panic, she did her business. She rose and zipped her black wool pants. As she washed her hands, more lights went off inside her and she knew . . .

They were talking about a cup.

His name means Son.

Something's going on here. Something not good. These guys are up to something.

She reached in her jacket pocket for her cell phone, and jammed in her home number. Her mother didn't answer. Then she glanced down at the faceplate and saw that her signal was very weak, here in the bathroom of the House of Caffeine.

Lilith-Mary Elizabeth put the phone back in her pocket and splashed cold water on her face. The light from her mind had moved in front of her eyes, and it was jittering and flashing, *ah ah ah ah, stayin' alive* is what it wanted her to do . . . *stay alive.*

The meds . . . antipsychotics . . . because she was the one who found him . . .

Proud like a satyr, but so horribly ashamed. His rheumy eyes—they had been drinking together first, the men—and that was what had thrown Mary Elizabeth over the edge. Not that Daddy had slept with men, but that his lust had shamed him.

Three days later, it was she, again, who had found

him. She had cut him down from the rafters where he had ineffectually dangled; she wanted to use him like a punching bag first and say, "Hanging was for Judas!"

But she realized that her father was Judas; he had betrayed the communion of the spirit not because he had loved men, but because he had repudiated the act. Acceptance of what he'd done, proclaiming the transcendence of eros, would have pushed his soul out of the burrow. If only he had seen his shadow, and embraced it . . . winter, yes, for six weeks—degradation, punishment—but then . . . the exquisite, longed-for sun would burst into glorious spring—resurrection, transfiguration.

Oh, Daddy, my Daddy . . .

The weakness and shame her father adopted like a foundling child had so infuriated her. . . .

"*First we'll tie her down,*" came a whisper through the bathroom door. It was Fils. "*She's out of it. Dunno how. She didn't even smoke any grass. But it's a lucky thing.*"

"*You're certain she's a virgin?*" That was Jackers. "*He'll only take virgins. If we offer him an unclean woman . . . remember what happened that last time?*"

"*Right. Like I could forget.*"

Her heart beat fast.

The bloom of light in front of her eyes beat faster.

"*She's unsullied,*" Fils responded. "*I can smell her purity. It's driving me crazy.*"

She thought about movies where hell breaks loose in the form of warning lights and blaring sirens. *Whoop, whoop, the spaceship's about to blow up! Whoop, whoop, the bomb is going to explode!*

Such screams rattled her cage in the bathroom. She

pressed herself against the wall by the sink, flooding with fear, working to keep it at bay as best she could.

Whoop, whoop! Wacko sacrificial Groundhog Cult!

Giddiness overtook her. Were they going to stake her out, let the giant evil groundhog devour her? Had she walked into the director's cut of *The Wicker Man*?

She massaged her temples. She had tamped down the memories of her psychotic break, how she had babbled to the intake counselor about the Corinthians, whose orgiastic practices had so alarmed St. Paul that he'd written them a letter asking them to tone it down. How proud she had been of her father that he had found his inner Corinth. How she had longed to follow him there . . .

. . . how he had denied himself the pleasure . . .

. . . *wait a minute; wait, my dad was having sex with men; my dad was a sinner . . . Satan is tempting me to approve* . . .

"You okay, Lilith?" Jackers called politely through the door.

Drop the act, Lilith whispered to herself. She waited a moment. She was numb from head to toe; lights were popping all around her. . . .

Drop the act.

Psychotic break.

She remembered those words; her therapist had styled himself like some Father Berrigan of the mind—a renegade activist for radical mental health. Joan of Arc burning away, we few, we unhappy heretics . . .

Below her feet, something roared. The floor shook. But the floor had been shaking for hours; the music had been pounding all day and all night; kids were jittering and shattering in the House of Caffeine from too much of a good thing.

The floor shook again, and as she watched, a large crack zigzagged its way across the black-and-white tile. She jumped back, gasping; the crack separated, and became a fissure about two inches wide.

Something moved inside the fissure, breaching like a dolphin above the surface of the ocean.

It was a claw.

She opened her mouth to scream. Then she remembered Jackers and Fils, waiting for her on the other side of the door. She stuffed both her hands over her mouth and forced back the sound.

Just as she had done when she'd discovered her father swinging like a church bell.

Is this happening? she wondered. *Am I having another break with reality?*

She kept as far back from the claw as she could, slamming against the wall, pushing hard with the tips of her shoes. She burst into tears as the fissure cracked yet again, and grew larger.

She saw the tip of a paw. Covered with coffee-colored fur, it spanned at least two feet across.

This time the roar shook the room.

"Help," she whispered.

Then she slid down on her knees and closed her eyes. Years of tenure as a PK took over, and she began to pray. But while she meant to say the words of the Lord's Prayer, the words of the medieval mystic St. Theresa formed on her lips.

Christ has no Body now but yours
No hands, no feet on earth but yours
Yours are the eyes through which He looks

The fissure slid apart, reaming the floor. With a ceramic thunk, the toilet broke and clean water gushed over the floor, swirling around Lilith's knees as she struggled to get back to her feet.

The little table with the incense and the candles fell over, into a small stack of toilet paper rolls in a wooden crate sprayed gold. The room was shaking as if it were a box the creature had a hold of—or some little animal's hidey-hole—and the creature was trying to get it out.

Fils and Jackers were both pounding on the door, shouting, "Lilith!" They sounded panicked, as if they didn't realize what was going on. As if they were pretending that they hadn't planned to sacrifice her to the very creature who was swiping at the air less than twelve inches away with its great paw and long, sharp claws.

Its fetid breath blasted through room, spewing ash and inferno, and she began to cough.

"Lilith!" Fils cried. "Open the door!"

Then the floor cracked wider, and the huge black snout of the beast pushed through. And then its teeth, yellow and sharp.

Lilith couldn't stop coughing. Doubling over, her chest billowed with smoke. Her eyes watered, twin trails of tears down her face.

The she heard Jackers shouting. "Fire! Call 9-1-1!"

For a moment, the light in her mind flared up again, reentering the great labyrinth the way it had come in.

Is that all this is? Did I knock over a candle and start a fire? I have been so sick. Devils lived in me and I saw so many things that were not there. . . .

Maybe I'm not here now.

But the therapist said one had to pick a consensual

reality, and stick with it . . . preferably one that allowed one to function . . . that whether it was real wasn't as important as whether it was a good place to be . . .

. . . and that's what I think Daddy meant about concrete symbols for goodness and mercy trending in the universe. . . .

The creature's enormous, furry front leg raised high above the fissure, then thwacked the floor. The tiles shimmied and flacked into the air like a pack of tarot cards. Its second reached and smacked down hard.

It eyes were black pits as large as the toilet.

She began to laugh hysterically. *I'm in a bad horror movie. The attack of the giant groundhog!*

"Lilitih!" Fils bellowed. "Open the door!"

The groundhog was rocking forward as if working to yank itself up out of the fissure. It appeared to take no notice of her, nor of the fire. From the toilet paper, flames had leaped to the walls, and were chewing rivulets of brilliant nonlectionary orange and scarlet into the black-and-white wallpaper, Aubrey Beardsley's *Salomé* theme . . . the man who had penned the play, Oscar Wilde, had been thrown into prison for sodomy, and died penniless.

Oscar Wilde had struggled with his faith all his life; his dream was to embrace Catholicism. . . .

The peace of Candlemas be with you.

And also with all unclean women everywhere.

"Lilith!"

She held out a hand, reaching it toward the door. If she made a run for it, tried to skirt around the groundhog as it emerged, could she do it?

What about the cup? What are they planning? What is happening? What is going to happen to me?

She threw back her head and screamed.

The groundhog whipped its head in her direction and eyed her as if for the first time. Its enormous eyes blinked; they were bloodshot from the smoke.

From somewhere deep among the brain folds, she remembered herself as a little girl of six. There had been furtive rustlings in the shadows of her house, papery whispers of men, and of her father admonishing someone Lilith could not see, saying, *"Ssh. Don't wake them up."*

She quivered, standing in the bathroom. Something flooded back—skin on skin, lips on lips—her father—

"They're all asleep. Don't wake them up."

Lots of men, in hoods, had it been? Gowns? Evening gowns or long white robes? She couldn't recall. But the memory had been a hedgerow in the labyrinth. . . .

And now her little light shone there, then and at the hour of her death.

Let he who is without sin . . . roll the stone away. . . .

She remembered being very afraid, creeping farther down the stairs to try to see what Daddy and the other men were doing . . .

. . . to Mommy . . .

Her father had said, "We have to catch it in the cup."

Another man had said, "Do you think we'll need more than one?"

And another: "She's pretty little. Are you sure that she's unsullied?"

And whatever she had seen that terrible night, she had cast in darkness. She had seen the shadow of that terrible act and retreated to her burrow.

Then Daddy had committed a great evil again . . . not an act of courage, but of evil . . . and I gave it a silhouette and chased that shadow down the rabbit hole and out the groundhog burrow . . . I'm either going to die from this or live again. . . .

The groundhog began to pant, its great head trembling. It looked at her as if for help.

She whispered, "I am the queen of it. I am the queen of all cups, and they will not be taken from me. . . ."

Slowly she approached the groundhog, her arm outstretched. She knew the tale of the virgin and the unicorn—only a virgin could lower that grand, erected horn to the earth. Virgins had powers to placate the gods, to birth gods . . . and to kill gods.

She touched its flanks with the tips of her outstretched fingers. The groundhog trembled and shivered, and lay passively. Its eyelids fluttered.

"Lilith!" Fils screamed. "Help is coming!"

She splayed her fingers against the fur. It was warm and nubby. As she coughed hard, she ran her fingers down its flank.

The groundhog waited.

She heard sirens. She heard Jackers shouting, "Everyone, *now*! Out!"

More curious than afraid, she looked around the room. The walls were ablaze. The ceiling had caught fire, and portions of the floor as well.

Lilith swung one leg up, then found purchase in the groundhog's fur as she inched herself up over its massive body. Hand over hand, she worked her way up to its broad, strong back.

Just as she reached the zenith of its spine, the door burst open. Fils stood framed by crackling tongues of flame, a fire extinguisher in his arms. He gaped at her.

She called to him, "Peekaboo! There will be six more weeks of winter!"

Then as he fell to his knees in utter disbelief, the groundhog easily made its way back off the shelflike outcropping of the floor.

Together Lilith and the creature sank beneath the flame, back through the basement, and into the warm burrow of the earth. There was no fire there, and no altar, and no men doing to her mother what no one else, not even in Corinth, would have been allowed to do to another human being.

And yet she stayed. All those years . . . Did she think she needed ritual purification? That she was that unclean?

No need to concern herself with that now. All the medications had worn off. She was free. And now she would begin to live out her reign as the goddess made flesh in the world of men.

Lilith and the groundhog continued to descend.

She smiled at the roots and the mud and the rocks as they slid past her; and said to the creature, "I love you."

Perhaps next year, the winter would be shorter.

It would all depend.

THE SECRET SYMPATHY

by Brian A. Hopkins

Four-time Bram Stoker Award winner Brian A. Hopkins is the author of several books, most recently El Dia de los Muertos, which James Morrow called "a searing journey into the mythic soul of Mexico and the intolerable heart of loss." Brian's story "Diving the Coolidge" was selected by Robert Silverberg and Karen Haber as one of the best fantasy stories of 2001. Darrell Schweitzer (Weird Tales) has called him "one of the most intriguing voices to emerge from the small presses since Thomas Ligotti." Brian has also been a finalist for both the Nebula Award and the Ted Sturgeon Memorial Award for science fiction. You can learn more about him by visiting his webpage at http://bahwolf.com.

> *True Love's the gift which God has given*
> *To man alone, beneath the heaven:*
> > *It is not fantasy's hot fire,*
> > > *Whose wishes soon as granted fly;*
> > *It liveth not in fierce desire,*
> > > *With dead desire it doth not die;*
> *It is the secret sympathy,*
> *The silken link, the silken tie,*
> *Which heart to heart and mind to mind*
> *In body and in soul can bind.*
> > > > —*Sir Walter Scott*, Lay of the Last
> > > > Minstrel, Canto v. Stanza 13

I FOUND a young man on my doorstep.

It was one of those last days of winter, in what I expected to be but a handful of winters left for me to endure. The sun was busy encouraging green things to suffer the pain of giving birth to spring. Gaunt squirrels were sniffing the dead, cold-trammeled grass, nervous tails twitching like thread-bare banners. It was a soundless, windless, cheerless afternoon, one in which the knock on the door came as a thunderclap too soon consumed by the silence of winter. There was no movement in the barren limbs of the trees. There was no shifting of dead leaves, for they'd all gone to rot in winter's callous cycle of freeze and thaw.

The contradictions—life-renewing sun versus winter malaise, young man in the prime of his life versus old man hunched in the doorway of an apartment in which he expected to die—were not lost on me. I had been passing the time with old photo albums, alternating between joy and heartache, with no discernible link between the long-cherished images and the emotions they inspired, tortured one moment by lost desires and lifted up in the very next by the fullness of memory.

He wrung his hands, this young man on my door-step, earnest and woebegone and not at all sure what he wanted. He looked to have lost his dog. Or his best friend. Or that one thing he cherished above all others in the world. But not his way—he knew where he was. And as he tried to remember what it was he'd meant to say when he knocked on my door, I caught him trying to peer around me into the dim confines of the small split-level apartment, as if what he'd lost might be found within.

So I asked him to step inside.

"Thank you," he said, morose and apprehensive, but appearing less lost than he had a moment before.

We sat on the loveseat while he rubbed sweaty palms to trouser legs and his gaze roamed the apartment. It was a modest dwelling: living area and combination dining room slash kitchen on the first floor; single bedroom and bath on the second; last in a row of a dozen identical abodes, all bricked and mortared together but crumbling at the corners, so they looked like a toppled tower. The entire complex had once belonged to the university, which had rented the units to married students. Budget cutbacks eventually eliminated all but the most rudimentary maintenance. In time, the university was obligated to sell the property to a slumlord in order that the apartments might complete their urban devolution without embarrassing university founders, administrators, and prominent alumni. After Virginia died, with little use for a home in the suburbs, I'd moved here.

"My wife and I started out here . . . in this apartment," the young man finally volunteered.

I nodded as if I understood the significance of that statement. Sometimes all it takes is the right expression and a willingness to listen.

"I thought . . ." An embarrassed shrug and a glance toward the low ceiling told me he wasn't sure how much he was really prepared to share with an old man addled enough to invite a stranger into his home without a second thought.

"I'll make some coffee," I told him. And while I made the coffee, just out of sight around the corner, he continued, less nervous, perhaps, when not confronted by my unwavering gaze.

"It's as if everything went downhill from the moment we left this apartment. We used to have a big overstuffed sofa right here. Chocolate brown. Most comfortable thing you ever saw. Had one of those papasan chairs in that corner, there where you've got a pole lamp. You know the kind of chair I'm talking about? Like a big cereal bowl. Made of rattan or bamboo or something like that, with a big round cushion."

I was amazed he'd managed to fit both of those items into the tiny living room. My loveseat and recliner left little room for anything besides a small entertainment center and a coffee table—and many's the time I'd barked my shins on the damn table.

"We lived here for four years while I went to college. By the time we were ready to move, the papasan chair was pretty ragged out and the sofa wasn't much better. We put the papasan out for the trash. We took the sofa with us, figuring it would do until we had the money for something new."

I brought him his coffee.

"Thank you." He sipped carefully, looking away as he continued his story. "We didn't have much, but this is where we were happiest. I thought if I came and saw the place again, maybe I could recapture some of what we felt when we lived here. It's as if once we left—no, even before that—it's as if once we started throwing things out and packing up what little we planned to take with us into our new life . . . well, things started going bad between us. When we set the papasan chair out on the street for the trash, a little bit of our love went with it. When we finally called Goodwill to come pick up the sofa, same thing. A part of who we had been and what we meant to each other was gone. And over the years, as everything we'd first owned in this tiny little apartment was replaced, we became different people. We lost our love for one another, one piece at a time." He finally looked at me. "That sounds crazy, doesn't it?"

I shrugged. "Not necessarily. People change."

"I'm not talking about change. I'm talking about having your life eaten away."

"They were just things," I told him. "Inanimate objects. I think it was Alexander Smith who said, 'A man's real possession is his memory. In nothing else is he rich; in nothing else is he poor.'"

"Who the hell is Alexander Smith?" he snapped, apparently annoyed that I'd stoop to tossing aphorisms at his pain.

"Doesn't matter. Do you still love your wife?"

"Yes."

"Does she still love you?"

"I . . . I don't know."

"Perhaps you should ask her. Perhaps you should tell her what you're feeling."

He looked away again. "We don't talk like we used to. I thought if I saw this place again, maybe I could go back and tell her about it, make her understand what was happening. We have everything we ever wanted now, but we were happier here when we had so little."

"For Ginny and me, it was never about the places we lived or the things we owned. It was just about being together." I reached out and opened one of the photo albums on the coffee table. "That's her. My wife, Virginia." The photo had been shot in Salvador during Carnival, last stop on our tour of the world, nearly eight years ago to the day. Ginny was sitting in a chair, arms wrapped around her knees, draped mostly in shadow—which was the only reason I could show it to him, since my wife was completely naked in the photo. Her head was back. Her eyes were focused on someplace a thousand lifetimes in the distance.

"She's . . . not here?" he asked carefully.

I swallowed. "Gone these last eight years. Waiting for me somewhere. I know that. I can feel it. True love waits. You know?"

"I'm not so sure I believe in all that true love and love-at-first-sight stuff anymore," he said. "Not since leaving this apartment."

"Then perhaps I should tell you my story—*Ginny's* story. Maybe then you'll believe."

He's nine years old, and because his father's business made a large contribution to the Kiwanis Club, he gets to ride on their float in the Mardi Gras parade and throw beads to the throngs of people along the route. This is Gulfport, Mississippi; not exactly the grandeur of New Orleans, but still the parade is an extravagant, highly-anticipated break from the mundane. The people lining the street are a half-dozen deep. She's in the very back, completely hidden behind adults and taller children. She's small for an eight year old, with long brunette hair and teeth that'll take her another couple of years to grow into. Though she's been trying for over twenty minutes now, she has yet to catch anything and has nearly been trampled several times already. She can't even see the people on the floats through the crowd in front of her. As he pulls a new handful of beads out of the large bag at his feet, he notices a necklace of hearts. Cherry red and delicate. He has a fleeting thought that it'd be nice to give them to his mother or—something he'd never confess—maybe to a nice, pretty girl. But the crowd is hollering and there isn't time to separate them from all the other beads. He slings the handful out into the forest of outstretched arms. The strand of plastic hearts catches on his little finger as the other beads leave his hand. A flick of his wrist frees them, but a little extra energy is imparted, causing the hearts to sail out over the front rows and vanish somewhere in the back. He doesn't see where they land. She doesn't see who threw them. But that first contact has been made. Unbeknownst to either of them, the universe is sorting itself out in a process that began at the dawn of time.

Initially, we fought it. When it was just breast cancer. Before it began to infiltrate other parts of her body. Even then, though it seemed hopeless, we did the chemo and the radiation, and we started out with the good intentions of a soldier committed to standing his ground to the very end.

But I'm not telling it right. I have to tell you about Gavin and Helen Rockford, because it was Gavin, after all, who convinced me to listen to Ginny when she said she was ready to quit. I was unable, you see, to accept the inevitable . . . until Gavin explained it to me. Gavin opened another door for me, one which I sometimes wish I'd never been shown, but, again, I'm getting ahead of myself.

Gavin and Helen were just one of many older couples we'd see at the cancer center, but there was an old world elegance and charm about them that caught my attention from the start. They had a certain ambience, a fastidiousness of dress and carriage and behavior—as if they were characters from an old black-and-white movie. Guessing, I'd say they were in their mid-seventies. The products of another age.

It was Helen who was ill: some rare blood disorder coupled with pancreatic cancer. Her immune system had long since given up the ghost, and the toxins they'd been pumping into her had left her frail and wasted, subject to fugues and frequent senility. Her treatment included a blood transfusion every three days and I don't know how many different drugs. Because of their caustic nature, her drugs had to be delivered over a period of hours so as not to burn out what fragile veins remained. She'd be there when Ginny and I arrived, and she'd still be there when we left, typically in a bed, covered with a blanket, closely monitored by instruments and nurses, with several bags of toxins connected to a catheter in her chest and tubes in her arms. Yellow-and-green bags with red warning labels hung from her IV pole. There'd be that bag of blood hanging there, too: thick as maple syrup, dark as blackberries. Mostly she would sleep, quiet as a mouse, with never any complaints or demands. I imagine the nurses thought of her as the perfect patient.

Gavin was *always* with her. He never just dropped her off and went to take care of things that he undoubtedly needed to do, even if she was asleep most of the time. Perhaps she *could* sleep as easily as she did, not just because of the drugs, but because she knew he'd be there when she opened her eyes, knew that he was watching over her the whole time. He never left her side except to make coffee in the waiting room— best damn coffee I've ever tasted.

I'm not sure what it was about Gavin and Helen, but they fascinated me. I think it was Gavin's unwavering dedication to her, the love that I could see in every touch and gesture and even in the simple way he wanted there to be coffee for whoever needed it, in the way that he saw that as a simple means of being useful during all those long hours at the clinic, of taking some small burden from the nurses who would have otherwise had to stop and make it. Or it could have been Helen's quiet elegance and bearing, the way she was holding up against such an aggressive and unpleasant treatment. It could have been the unspoken, the unseen, the intuited aura that emanated from the two of them together. Ginny and I were seated next to them in the chemo room one day—next station over—when she said, not complaining but merely acknowledging, that she just didn't know how she would find the time that week to get her hair done. Gavin leaned over, kissed her forehead, and said, "Don't you worry, sweetheart. I'll make sure you get your appointment. I'll make sure you get your hair done." And you just knew, sitting there and watching them, hearing the devotion in his voice, that he would find some way to keep that promise, even though nearly all of their time was spent in the clinic. He would take her to the beauty salon after carefully arranging the whole thing with the beauticians and the friends she'd spent a lifetime meeting there, and they would pamper her and wait on her and visit like they'd always done . . . and never once let on that dear, sweet, senile Helen had long since lost all her hair.

You knew this wasn't a man to break promises, at least not to her. In his voice and in the simple way she nodded and smiled, without ever opening her poor tired eyes, you knew that she knew it, too, that he'd been making and keeping such promises for a *very* long time. You just knew he'd trade places with her if he could, that there was nothing he wouldn't do to make her well.

And watching them, I wondered what he'd do, who he'd be, how he'd cope . . . without her.

She's thirteen, and though she told her mother she was walking to the movie theater with her best friend Tammy, the truth is that as soon as Tammy and she arrived they split up, each to be with a different boy. But the boy she's with its rude and obnoxious. Twice he tries to stick his tongue in her mouth. The final straw, however, comes during the last few minutes of the film when he shoves his hand down the front of her shirt. She runs from the theater, completely forgetting her coat until the cold air outside hits her in the face. She stands there for several long minutes, wondering how to face going back into the theater after her coat, wondering what she'll tell her mother if she walks home early. The theater finally lets out. She stands to one side so her erstwhile date won't see her. She's watching for Tammy, planning to have her friend go back into the theater with her so they can retrieve her coat, but then the theater manager comes out the door with her coat in his hands. "A nice young man said that you left without this," explains the manager, and all she can think about is the boy she'd run away from. "No," says the manager, "not the boy you were sitting with, but another boy—nice, clean-cut lad. Fourteen or fifteen." The manager searches the crowd for the boy who had turned in her coat, but apparently he's already left. She never sees him. Never knows how he'd held the coat to his face, sniffed the rich lavender of her perfume from around the collar and imagined he was actually holding her, and wished he had the courage to walk up to her and introduce himself. The myriad particles comprising the universe continue to resonate with that singular chord of creation, shifting nearer their ultimate positions, chaos striving for order.

The end of our days at the clinic came on a Wednesday, predicated by the tears of a lonely woman whose name I never even knew and Gavin's last pot of coffee. It started with an argument. Virginia had had enough. The treatments weren't working. As far as she was concerned, all they were doing was robbing her of her last year. She was too sick to do *anything*. When we weren't at the clinic undergoing a round of chemotherapy or radiation, we were at home recovering, building up the strength to face the next round, all the while watching the oncologists struggle with what they knew was a hopeless case. Ginny couldn't eat, couldn't sleep, couldn't enjoy any of the things that had so enriched our lives together.

So we were arguing in the waiting room, Ginny insisting that she wanted to get up and leave. Just walk out. Surrender. "I might only have a year left," she said. "There are a million things I've never seen. I'd like to travel the world, see as much as I can. We could sell that property your father left us in Nashville. Cash in our stocks and bonds. Use some of our life savings. There's more than enough. And there'd be enough left for you after—"

"Shhh," I said, putting my hand over her mouth. "It's not me I'm worried about. And the money means nothing. I just can't bear thinking about life without you. If there's even the slightest chance that these doctors can save you . . ."

It was then we saw a woman across the room crying. She was forty or forty-five, heavyset, bald, frumpy, and unattractive. Clearly she'd lost one breast, but made no attempt to hide that fact—no reconstructive surgery or prosthetic brassiere or any other attempt to cover up the mastectomy. This was perhaps in keeping with her attitude regarding her cancer and her appearance. She never wore a wig or scarf or anything, didn't feel the need to hide what was happening to her. "Stare at me if you want," I could imagine her saying, "but I refuse to hide my condition as if it was something I'd done wrong, something I should be ashamed of."

That day she was wearing an old baseball cap and sweats. I had seen her plenty of times before, coming in for chemo or for follow-ups. She would sit by herself and never talk to anyone. Ginny had commented more than once on how sad she looked, how desolate and alone. We had *never* seen this woman with anyone else. All the patients had someone with them, from time to time if not *all* the time. A spouse. Children. Siblings and parents and just good friends. I couldn't count the number of times I had seen entire families invade the chemo room in support of one of their own.

But this woman, the one that I want to tell you about, was *always* alone.

She was quietly sobbing to herself. She was sitting with her back to the counter, so none of the people in the office saw her. I'm sure they'd have done something. There was a receptionist, a counselor, doctors and nurses and lab technicians, and who knows who all else working the clinic, all of whom would have done something if they'd seen her. The poor woman just sat there sobbing. She pulled a tissue from her purse and drenched it. Not making any noise. Holding it all in. Brave, silent tears that said, "I don't want to cry in front of these people, but I'm truly at the end of my rope." Or worse, and what I suspected, she'd probably just been told that her cancer was back, that it had metastasized into the bone or into her organs or into her brain, the same sort of invasion before which my sweet Ginny was retreating.

This woman sat there and no one did anything. The tissue was falling apart in her hands, and all I wanted to do was go over there and hug her, to tell her that it'd be okay, even if that was a lie . . . but, well, she was a stranger and I didn't know her or what was wrong with her and there's that whole barrier of privacy and . . . well, what do you do? The tissue disintegrated, and she was still crying, hopeless tears that spilled down her face and dripped from her chin, leaving spots on her rumpled sweatshirt, the one that lay so flat and wrong against the right side of her chest. The waiting room had gone quiet. It had taken on the tableau of an auto accident. We were standing before the scene of a dreadful accident and didn't know how to fix it. In that silence, this woman's desperate sobs were heart-wrenching. If I were to get up, cross the room, and hug her, I would break down and cry myself.

So I walked to the counter where there was a box of tissues. I pulled out half a dozen and carried them back to her, put them in her hand. She looked up from under her baseball cap and thanked me, barely a whisper. I caught and squeezed her hand as she took the tissues . . . just to let her know someone cared, just to let her know I was right there if she needed me. Then I went and sat back down with Ginny, our argument forgotten. A minute later, an MA came out from the back for the weeping woman, put an arm around her, stroked her back, and led her somewhere more private to discuss her options. I don't know how many times I had seen that woman sitting alone, reading a book or just staring off into space. Don't know how many opportunities I had wasted to sit down beside her, extend my hand, and say hello. I promised myself that if I did see her again, that was exactly what I'd do. But I never saw her again.

What I realized that day, however, was this. No one should ever have to cry alone. No one should face a debilitating illness alone. And there's value and beauty in each and every one of us. We all deserve to be loved.

Shaken, I went to get a cup of coffee. To my surprise, because I hadn't known the Rockfords were even there that day, I found Gavin standing over the coffeepot. "Gavin," I asked, "where's Helen?"

"Gone," he whispered, as he filled my cup.

It felt as if someone had just kicked me in the gut. My legs went weak. "Oh, Gavin, no. I'm so sorry. Please come sit with Ginny and me. Let us—"

"Don't let her go this way," he told me, suddenly gripping the lapel of my jacket.

"What? What do you mean?"

"I overheard the two of you arguing. Give your wife what she wants. Don't make the same mistakes that I did."

"Gavin, I . . . I can't."

"You must. If you love her, you'll do what she wants. This is no place for your Ginny to spend the rest of her life. God, how I wish I'd gotten Helen out of here in time."

Then he turned and left the clinic, while I stood there trembling, unable to call him back, for the first time realizing that there was nothing to hope for, that my wife was truly dying, and that all I could do was try to help her enjoy whatever time remained to her.

I went to the reception desk and asked about Helen Rockford.

"I'm sorry," said the girl behind the counter, "were the Rockfords friends of yours?"

I explained that we'd met them here at the clinic

and over the last four months had become quite close. "When did she die? And do you know where the services will be held? I suppose I could call Mr. Rockford, but—"

"Sir? Didn't you know? Helen Rockford passed away at home the night before last. Afterward, her husband took an entire bottle of sleeping pills and lay down beside her. When they didn't show up yesterday for her treatment, we called and called, and finally had someone go by the house to check on them."

"I don't understand," I stammered.

"Sir, *both* the Rockfords are dead."

"That can't be."

She reached across the counter and touched my hand. "I know. It's hard for us to believe, too."

"No. I mean . . . it can't be, because . . ." But what was I going to tell her? That I had just accepted a cup of coffee from a ghost? That Gavin Rockford had made one final call on the clinic to give me a last piece of advice, to warn me against making the same mistake that he had?

"Sir?"

"Thank you," I mumbled. Then I went and helped Ginny to her feet.

She could tell something was wrong by the look on my face. "What is it?"

"This trip around the world," I asked, "where would you like to start?"

And so it continues: an item touched by both in a department store not fifteen minutes apart, the movie they both enjoy; a favorite novel checked out of the same library, their names scrawled intimately close together on the card in the back, the loops and swirls of ink intertwined; a bouquet of flowers delivered to the wrong address; a wrong number dialed and the briefest of hesitations before she apologizes and hangs up, wondering, despite the absurdity of it all, wondering what if she's meant to talk to the person on the other end of the phone; and he, often remembering the girl he'd seen in the movie theater and the fragrance from the collar of her coat. When he's sixteen, he buys a used Mustang and spends a year restoring it, then sells it for twice what he's invested so that he can buy a brand-new Corvette, paying the balance by teaching computer courses to the elderly. He's only seventeen, but he's already established himself as hardworking and intelligent. The Mustang is confiscated in drug bust and eventually auctioned off to a used car dealer. The car dealer takes a liking to the Mustang, drives it himself for a while, but then gives it to his daughter as a birthday present. Gripping the steering wheel, her hands resting exactly where his once did, does she feel it? Does Fate leave a fingerprint of recognition? A warm tremor of intuition waiting for just the right trigger?

So we traveled, making the most of what time we had left together: Rome, Paris, Sydney, the Great Wall of China, the pyramids at Giza. I watched the sun brown her skin on the beach in Cancun. Watched a morning frost highlight her hair on the bow of a cruise ship in the Arctic. We swam with a dolphin off the coast of Ireland. Met the Princess of Monaco, stood in Dracula's castle, crossed the tidal flats of the English Channel to Mont Saint Michel in France, and rode elephants in Côte D'Ivoire.

Though I knew I was losing her, I never gave up. As we traveled, I sought out local remedies, from the practical to the extravagant to the outright ludicrous. It became something of a joke between us, the vari-

ous potions and witch-doctoring. None of it helped
her. Not herbs from special clinics in Mexico. Not
rhino horn or shark cartilage or the venom of cobras.
Not the spells of Haitian *hougans.* Not the blessings
of Tibetan monks. I prayed to every god I came
across, left offerings in holy shrines from the Fiji Is-
lands to Lima, Peru.

Nothing helped.

We came at last to Bahia in Brazil and the city of
Salvador simmering between the deep indigo of the
Atlantic Ocean and the cobalt blue of the Baía de
Totos os Santos—All Saints Bay. *"Seja bem vindo à
magia da Bahia!"* people called to us from the streets
just outside the airport. The palm-lined boulevards
were in a state of confusion, as everywhere we
looked people were decorating for Carnival. The festivities would officially start that very night when the
keys to the city would be given to the Carnival King.

While the city made ready for Carnival, we rented
a car and ventured inland into the Recôncavo, the
most fertile farmland in Brazil. We drove through
fields of sugarcane, coffee, and tobacco, by midafter-
noon finding ourselves at a gorgeous little eighteenth
century chapel called Our Lady of Guadalupe near
the town of Cachoeira. It was there I first heard about
Omolú, a powerful African Orixá alternately known
as the Plague Doctor or the God of Infectious Disease. Omolú was something of a paradox, for he was
credited with both causing and curing highly conta-
gious diseases like smallpox, hepatitis, hemorrhagic
fever, and AIDS. In Dahomey, it's forbidden to speak
his name for fear of invoking illness, but in most of
Africa he's the target of millions of prayers for a cure
to HIV.

Omolú was just one of hundreds of Orixá brought

to Brazil by African slaves who sustained their Yoruba and Kongo divinities by matching them with Catholic saints, creating the Afro-Brazilian religion Candomblé. Omolú was paired with São Lazaro—Saint Lazarus. Omolú is depicted as a bent old man, his face concealed by a raffia and cowrie shell mask, a palm broom in his hands for sweeping away illness.

"Is there a shrine to this god?" I asked the Brazilians at the chapel. "Some place I can leave an offering?"

"One does not simply leave an offering for Omolú," said a young man who introduced himself as Francisco Santos. "You must attend a *bembe*, a Candomblé gathering with drums and dancing and singing, conducted by someone who knows the old Yoruban ceremonies."

I asked who conducted such ceremonies.

"Many of the old Yoruba interpret for Omolú," Francisco said, "but the best is Madam Oliveira Olindo de Silva. She lives in a *favela*, a—how you say? Shantytown? Yes, that's it: a *favela* on the east side of Salvador, near the Praia do Forte beach. For fifty dollars, I will show you the way."

So, while Ginny rested in our hotel that evening, I went looking for Madam de Silva, guided by Francisco Santos, whose wavy brown hair, midnight eyes, full lips, and cocoa skin hinted at the mixed heritage of the state of Bahia. His great grandparents might have been slaves from Africa, but there was also blood in his veins that had originated with Brazil's Portuguese colonial period.

"This is the Pelourinho district," he said as we drove through streets lined with pastel stucco homes and modest businesses, "named for the pillory where slaves were whipped. There's a museum—down that side street there—dedicated to the famous Brazilian novelist Jorge Amado."

Most of the boxlike, two-and three-story buildings had wrought-iron balconies on which people were already gathering in anticipation of Carnival. The enormous *trios electricos*, massive sound trucks carrying musicians and performers, would soon be winding their way through the streets surrounded by millions of revelers. The *Afro Blocos* drum troupes would soon be rattling the foundations of these homes, the monstrous *surdo* drum said to make a sound capable of waking the dead. I had been told that the traditional Carnival route ran from our hotel, the Tropical Hotel da Bahia, along Campo Grande to the Praca Castro Alves in the old part of town. It's said during the six-day festival that there are over a million and half people dancing in the streets at any one time.

"Who is sick?" Francisco asked as the streets and homes took on a more run-down appearance on the outskirts of the city.

"My wife," I answered, amazed that he hadn't noticed. Virginia had been lethargic for several weeks now. She was barely eating and had been sleeping perhaps sixteen hours a day. In fact, she had slept in the car while I toured the chapel and talked to Francisco, as well as all the way back to the hotel. Perhaps Francisco had attributed her fatigue to jet lag.

"I am most sorry," he said.

By the time we reached Madam de Silva's, the sun was drowning in the bay on our left. The decrepit homes and businesses in this part of the city cast long, sinister shadows, rife with the jagged edges of broken glass and nooses of barbed wire, and I was rethinking my visit to the Cadomblé priestess, wondering if I'd been wise to trust Francisco, regretting the time spent away from my wife. The festive lights and decorative colors of Carnival had been left behind us, replaced with Brazilian graffiti. The narrow streets were crooked, slightly out of focus, besieged with buildings that all seemed to warp inward, as if a child had built them with discarded scraps of plywood. The place was deserted, save for an old cur who raised his head and bared his teeth as we passed.

"Everyone has left for Carnival," Francisco explained as we parked in a dark alley.

"What about Madam de Silva?"

"She will be here," he assured me.

There was an old man seated on the steps of Madam de Silva's tiny chapel, his arms wrapped around his knees, face lost in shadow, long gray hair and beard a wintry silver in the last of the daylight. Francisco passed him by as if not even seeing him. Intent on meeting de Silva, I might have passed the old man by as well, but as I neared him, he spoke.

"What?" I asked.

"A gift," he rasped. "A gift for an old man?"

He extended his hand, and I saw that it had suffered some accident. The last two fingers were gone, leaving but three alien-looking digits splayed in the traditional beggar's gesture. I checked my pockets, but I had no coins. The smallest Brazilian bill in my wallet was the equivalent of about sixty dollars US, hardly suitable for a handout, especially since Ginny and I had very nearly spent our entire life savings touring the world. But what to give the old man? The only other things of value on my person were my wedding band and my watch. I looked at my watch, which had stopped at three o'clock. Since we'd started traveling, knowing the time had become less and less important to me, and I was constantly forgetting to wind my watch. These days, the passage of time was measured not in minutes and hours, but in how much weaker Ginny was each day, in how much more sleep she needed, in how often I sat wondering if she would wake up. Sure, there'd been flights, buses, and trains to catch, but often missing one mode of transportation had simply led to an intriguing alternative. We'd been carefree, letting Fate blow us where it would. My wristwatch was part of a life I'd walked away from a year ago.

I slipped off the watch and placed it in the palm of his hand, then stepped around him to enter the chapel. He caught the leg of my trousers, tugging me back, gesturing that I should lean close.

"It is sweet to die in the sea," he sang in a low voice clotted by many hard years, *"in the green waves of the sea."*

"Were you a fisherman?" I asked, knowing the peninsula of Bahia had served as Brazil's largest seaport for centuries.

"Mother of all life," whispered the old man, his rheumy eyes retaining a ghost of blue beneath milk-white cataracts.

"Hurry," Francisco called from within.

Somewhat reluctantly, I pried loose the beggar's fingers and followed Francisco inside.

The chapel consisted of a simple arrangement of pews facing a shrine to what I thought at first was the Virgin Mary. Though the face and arrangement seemed right for Mary, there were obvious differences. This version of Mary was holding a comb that shimmered like mother-of-pearl and a mirror made of seashells. Her brow was adorned with a crown of silver, decorated with shells, starfish, and pearls. She was seated in a massive oyster shell.

Madam de Silva was waiting in an old rocking chair. I expected her to be alone, but there was a host of people, all standing quietly along the walls of the chapel. She was old and withered, but her eyes were an intriguing turquoise, completely out of place in her ebony face. She motioned for us to sit on a pew near her, then she spoke in a soft, lyrical language that I guessed was Portuguese.

"She does not speak English," Francisco explained. "I will translate." He spoke with her for several minutes, while I grew nervous under the stares of the people gathered around us. "I have explained why you are here," Francisco finally said, "but she says she cannot help you."

"Tell her she must help me. I would like to ask Omolú to cure my wife. I will pay her to summon him for me."

Again he spoke in Portuguese with the old woman, while I stared back at the dour people lining the walls, wondering why they didn't speak, why they were waiting here. "Will the *bembe* start tonight?" I asked, interrupting Francisco. "Is that why they're waiting here?"

Francisco looked confused. "Who?" he asked.

"Them," I said, nodding toward the people.

Madam de Silva leaned forward in her chair. "What do you see?" she asked in perfect English.

"What do you mean, what do I see?" I asked angrily, realizing that their translation game had probably been nothing more than a sham to milk me of more money. "I see you. I see them. I see this chapel

and the Virgin Mary on the altar and the old beggar
out on your front porch and—"

"There was no one on the porch," insisted Francisco.

Madam de Silva quieted us both with the wrinkled
palms of her hands. "Wait. Slow down." She gestured
to the altar. "This is Yemanjá, mistress of the waters
of life, siren of the five names: Janaina, Ynaê, Iyá,
Queen of Aiboká. Jorge Amado called her 'she of the
perfumed tresses and shipwreck eyes.' She reigns over
the watery empire—the sea, the lakes, and rivers—
commands the winds, and unties the tempests. Because all life originated in the sea, we who follow the
ways of Cadomblé consider her the mother of life.

"Now tell me about the beggar you saw on my
porch."

"I gave him my watch. It had stopped anyway. He
only had three fingers . . ." I showed her with my
hand. "And he sang something to me, something
about the sea."

She looked at Francisco. "And you saw no one?"

He shook his head.

"I believe that was Exu," she said. "No beggar. He
is a messenger between men and Orixá. He is typically found at a crossroads, in this case perhaps not
a physical crossroad, but rather a choice for you. Exu
is always represented by the number three—"

"My watch had stopped at three o'clock."

"—and is only to be trusted when appeased with
a gift."

"My watch."

"Yes. What did he sing to you?"

I tried to remember the words, but they were gone.
"It was some sort of fisherman's song. I don't remember the words."

She nodded. "He's telling you to seek help from Yemanjá."

"Why? What can she do? I thought Omolú was the Cadomblé god of disease?"

She rose from her chair and took my hands in hers. "Tonight. At midnight. I will lead a procession to the beach where we will make offerings to Yemanjá. This is the *Lavagem do Porto da Barra*, a Carnival tradition when people dance and sing on the beach. Bring your wife."

"I don't understand."

She squeezed my hands and released them. "You will. Now go."

I turned toward the door, Francisco following quietly, but then something else occurred to me. "These people," I asked her, gesturing to those who lined the walls of the chapel, "what are they waiting for?"

"They are also waiting for me to lead them to Yemanjá."

Francisco tugged me out the door and down the steps of the empty front porch.

"But why were they so quiet?" I asked him.

I saw him shiver. Watched him make the sign of the cross.

"Francisco?"

"There was no one else there," he stammered. "Just the three of us: you, me, and Madam de Silva. Other than that, the chapel was empty."

Her Mustang breaks down one day, leaving her stranded on the side of the road. Not knowing what else to do, she gets out, raises the hood, and stands there staring at the mysteries of the internal combustion engine. He's on his way to a job interview, already running late, and decides to take a roundabout route in order to avoid traffic, hoping it'll be quicker in the long run and get him there on time. He passes the car with its hood up on the side of the road and wouldn't have a given a moment's thought to stopping because he's late and really needs this job, but then he realizes that it's his old Mustang. He pulls to the side of the road, puts his car in reverse and backs up. In his side-view mirror, he sees her relieved yet apprehensive face there above "Objects in mirror are closer than they appear." He doesn't recognize her from all those years ago at the movie theater, but the universe adjusts its secret symphony, now just that much closer to perfection, as these elements settle at last into their proper position.

I returned to the hotel, weaving through streets crowded with costumed merrymakers, buffeted by the deep samba rhythms of music that might be indigenous to Brazil but was clearly African beneath the surface, transplanted as surely as Omolú, Yemanjá, and Exu. I let Francisco Santos out on a corner where he said he would meet some friends. He leaned on the car door and extended his hand before the crowd swallowed him up. "I'm sorry about your wife," he said, and I told him that I still didn't understand. "Sometimes a door is opened," he speculated, "and a link is formed between this world and the next. I don't know why. I don't even think Madam de Silva knows why."

"How do I close this door?"

"I don't think you can. Someone reached out to you once—for whatever reason—and now you'll always have that connection, that ability to see."

And I understood that even though Gavin had

given me this last year with Ginny, he had also cursed me for life. Once you've seen one ghost, you can't help but see others.

Mounting the stairs to our hotel room, I nearly crushed a lone ant on the banister, pulling my hand back only at the last second. It occurred to me that most of us are like that ant, apparently lost and alone, wandering chaotic and undirected through our lives. Step back and see the whole picture, though, see the whole of the ant colony from a universal viewpoint, and maybe everything fits in some hive-like orchestration, each piece of the puzzle moving in divine coordination. The world resonates to its own song, a chord of creation born millennia ago, each atom vibrating and calling out to the others, seeking that perfect match, that exact position in the pattern of the cosmos.

I opened the door, entered our room, and found Ginny sitting naked in the chair by the window. The lights and music of Carnival reverberated against the closed blinds, but Ginny's focus was on a horizon I couldn't see. Our camera lay on the dresser where I'd set it down earlier that evening. I picked it up and snapped her picture, not really understanding why, just knowing that I had to capture that singular fragile moment in time.

I went to her and gathered her in my arms, feeling the warmth and the weight of her, the electric shiver of her skin exchanging energy with my own. I could smell lavender on her neck. Could feel the whisper of her breath on my cheek as we shared the very same air.

"How long have I been keeping you here?" I asked, tears running down my cheeks.

Her lips on mine forestalled any other questions.

It wasn't necessary that we talk, and perhaps there was nothing to be said.

I held her for several hours, until the clock on the nightstand clicked over to midnight. Then I wrapped her in a bathrobe and walked her down to the beach, through the waves of dancers to the tidal wrack and into the surf . . .

. . . where she left me without ever breaking the waves, slipping out among the thousands of tiny offerings candle-flickering on the sea, each a tiny prayer to whatever gods or natural forces govern our destiny.

"I love you," I whispered to Yemanjá's endless susurration, to the music that echoes within conch chambers, to the endless cycle of waves and the caress of each tiny particle of sand on its neighbor.

"I don't know how," I told the young man seated in the living room of my tiny apartment, "it's possible to accept a cup of coffee from a ghost or—" I touched the photo on the open page of the album. "—take one's picture, but I do understand that life's a greater mystery than we will ever truly know. We are all the dust of stars, seeking and maybe one day settling into proper position and alignment in some great sympathetic kaleidoscope of matter and energy."

He said nothing—had said nothing throughout my story—but there were tears in his eyes that said he understood.

"Somewhere out there, the essence of my Ginny is even now embarking on a great quest toward a reunion with me. I believe that. I have to believe that. And if you still love your wife, then that same journey waits for you."

I reached out, touching him for the first time, and squeezed his arm.

"Let people who never found true love, people who never experienced love at first sight, say such things don't exist. Their lack of faith will make it easier for them to live their lonely lives and die never having experienced such things. You and I know different."

He set his empty coffee cup on the table and rubbed at his eyes. "I thought it was too late," he said, "but perhaps you're right. Maybe there's still time to make her understand. And maybe there'll be a time and place for us to love one another again."

As I pondered what he really meant by this, he stood and went to the door. "Thank you," said the young man, "I didn't mean to take up so much of your time." Then he closed the door behind him.

I rose from my chair, crossed the room, and pulled back the curtains to watch him leave. But the street was empty. I opened the door and stepped out onto the porch. There was no sign of him. No fading echo of his vehicle's tires on the pavement. No barking dogs. Nothing.

Just the chill embrace of winter.

For Betty

Tanya Huff

Smoke and Shadows

First in a New Series

Tony Foster—familiar to Tanya Huff fans from her
Blood series—has relocated to Vancouver with Henry
Fitzroy, vampire son of Henry VIII. Tony landed a
job as a production assistant at CB Productions, ironically working on a syndicated TV series, "Darkest
Night," about a vampire detective. Except for his
crush on Lee, the show's handsome costar, Tony was
pretty content...at least until everything started to fall
apart on the set. It began with shadows—shadows
that seemed to be where they didn't belong, shadows
that had an existence of their own. And when he
found a body, and a shadow cast its claim on Lee,
Tony knew he had to find out what was going on, and
that he needed Henry's help.

0-7564-0183-6

To Order Call: 1-800-788-6262

Tanya Huff

Victory Nelson, Investigator:
Otherworldly Crimes a Specialty

BLOOD PRICE
0-88677-471-3
BLOOD TRAIL
0-88677-502-7
BLOOD LINES
0-88677-530-2
BLOOD PACT
0-88677-582-5